...fina

..k Mofina."
—Fresh Fiction on *Full Tilt*

"Mofina's novels are guaranteed to be exciting, thought-provoking and full of surprises. Another stellar read that demonstrates Mofina's one of the best thriller writers in the business."

—*RT Book Reviews* on *Whirlwind* (Top Pick)

"With the exciting plot and a conclusion that is a true surprise to one and all, this is one book that has to be seen ASAP."

—*Suspense Magazine* on *Into the Dark*

"Mofina is one of the best thriller writers in the business."
—*Library Journal* (starred review) on *They Disappeared*

"Rick Mofina's tense, taut writing makes every thriller he writes an adrenaline-packed ride."
—Tess Gerritsen, *New York Times* bestselling author, on *The Burning Edge*

"A blisteringly paced story that cuts to the bone. It left me ripping through pages deep into the night."
—James Rollins, *New York Times* bestselling author, on ...peration

"Taut pacing, rough action and ... a relentless pace. *The Pan...* intent."
—...tor

"*Vengeance Road* is ...nt! It's a great read!"
—Michael Connelly, ...*Times* bestselling author

"*Six Seconds* should be Rick Mofina's breakout thriller. It moves like a tornado."
—James Patterson, *New York Times* bestselling author

Also by Rick Mofina and MIRA Books

Other books by Rick Mofina

RICK MOFINA

EVERY SECOND

MIRA®

ISBN-13: 978-0-7783-1751-7

Every Second

To the memory of my nephew, Matt.

EVERY SECOND

1

Lori Fulton woke in the darkness of her bedroom to a strange pressure covering her mouth, forcing her head deep into her pillow.

A hideous face glared down at her.

Straining to breathe, Lori thought: *I'm dreaming!* Then her eyes flicked to her husband's side of the bed. It was empty.

Where's Dan? What's happening? Wake up!

At the peel of duct tape and the guttural noises of a struggle nearby, Lori's brain thundered awake with the horrible realization that the man above her was real. Again, she thought of her husband and her son.

Where's Dan? Where's Billy?

She thrashed against her attacker, who countered by seizing her throat.

"Don't move!"

The lights switched on and she saw Dan was across the room in his T-shirt and boxers, on his knees, hands bound behind his back. A band of tape sealed his mouth. Blood webbed down his cheek. His eyes met hers.

A gun was being held to his head.

Dan! Oh God, where's Billy?

The two men in her room wore loose mechanic-style coveralls over top of hoodies and white masks with grotesque faces. In an explosion of terror and rage, Lori fought back, shaking her mouth free to shriek.

"Billy! Where's my son? Billy!"

Lori's assailant pressed a strip of duct tape over her mouth then yanked her by her hair from her bed. Dan moved to protect her but was stopped when his attacker smashed the butt of his gun against his face. Lori was shoved to the floor, her nightshirt hiked up to her waist in the scuffle. Her attacker—Thorne, according to the name embroidered on the patch on his chest—paused to take in her body before dropping his knee hard on her stomach, knocking out her breath. He clamped her wrists in one gloved hand then reached for the duct tape.

Through her pain Lori noticed him fumbling, unable to find the start of the tape. He cursed, shook off his glove, peeled a lead and quickly wrapped her wrists like a rodeo cowboy in a calf-roping competition.

Thorne replaced his glove, then pulled Lori to her knees positioning her next to Dan, both of them now bound helplessly. Lori wheezed, her need for air contending with the ache in her gut. A muffled whimpering sounded through their open bedroom door. Shadows moved in the hallway as two more figures approached, dressed the same as the first two. Their name patches read Cutty and Percy.

Cutty, the largest of the four, carried Billy on his hip as if he were luggage.

Dan's muzzled growl nearly burst through his tape as Lori screamed under hers. Billy's hands and mouth were bound, his eyes wide with terror as Cutty tossed him on the floor next to them. Lori fumbled closer, feeling Billy's body trembling against hers as he sobbed.

Who were these monsters?

The man who'd been holding on to Dan—Vic, by his name patch—took charge. He sat on the foot of Lori and Dan's bed, casually contemplating his gun, then the family.

Lori, Dan and Billy were on their knees before him, their armed attackers looming behind them— a portrait of contrasts. Dan was in his favorite Jets T-shirt, now bloodstained, and Billy in the new Spider-Man pajamas Lori had bought him for his ninth birthday last month. They'd been torn in the struggle.

Why had these people violated their home?

Vic tapped his gun to his knee as if coming to a decision.

"Are we calm now? Do we have your attention?" he asked. "I'll make it simple. If you do what we say and do it right no one gets hurt and this will be over tomorrow. If you fail at any stage, you'll die."

2

Lori's pulse pounded.

As the invaders marched her, Dan and Billy downstairs, fear and questions burned through her mind.

Why didn't the home security alarm work? Why isn't someone helping us? Please, God, don't let them kill us! We have to fight back. What can Dan and I do without guns?

Overwhelmed with panic, Lori drew a few deep breaths to calm her nerves and focus. The attackers had moved them to the living room and put them on the sofa. A duffel bag, zippered shut, sat on the hardwood floor in the middle of the room like an unanswered question. The invaders closed the curtains, kept the main floor lights dim then browsed around as if they were interested buyers at an open house.

Thorne inspected their paintings, the crystal figurines and their furniture.

"You got a lot of nice stuff," he said from behind

his mask. "So much suffering going on, so many people in trouble in this world, but why should you care, huh? You're living the American dream."

Lori watched as Cutty and Percy went to the kitchen, opened the fridge and helped themselves to leftover takeout—pizza and Chinese food Dan and Lori had ordered when they'd worked late this week.

Lori saw them opening soda cans, lifting their masks to eat and drink. She couldn't make out their faces in detail, but she could see they were white males in their early twenties.

Like college kids snacking after a late night.

"It's goin' good," Cutty said between bites. "Like you said it would, Jake."

"Shut up! My name is on my patch!" Vic said.

One of them was named Jake. Lori glanced at Dan as they both noted the slipup before a new fear dawned on her. She looked around for Sam, Billy's golden retriever. He wasn't a barker or a good guard dog at all, really. He was just gentle, loving Sam.

What've they done with him?

Vic sat in the chair opposite the sofa, placing his gun on the arm and staring at her family from behind his mask.

"We've been watching you for a long time," he began. "We've been doing our homework. We know all about you. Billy Fulton, fourth grade at Eisenhower Elementary, dog lover, Little League, shortstop for the Roseoak Park Wild Tigers. Lori Fulton, age thirty-four, devoted mother. You never miss one of Billy's games. You work at Dixon Donlevy Mutual Life Insurance investigating insurance fraud. Someone in this house is partial to Ben & Jerry's ice cream. Cherry Garcia, judging by what we found in your trash.

"Dan, age thirty-six. You were in the National Guard, army, when you guys lived in Southern California. You work for SkyNational Trust Banking Corp. A few years ago, you were transferred to New York. Now you're the manager of a suburban branch here in Roseoak Park. You like the Jets, but you're still loyal to the Dodgers, according to your Tweets. You both volunteer with charities. How we doing so far? We've got you nailed, right?"

Lori's stomach clenched at Vic's accuracy. She glanced at Dan. He remained tense, keeping his eyes on Vic as he continued.

"Tomorrow's going to be a long day. We know Dan's branch is one of the earliest-opening branches in the state, opening its doors at 6:00 a.m., to serve commuting customers. This is what's going to happen. Dan, you'll be going to work in the morning, as usual, while we stay here with your wife and son. But tomorrow you're going to remove a quarter million dollars from the vault. We know about cash inventory in a branch like yours. You'll place the money in a bag like this one here." He motioned to the duffel on the floor. "No dye packs, no radio transmitters, no bait, no silent alarms. You'll leave the bank, follow our instructions. Once that's done and we have the cash, everyone is let go unharmed. You got that?"

Dan didn't move. His face was expressionless but for a twitch in his jaw.

"You need more incentive, Dan?"

Vic nodded toward Thorne, who came forward and unzipped the duffel bag, removing what looked like a small vest bearing thin, brick-shaped items connected to wires. Cutty then yanked Billy from the sofa. He sliced the tape from Billy's hands and, with Thorne's help, slipped the vest over Billy, then resealed his hands.

Lori screamed into the tape.

"No!" Dan roared into his.

Vic leaned forward.

"That's right," he said, pointing with his gun as he continued. "That's a suicide vest. It's loaded with C-4 and all sorts of good stuff. Any of us here can detonate it simply by dialing a cell number."

Thorne and Cutty pulled another vest from the bag, cut the tape from Lori's hands, and forced it on her. She struggled in vain when they retaped her wrists, her mind reeling. As she stood next to her son, each of them now wearing a bomb, her knees weakened at the thought of Billy in danger, and she inhaled sharply. They were living and breathing second by second. Their surroundings—the curtains she'd sewn herself, the sofa set they'd bought on sale, the antique coffee table they'd gotten in Williamsburg—their sanctuary instantly took on an unspeakable dimension as images blazed before her.

She imagined their viscera splattered over the living room walls, mingling with the paint color,

Coral Sunset, she and Dan had finally decided on. Blood obscuring the paintings they fell in love with on their vacation in Maine. It all seemed silly now.

"Now, I'll ask you again," Vic said. "Are you going to cooperate, follow our instructions and get us the money?"

Dan looked hard at Lori and Billy, his eyes filling with tears, and nodded.

3

Cutty, Percy and Thorne took Lori and Billy to the basement.

Their captors switched on the stairway light and marched them down the stairs. With every creaking step, Lori felt time ticking on their lives. The heavy vests enveloped them with the threat of death. Her skin prickled as adrenaline burned through her body, but she moved slowly, terrified that a sudden action might trigger the bombs.

The sound of her own blood rushing in her ears was deafening, but a steely clink and jingle caught her attention. Cutty carried a coiled chain with locks. The heavy fragrance of powdered detergent filled the damp air when they reached the laundry room, stopping at the wall before the washer and dryer.

"Lie down there." Thorne pointed to the shag mat that Lori had made herself when they'd lived in California. There were mistakes in it that she noticed every time she looked at it, but Dan loved it and had insisted she not throw it out. Heaped on the mat were the sheets and towels she'd planned to wash the next day. As Lori and Billy eased themselves carefully on to the pile, Lori could feel the components of her vest digging into her side. She held Billy's terrified gaze, hoping to reassure him despite the fear that bubbled inside her.

The chains jangled as Cutty and Percy worked fast, fixing them to a shackle they'd secured to their ankles, grunting as they looped them around the joists in the ceiling and a naked, load-bearing beam.

Padlocks clicked.

Then the three invaders moved the snow tires for Dan's car. She always hated that he'd stored them in the already cramped laundry room, and now the men moved the tires toward Lori and Billy, building a makeshift wall. The rubbery smell was strong. Atop the tires, they piled dusty cushions from the old sofa at the other end of the basement, then worked together to heave the washer and dryer closer to them, pulling the hoses taut.

Why?

The answer suddenly dawned on Lori. The men were building a barrier to absorb an explosion—something to protect themselves if they detonated the bombs while they were still in the house.

She blinked rapidly, struggling to process the reality of the situation.

Thorne moved close to Lori, lowering himself until he was squatting before her. He drew his horrible mask to within an inch of her face.

"You deserve what's going to happen to you."

Without another word, Thorne and the others left. They switched off the lights at the top of the stairs and closed the door.

In the cool darkness Lori felt the warmth of Billy's body against hers. *How could anyone deserve this?* Billy was crying softly. She could hear his muffled calling for Sam. As she nestled closer to comfort him, she tasted the salt of her own tears that had seeped under the tape covering her mouth. Her eyes adjusted to the dim basement light and she searched through the cracks of their crude enclosure for any sign of their dog that might reassure Billy. She couldn't find anything, and she hoped he'd managed to escape through his door in the kitchen. She was suddenly thankful for her bad habit of leaving it unlocked.

Lori's attention went to the basement window, the night sky and a corner of the Millers' roof next door.

Lori thought of Grant and Monica Miller sleeping peacefully a few feet away, unaware of the horror playing out in the house beside them. Grant was a mechanic, Monica a nurse. They had little girls. Grant had loaned Dan his generator when they lost electricity in that storm last month. In the spring, Monica had come over to check on Billy when he was running a fever. The Millers were the kind of people who'd go out of their way to help you.

They'd call the police, if they only knew.

In the Tudor home across the street, their neighbors were Ward and Violet Selway, a retired couple.

The kindest people you could ever meet. Ward had been an accountant years ago. Violet had managed a clothing store at the Roseoak Mall. Their son lived in Oregon and they spent winters in Clearwater, Florida. Lori had always admired their beautiful yard, and Ward would give her gardening tips. Violet was always baking cookies to share with Billy.

Oh God, if our neighbors only knew!

Lori ached to wake from this nightmare and return to the normal life they'd been living less than an hour ago. It wasn't perfect, but they'd been doing okay since everything they'd been through in California. They'd finally been moving on.

Lori's attention shifted to the storage area on the far side of the basement. *Pieces of our lives.* There was the closet filled with clothes, Dan's old shirts and suits and some things of her own. Things she was certain she'd never wear again. *Why do I keep them?*

But she knew the answer. *Because of Tim.* She reminded herself she had to give all that stuff away, as if any of that mattered at this moment.

Beside the closet was a shelving unit jammed with boxes of board games, lamps, radios, computer keyboards, extension cords, cables and replacement bulbs for the Christmas tree. Rows of old books and stacks of ancient magazines cluttered the rest of it, along with photo albums containing a record of every year of their lives.

Except for...

Lori shuddered. Stress had always been a trigger

for these memories, pulling her back to a darker time. In a flash she saw herself…

Sitting in the street, covered with blood, helpless to do anything...

Up until then she had been a whole person—a confident, strong woman who could handle anything the world could throw at her.

Until that night six years ago.

Lori flinched at the sound of movement above them, snapping her mind back to reality.

She was as familiar with the noises and rhythms of her home as she was with the back of her hand. The strain and measured creaking of the floor indicated that the men had gone to the top floor. *Maybe they've taken Dan back to the bedroom?* Soon, more groans and squeaking indicated the invaders had returned to the main floor. Next she heard muffled conversations, though she couldn't make out the words. But as the voices echoed through the vent nearby, Lori guessed they were discussing a strategy. No matter what their plan was, she didn't believe it included letting her family live.

She pressed her cheek to the top of Billy's head, then examined their vests more closely. There was a small red light blinking from a battery pack on each of them, flashing in time with her heart, ticking down, second by second.

4

Roseoak Park, New York

Dan's heart hammered against his rib cage.

He stared at the ceiling, his hands bound and his mouth still covered with tape. His feet were now chained to the footboard of his bed. He wrenched against the shackles until the metal cut into his skin, drawing a rebuke from Percy, the captor guarding him.

"You need to be sharp in the morning. Be smart and sleep."

How could he sleep knowing bombs were strapped to his wife and son? Again, Dan raged against the chains, but they held him firmly in place, and soon he slumped back into the mattress, exhausted and defeated.

These animals invade my home and what do I do? Do I protect my family and fight? No, I watch them become weapons.

The images of Lori and Billy in suicide vests tormented him. Each passing second threatened an explosion that would kill the two people he loved most in this world.

As the hours slipped by, the quiet of their suburb mocked the reality of his situation. His pulse roared in his ears. No matter how hard Dan tried to find a way to fight back, he came up empty.

It's because I'm a coward.

Once he'd been a trained soldier, a "weekend warrior" with the California National Guard. But that was years ago. The only action he'd seen was wildfires and mudslides. He hadn't been deployed to Afghanistan or Iraq, like other units who'd been tested in battle. He'd often been told he was on standby to go—and during those weeks tension had knotted his stomach.

Because deep down, he was afraid.

It wasn't the risk of dying that had overwhelmed him; he'd accepted that being a soldier might mean not coming back. In fact, coming back was what actually terrified him, the possibility of being permanently damaged—not just physically, but mentally—and not being able to deal with it. He'd never told anyone about his secret relief at not being deployed.

Now he was being tested again, and he was failing.

His home was under attack and he'd done nothing to stop it.

Trained soldier, my ass.

He didn't even have a gun in the house because Lori didn't want one. Dan understood. After everything she'd already been through and the price she'd paid, she was justified to feel that way. And back then, in her time of crisis, she'd taken action.

His faced burned with shame, knowing she was stronger than he was.

A bark from somewhere outside made him think of his neighbors. They'd know what to do if they were in his shoes.

Miller, a mechanic covered in tattoos—that guy could fix anything, and Dan knew he would've fought back against these men. So would Ward, a retired accountant who'd done two tours in Vietnam.

That's the kind of men they are.

Dan stared at the ceiling.

The seconds ticked by.

And what kind of man am I?

By sunrise Dan was grasping for hope, telling himself that his chance to act might come later, and he had to be ready for it.

After hours of dark silence, he jumped when the door opened and Vic kicked his bed.

"Time to get ready."

As Percy unshackled Dan's feet, Vic stood over him.

"You look like hell. Get up."

Dan stood, but shakily. His head was still sore from being pistol-whipped.

"You're going to go through your routine like this was a normal day," Vic said. "We're going to free your hands and mouth first. You're going to shower, shave, get dressed, have breakfast and go to work like any other day, and you're going to follow our instructions to the letter."

Vic motioned toward Percy, who held up a cell phone.

"If you try anything, anything at all, Percy will hit Send on a speed dial number and your wife and son are gone. There are no second chances. You got that?"

When Dan nodded, they removed the tape from his wrists and mouth.

As soon as his mouth was free, Dan rushed to speak. "Please—I want to see my wife and son."

Vic held up another phone, showing a grainy video of Lori and Billy, bound and afraid. Given the quality, Dan couldn't determine where they were, if it was real time or recorded.

"When was this taken? How do I know they're still alive?"

"That's all you get!"

Vic pulled the phone away before they forced Dan into the bathroom, leaving the door open. As they stood guard with their guns, they watched him relieve himself and then climb into the shower. His body was stiff and numb from being tied up all night, and he welcomed the needles of hot water, bringing back some of his adrenaline from earlier. He kept his thoughts on Lori and Billy, praying they were still safe.

Stepping from the shower, he glanced at Percy, who passed him a towel. After drying himself, Dan wiped steam from the mirror and lathered his face. His hand shook as he shaved, nicking his chin with the razor. He stemmed the blood with a dot of toilet paper then put a bandage on his temple where he'd been struck with the gun.

After shoving Dan's robe at him, the men took him to the kitchen where they watched him gulp two cups of black coffee and forced him to eat a bagel. It would be a long day, and they didn't need him hungry and light-headed. "We don't want your stomach growling at the bank."

In the early morning quiet, Dan heard no sign of Lori and Billy, or the two other invaders from the night before. He wondered if they were still in the house—maybe the basement? Or the garage? As he ate, he found it difficult to absorb the bizarreness of his situation: his family's lives suddenly at stake; the armed invaders with their freakish masks; the way they watched him and then checked on neighbors at the windows with blinds drawn. As they monitored their phones for messages, Dan noticed Vic checking a duffel bag and the way he kept an eye on the clock over the fridge. If, as they said, they knew everything about his family, then they were aware of their routine. Dan went to work first, and concerns at Lori's office or Billy's school about their absences would not surface for a few hours yet.

When Dan finished, Vic and Percy took him back to the bedroom to brush his teeth and dress, bringing the bag with them.

On the bed, Dan laid out his navy gabardine trousers, his navy wool blazer, a silk tie and his powder-blue dress shirt. He'd got as far as pulling on his pants before they stopped him again.

Dan's heart skipped a beat as he watched Percy reach into the bag for a vest just like the ones they'd strapped to Lori and Billy. They placed it on his chest, the Velcro fasteners crackling as they adjusted it. Dan saw the thin bricks and the wires connecting them to the power source. He could smell the nylon mingling with the scent of vanilla and plastic. They activated the power source and the timing light blinked red. Then they helped Dan tug on his shirt—a snug fit with the vest, but it worked.

Sweat beaded on Dan's brow and his fingers trembled as he knotted his tie in front of Lori's full-length mirror.

"Relax, Dan, and pay attention."

Vic held up Dan's glasses, black with rectangle frames.

"We did a little work on these, see?"

Looking closely, Dan noticed a small metal button no bigger than the head of a pin fixed to the bridge. On the inside of the arms, they'd attached two more small metal buttons.

"The one in the front is a camera lens. The ones on the sides are microphone-earphone receiver transmitters. They let us see remotely on our laptop what you see, hear what you hear. And they let us talk to each other. Put them on."

Vic showed Dan the image he was seeing on their laptop.

"So don't think about being a hero today. We're watching every move. If you deviate from our instructions, we'll detonate the vests, all three at once. Do you understand?"

He understood.

They helped him pull on his blazer, adjust his hair, slip on his glasses.

Vic checked the time, then handed Dan his briefcase containing an empty, folded duffel bag.

"Okay, Dan, let's go to work."

5

The house is too quiet.

As they walked Dan through the back and into the garage, his fear mounted.

"Are Billy and Lori in the basement?"

"Shut up!" Vic said. "Focus on what you need to do."

Dan's eyes went around the garage, taking quick inventory. Suddenly the everyday items took on a new and desperate significance, a reflection of their lives before the attack. Billy's bicycle, his goal net, his bats and hockey sticks, and up in one corner, his old tricycle.

Stacked on the bench were cardboard boxes of clothes Lori was preparing to donate to the church. Nearby were her clay planters, her gardening tools and her flower-printed gardening gloves. Looped neatly on a hook was the hose and, near it, Dan's John Deere mower. He did his best thinking and problem-solving when he mowed the lawn.

I've got to do something.

Vic nudged him. Dan opened the door to his Ford Taurus and got in alone. As he sat behind the wheel, he glanced at Lori's Dodge Dart, parked next to him.

"Step it up!" Vic said.

Dan inserted the key and started his car. Vic tapped the window with his gun. Dan lowered it and Vic leaned into the driver's door, resting his gun on the frame. For an instant Dan contemplated grabbing it, but he was distracted when he saw that Percy had vanished.

They must've parked their vehicle nearby.

"Remember," Vic said, "all you have to do is follow our instructions. You're doing good so far. It'll be over before you know it, so don't mess this up. We're watching you every step of the way. Now get going."

As Vic stepped away from the car, Dan backed out of the driveway and wheeled down the street. The vest was hot and cumbersome. His skin tingled with each bump and pothole for fear the thing might go off.

On the console he saw the receipts from the recent weekend he and Lori had spent in Boston. His chief worries then had been finding good parking and the price of gas. Dan adjusted his grip on the wheel.

What the hell's happening?

He rolled through their corner of Roseoak, a middle-class community of tree-lined streets with Tudor, ranch and Colonial houses. Flanked by Douglaston, Little Neck and Oakland Gardens and bordered by the Long Island Expressway and Grand Central Parkway, Roseoak Park was a desirable enclave of Queens. With good schools and no crime, it was considered a safe place to live.

A clear radio voice sounded in his ear.

"Looking good, Dan."

He checked his mirrors in an effort to spot their vehicle. But there was nothing to see. It was futile.

"Stick to the plan and no one gets hurt, Dan."

Dan prayed that Lori and Billy were still safe—or as safe as they could be wrapped with a bomb—and racked his brain for a way out.

Glancing in vain in his rearview mirror, he wondered again who they were—and why they'd chosen him. He crawled through traffic, knowing he had little time to act.

I could drive to the police—go right to the 111th Precinct in Bayside. Tell them everything!

He thought of Lori and Bill, and how Vic had vowed to kill them.

If I go to the police I could save them.

Sweat trickled from his temple, nearing his eye.

Or...I could kill us all.

6

Kate Page stood on the southbound platform of the 125th Street subway station.

Waiting for the next train to get her to Midtown and Newslead, the global news service where she was a reporter, she reviewed the messages on her phone again and let out a long breath.

She hadn't even set foot in the newsroom, but her exchange a few minutes ago with Reeka Beck, her editor, had already set the stage for a bad day.

You're covering the conference of security experts at the Grand Hyatt for us today, Reeka had texted her.

But Chuck told me I was clear to enterprise today.

Change of plan. A lot going on today. Randy Kent's wife went into labor, so you're going to the Hyatt this afternoon.

What about Hugh? He's backup on security?

It's you, today. End of discussion.

The tunnel grumbled with distant vibrations of the approaching train. Its bright headlights shot from darkness as it rattled into the station. With a rush of hot, dank air, the brakes squealed and the train came to a stop. The doors opened. Kate boarded and found a seat under the large MTA subway map and ads for the addictions hotline and STD awareness.

As the train rolled south, Kate resumed panning for a story. For the past few weeks she'd been trying to nail down some long-shot leads, one about stolen satellite technology and one on human trafficking. She didn't have much on either of them, and she'd wanted to pursue them today, unless something fresh broke. She'd sent out some notes to a few trusted sources to see if anything new was going on, but the messages that trickled back were not promising. Kate looked up from her silent phone, wishing for a good story.

It's Deadsville out there.

She could not escape the fact that times were tough in the news business. More and more newspapers were shedding jobs. Newslead was losing subscribers, and rumors of cutbacks were swirling. But as the train grated and swayed, she did her best to stay positive. Whatever happened, she would survive.

I made it this far.

Kate stared at her translucent reflection in the window as the drab tunnel walls rushed by, pulling her back through her life. She was a thirty-one-year-old single mom with an eight-year-old daughter. Kate had been seven years old when her mother and father died in a hotel fire. After the tragedy, Kate and her little sister, Vanessa, had lived with relatives and then in foster homes. A couple of years later, Kate and Vanessa's foster parents had taken them on a vacation to Canada. They were in British Columbia, driving through the Canadian Rockies, when their car spun out, flipped over and crashed into a river.

The images of that moment were seared in Kate's mind.

The car sinking...the windows breaking...the icy water...grabbing Vanessa's hand...pulling her free...to the surface...the frigid current numbing her body...fingers loosening...Vanessa slipping away...disappearing...

Kate was the only one who'd survived.

They'd found the bodies of Kate's foster parents, but Vanessa's body was never recovered. The search team reasoned that it got wedged in the rocks downriver, but Kate never gave up believing that Vanessa had somehow escaped the rushing water.

She never gave up searching for her.

After the tragedy, Kate had bounced through foster homes, eventually running away for good. She spent her teen years on the street, taking any job she could find to put herself through college, where she'd studied journalism. She'd worked in newsrooms across the country. Then, in San Francisco, she'd had a baby girl by a man who'd lied to her about being married and had written her off when he'd found out she was pregnant.

Kate named her daughter Grace and raised her on her own in Ohio where she'd worked at a newspaper in Canton, before downsizing cost her that job. But she hung on. She found a short-term reporting position in Dallas, and now here she was: a national correspondent at one of the world's largest news organizations.

I've come a long way, and I never, ever, give up.

The proof smiled back at her from the photo on her phone's screen.

Grace and Vanessa.

Kate blinked at them.

It nearly cost her everything, but eventually she'd found Vanessa.

Kate smiled to herself. It'd been a year since she'd had her sister back in her life, living with her and Grace. Vanessa was a fighter. She'd made remarkable progress with her therapy; she was going to school and working part-time as a waitress. Last month Kate and Vanessa finished a book on their lost years, Kate's search for her and their reunion. It was titled *Echo in My Heart: A Relentless Story of Love, Loss and Survival*, and it was going to be released in the fall.

We're doing okay. We're living our lives.

Kate was also blessed to have Nancy Clark in her life. The retired and widowed nurse lived alone on the floor above them. Ever since Kate had moved into the building, she and Nancy had become more than neighbors. Nancy had never had any children of her own and had opened her heart to Kate, Grace and Vanessa. She was so kind and warm she'd practically adopted the three of them, insisting on helping them whenever she could.

A steely scraping pierced Kate's ears and the train decelerated. The blurring dark tunnels were quickly replaced by the bright tiles of the platform walls of Penn Station.

She stepped off, remembering to breathe through her mouth and avoid inhaling the humid, musty air while navigating the pandemonium of the crushing commuter crowds. Kate had become adept at threading her way through the vast low-ceilinged warren, up to the doors and outside.

She'd surfaced in front of Madison Square Garden, across from the post office, when her phone vibrated. A man bumped her, snickering something, when she stopped to read a message from a source, a detective with the NYPD.

Nothing going on, he texted. But stay on your toes. Never know what's coming around the corner.

That was it.

Kate put her phone away and hurried toward Newslead's world headquarters, a few blocks away in a fifty-story office tower on Manhattan's far West Side.

7

Roseoak Park, New York

Dan stopped at a red light two blocks from his bank, paralyzed with indecision.

Then he saw the cop.

A white guy, mid-twenties, sipping coffee from a take-out cup behind the wheel of an NYPD car in the opposite lane.

Drive into the intersection! Now! Block him and tell him!

As Dan tightened his grip on the wheel, Vic hissed in his ear.

"We see that cop, too, Dan. Don't try anything stupid. You've got a lot of lives in your hands right now. You want to risk killing Lori and Billy?"

Dan hesitated.

He heard shuffling in his ear, and then Lori's voice filled his ear.

"Dan, oh God! If you can hear me, please, do what they say!"

"Lori! Lori, did they hurt you?"

More shuffling, then Billy: "Dad, please, do what they want!"

"Billy! Are you okay?"

A beat passed, and Vic's voice returned.

"You heard them, Dan. Just stick to the plan, and no one gets hurt."

The light turned green.

Dan's pulse was hammering as his foot twitched on the brake pedal.

The cop rolled through the intersection and down the street in the opposite direction. A horn tapped behind Dan, and he continued driving, dragging the back of his hand across his brow as he let out a breath.

Moments later he came to Branch 487 for Sky-National Trust Banking Corp., a small one-story building constructed in neo-art-deco style. Its floor-to-ceiling glass walls gleamed in the morning sun, with a curving clean-lined flat roof extending over the three drive-through ATMs. The property was bordered with shrubs, plants and flowers that were professionally maintained. SkyNational had given Dan awards for exemplary management of his branch.

He turned into his usual parking spot. The lot was empty except for the two cars of the staff who'd arrived first and were in charge of opening. Dan was versed in branch opening procedures and ensured his people complied with, and adhered to, all security standards of the Bank Protection Act.

The bank's policy required two people to arrive at the same time for opening. First, they scanned the area for anything suspicious. Then the first employee entered while the second one stayed in the car, waiting for an all-clear signal or cell phone call. These steps guarded against "morning-glory robberies," whereby criminals lay in wait for staff prior to opening.

Once it was safe to proceed, the two staff members used the dual control system to open the vault and obtain daily cash boxes for the tellers. Then they opened the night depository and collected the overnight deposits. An armored security company collected deposits from the ATMs. Aside from a few additional matters, those were the key steps before unlocking the front doors for daily business.

Until today, the branch had never been robbed.

"Time's ticking!" Vic said. "Get your ass in there!"

Dan grabbed his briefcase. Heading across the lot to the rear entrance, he heard a metallic clanking and looked up at the flag poles. The Stars and Stripes, the state flag and SkyNational's corporate flag waved dutifully in the breeze.

At the door's lockbox, he swiped his manager's card and pressed his security code on the keypad.

Nothing happened.

His hands were a bit shaky. He took a breath, repeated the process. The door opened, and he was greeted with the aroma of fresh coffee.

"Morning, Dan." Annie Trippe, the head teller and soon-to-be assistant manager, smiled from behind the counter where she was topping up supplies for tellers.

"Annie."

"Hi, Dan," Jo Ballinger called out. Jo, one of his best tellers, was arranging an assortment of pastries the branch offered to morning customers.

"Morning, Jo."

Dan glanced around. They would open the doors in twenty minutes.

"How'd your opening go, guys?" he asked.

"Tickety-boo," Jo said. "All tickety-boo. Except…"

"Except what?"

"These 6:00 a.m. openings are killers, Dan."

"I know." He smiled sympathetically, trying to look as natural as possible. "But central selected us to be a pilot branch. It's all about serving the needs of our early-bird commuters. Now, I've got some urgent business to take care of, then I have to step out."

Annie's head shot up, and she took a longer look at Dan as he headed for his office.

"Hold on, there, Dan. What happened to you?"

"What?"

Annie touched her temple indicating where Dan had a large bandage.

"Knocked my head against the door. Getting clumsier, I guess."

The concern on Annie's face was slow to melt as Dan shrugged and stepped into his office. He switched on the lights, set his briefcase down on his desk and logged into his computer.

Vic's voice rumbled quietly in his ear. "You're doing good so far, Dan."

He immediately set to work, his keyboard clicking as he typed, but he stopped when a shadow fell over him, followed by the soft thud of a ceramic mug of coffee set on his desk.

Annie stood before him.

"What's going on, Dan? You don't look so good."

He licked his lips, aware that Vic would hear and see everything.

"Shut the door," he told her.

"Careful, Dan," Vic reminded him.

After closing the door, Annie turned to him. She was in her midforties, with high cheekbones, dark eyes and a warm smile. Her husband was a fire captain, and her son was starting Hunter College. Annie had been with SkyNational fifteen years. She was devoted, dedicated—an intelligent woman who was not easily fooled.

"Something's up, Dan. What is it?"

"This is completely off the record and stays between you and me."

"Of course. What is it?"

"It's South Branch—seems Mort's got a little crisis."

"Odd. Mort's such a perfectionist. What sort of crisis?"

"His cash inventory is low, so I'm issuing a directive to transfer two hundred and fifty thousand from our vault to South Branch, which I will personally deliver to them this morning."

"You can't be serious!"

"Believe me, it has to be done this way." He input several commands, and his printer came to life. "I'll need you to cosign the directive."

Dan grabbed the pages and his pen.

"What you're doing isn't right," Annie said. "We use armored car services for interbranch transfers. They're directed by the Central Branch. Dan, there are strict rules for this. You know that. Mort has to call Central with his inventory issue. Besides, this would drain us. It makes no sense."

"This is an emergency, Annie." He put the directive in a file folder and hunched over it slightly as he signed it. All the while he kept his head up, looking at her. "Believe me, you'll understand later why I had to do this." He closed the folder on the paperwork, turned it over to her and, leaving it on the desk with the pen, stood and picked up his briefcase. "Please cosign it after you read it carefully. I have to go."

"No, I won't sign it." She turned from the desk without looking at the folder. "This isn't right. Dan, wait!"

Dan went to the vault, opened his briefcase and began filling the duffel bag with bundles of cash, pausing to look at them and mentally counting.

"Dan, please, stop, I don't understand what you're doing! Tell me what's going on."

Just as Dan was scrambling to come up with something to tell her, Vic whispered, "Tell her it's a security exercise, that she's not technically supposed to know anything and that she'll get a call fifteen minutes after you leave."

"Listen to me." Dan dropped his voice, continuing to load the bag. "This is part of a secret security drill. Everything's all right. You'll get a call from security fifteen minutes after I leave."

Annie's face creased with fearful disbelief.

Dan zipped the bag, hoisted it over his shoulder, left the vault and strode out the rear entrance to his car.

8

Roseoak Park, New York

Annie Trippe stood inside the bank's rear door.

She watched her manager drive away, her hands pressed against her mouth and tears stinging her eyes. She jumped when someone touched her shoulder from behind.

"Annie, are you all right?" Jo asked.

Shaking her head and regaining most of her composure, Annie turned.

"Something's very wrong with Dan."

"I got the feeling something wasn't right. What's going on?"

"He just walked out of here with a bag full of cash—a quarter million."

"Are you serious?"

"He was talking about low inventory at South Branch, made a transfer directive for me to sign, then said something about a security drill."

Jo's brow creased. "But…none of that makes any sense."

"I know." Annie pulled herself to her full height,

looked around the empty lobby and took charge. "We've got to do something—fast. Jo, don't open the front doors until I tell you."

Annie hurried to her desk, picked up her phone and called Dan's cell phone. As it continued to ring, she tried to come up with a reasonable explanation for what he'd just done. He clearly wasn't himself, and she hoped she could get him to come back to the branch before things escalated any further.

When his voice mail picked up, Annie called Dan's home and got the same result.

Her mind racing, she pulled up Dan's full contact information, hoping she'd have some luck with his wife's cell phone.

Maybe Lori knows what's happening. Maybe she can help.

It rang through to voice mail. Out of options and out of time, Annie called one more number.

"SkyNational, South Branch. How may I direct your call?"

"Sally, its Annie Trippe at Roseoak."

"Hey, kiddo."

"Is Mort there? I need to speak to him, now."

"He's got someone in his office."

"Can you just get him on the line, Sally—please!"

"I will, dear, just as soon as he's free."

"No! I need to talk to him now!"

"Whoa, what's going—"

"I'm sorry, Sally. Just, please, get Mort. It's an emergency."

Annie heard a few muffled voices, then the line clicked.

"Annie, what's going on?" Mort Frederick asked.

"Do you have an inventory issue, and did you ask Dan to personally make an interbranch transfer to you first thing this morning?"

"What the hell? No! Of course not."

"Mort, swear to me."

"I swear! What is this?"

"Are you aware of any secret security exercises, anything involving cash transfers?"

"Hell, no! Annie, what's going on? Where's Danny— Is he there?"

"No!"

"What's this all about?"

"Mort—" Annie's voice broke "—Dan just walked out of the branch with a bag filled with two hundred and fifty thousand!"

"He *what*?" Mort cursed under his breath.

"What do I do?"

"Annie, call the police!"

9

FBI special agent Nick Varner held out his ID to the NYPD officer whose patrol car blocked the entrance to the bank's parking lot.

Marked NYPD units from the 111th Precinct dotted the lot and the area surrounding the SkyNational Trust branch. A heavy-duty response, Varner thought, but then this was Roseoak, middle-class neighbor to upper middle-class Douglaston, with its winding hilly streets and waterfront mansions on Little Neck Bay. The entire region was an appealing, sleepy corner of Queens where not much happened, and residents here wanted it that way.

"Yeah, take it over there, pal," the officer said.

Varner parked his Bureau car, collected his notebook, his recorder and organized his thoughts. He knew the drill. He was thirty-nine and had put in twelve years with the FBI that had included a tour at headquarters in Washington, DC, assignments in Los Angeles, Phoenix and, for the past seven years, the New York Field Office in Manhattan, where he'd been a member of several task forces. Now he was pulling double duty, assigned to Violent Crimes and the Joint Terrorism Task Force.

He sized up the building. Typical suburban detached box. All the blinds had been drawn. A sign had been posted at the front doors. Printed by hand in block letters, it said the branch was closed. It directed customers to the nearest branch and ATMs in the area.

Varner went to the rear entrance and showed his ID to the uniformed officer there. She nodded and handed him some tissue-paper shoe covers. Varner tugged them on and entered.

The lobby was active.

Investigators with the NYPD's Crime Scene Unit were just setting up to go into the vault and start processing it. Two others were talking to a guy in a suit who Varner took to be a bank security chief.

"Nicholas Alfonso Varner. Well, I'll be damned."

Varner found himself shaking hands with a familiar big-chested man in his fifties, a badge hanging from his chain: NYPD detective Marv Tilden. They'd worked together during the final years of the Joint Bank Robbery Task Force before the NYPD pulled out. They'd spent enough long hours as partners for Tilden to know Varner's middle name was Alfonso, and that a few generations back, Varner's family had come to America from Italy. Officials at Ellis Island had changed their name from Varnisanino to Varner.

"Morning, Marvin," Varner said. "You must be close to hanging it up."

"One more lousy winter, then we move to Nevada. Hey, you're alone? You feds never come alone—and you got here pretty fast."

"Traffic was kind to me, and the others are on their way. What do we know?"

"Not a lot. We've barely started."

"What can you tell me?"

Tilden described how Dan Fulton, the branch manager, came to work alone talking up an emergency branch transfer. "Then he violates security procedures, fills a bag with cash and disappears. No GPS, dye packs, transmitters or bait bills."

"The tally?"

"They're still calculating, but it looks like two hundred and fifty thousand, which would just about clean them out of cash inventory."

"What've we done so far?"

"Like I said, we're just getting started. We've alerted the Real Time Crime Center, put out a BOLO for Fulton's car, a 2015 blue Taurus SEL. We're calling on traffic to put people at toll plazas, but that's a resource matter—we can't cover them all. We're checking to see if the car has anything we can maybe get a signal on, like a GPS. And we've got people heading to his house. Whit Tallbreck, SkyNational's security guy, is just getting his legal department's blessing to volunteer the cameras, and he's got people pulling Fulton's file. We already ran him and nothing lights up."

"What'd you think, Marv? Duress, drugs, debt—
he just flip out?"

"Any of the above. Look—" Tilden nodded to
a desk in a far corner "—my partner, Betsy Men-
delson, is talking to one of the two tellers who
were here when it happened. I'm about to interview the other one. Why don't you join me, be like
old times?"

Annie Trippe sat alone in the lunchroom at the
back of the bank.

She was holding a mug of hot tea to keep from
shaking. When she wasn't dabbing her eyes with a
tissue, she traced the words *World's Best Mom* on
her mug between glances at the staff bulletin board
next to the fridge. It was feathered with notes, self-
ies from vacations and a group shot from the tug-
of-war for charity.

Dan Fulton was smiling with his arm around her.

Looking at it, Annie's lower lip started to trem-
ble.

"Hello again," Tilden said as he entered the
room. He held out an arm toward another man
Annie hadn't met yet. "This is Nick Varner with
the FBI. We'd like to talk to you about what happened."

Chairs scraped as the two men sat opposite
Annie at the table. They flipped through their notebooks to clear pages, logged the time and copied
Annie's information from her driver's license before starting their recorders.

"Can you start by giving us a time line and step-by-step account of your actions?"

Annie steeled herself then related details of the morning; how she and Jo Ballinger arrived, followed branch opening procedures and what had transpired when Fulton got in. Varner and Tilden took notes, nodded, asked occasional questions.

"Everything was by the book and routine until Dan arrived."

"And you say he seemed a little off center?" Tilden asked.

"Anxious, distracted, troubled even."

They made a note.

"And he insisted you violate policy with the transfer directive that he'd created on his computer and demanded you sign it after reading it carefully?" Varner asked.

Annie nodded.

"Did you read it?" Varner asked.

"No. It was a policy violation and I refused to sign it."

"Where's this directive?" Varner asked.

"Still on his desk in his office, I think."

"Did your people look at it, Marv?" Varner asked.

Tilden's chair scraped as he stood and left the room. A short time later he returned wearing latex gloves, a file folder in one hand and the transfer directive in the other. He looked grim as he laid the printed form on the table for them. Annie went still as she read the note Dan had scrawled on the signature line: *Family held hostage at home! Strapped bombs on us!*

She suddenly felt sick, but before she could say anything, Tilden reached for his phone.

"We need ESU on the Fulton house ASAP!"

10

Roseoak Park, New York

It's almost over. Stay calm.

Dan's scalp was prickling as he drove back toward his house.

The bag with cash sat on the passenger floor. He'd done exactly what they'd forced him to do. He'd walked into his own branch and robbed it.

Now this nightmare can end. They've got to release Lori and Billy. You just need to get home.

He'd expected further instructions when he'd gotten back in the car, but Dan had heard nothing from Vic since he'd left the bank.

"Hello?" Dan said aloud. "I've got your money."

Nothing but silence, making him worry their communication system had malfunctioned. He gently pressed the arm of his glasses to his ear.

"Are you there? Look, I did what you wanted. I've got your money. You've got to release my wife and son, now!"

Silence.

As the shaded boulevards of Roseoak rolled past,

Dan's mind raced with images of what had happened and scenarios of what may be playing out. He pictured Annie at the bank, how he'd shocked her, how he'd hated seeing her grappling with unthinkable events.

I know she'll come through.

Annie was smart, and she was strong. He trusted and believed she'd know what to do.

She'll find my message. She has to.

In the bank he'd been careful not to lower his head, pulling the directive close to his chest so it was out of the camera's view as he wrote. He imagined Annie and Jo finding it, making calls, showing it to police, and people jumping into action to help.

Maybe that's why no one is answering, he thought hopefully.

Maybe police had raced to his house and rescued Billy and Lori. Maybe they'd arrested Vic and the others. Would it happen that fast? He had no way of knowing. They'd taken his cell phone, and it would be too dangerous to call, anyway.

Still, Dan couldn't convince himself that he was off the hook. He grew anxious about what he'd done at the bank.

Maybe I shouldn't have left the note. Maybe they know, maybe they saw and—

"You did good," Vic said.

"I've got your money! Now release my family!"

"We're not done, Dan. I need you to pull into the Empire Coastal Mall up ahead."

"Why?"

"Do it, right now!"

Empire was one of the state's largest malls, and the marquee for the north entrance towered just ahead of the traffic light. Dan got in the turning lane.

"Go to zone fourteen. Park near the lamppost with green flags."

Fourteen was the outermost zone, far from the congested parking lanes closer to the mall. Not many people had parked here. A few abandoned shopping carts kept a lonely vigil. After Dan parked, Vic told him to turn his car off, leave the keys and grab the duffel bag filled with cash.

"See that green Chevy in the lane directly across from you? It's unlocked, the key's inside. Get in."

Dan remained frozen where he stood.

Alone in the lot with the heavy bag, he considered running into the mall for help. For the hundredth time this morning he wondered if he should end it here. There was always a chance they'd been bluffing the whole time. Maybe they never intended to kill anyone. Maybe the bombs weren't real. But could he risk it? What if it backfired? Could he live with himself if they killed Lori and Billy because he screwed up?

"Get in the Chevy now, Dan!"

Reaching the car, he opened the front passenger door, dropped the bag on the floor, then walked around and got in behind the wheel.

He noticed the faint hint of men's cologne and cigarettes. The car's interior appeared to have been cleaned, as if all traces of the previous user were hastily obliterated. There were gouges and scratches around the ignition switch, some wires were hanging down. A single key had been inserted into the switch.

It's a stolen car!

Dan's fear suddenly deepened—Vic and his crew were not planning to end this soon. This meant they wanted something more.

"Start the car, Dan."

"No. Please… I—I've got your money! Just take it, release my family and leave us alone."

"Start. The. Damn. Car. Now!"

Dan hesitated.

"Don't test us, Dan!"

The Chevy's motor came to life.

"That was smart. Now drive back to the street, get on to the Cross Island Parkway north to the Throgs Neck Bridge."

"Why?"

"We're not done, yet."

"Yes, we are! I've got your money, and I'm driving home to give it to you!"

"Get on the parkway now!"

"No. I've got your money! You're going to take it and release my family!"

A long moment of silence passed before Dan wheeled back to the street, but he didn't head to the Cross Island Parkway. Instead, he headed home.

"Where're Lori and Billy? I want to talk to them!"

"You're disobeying us, Dan. There'll be consequences."

"You already killed them, didn't you?"

Silence.

"Put them on, or I swear I'll ram this car into a bus!"

Still nothing from Vic.

Sweating, gasping for air, Dan searched the streets, the strip malls, the corner store, the retirement home, the gas station and the houses as he passed by. People were just going about their daily lives while he was barely hanging on to his, helpless to do anything.

Suddenly his vest vibrated, and his entire body contracted. He gripped the wheel as hard as he could, preparing for the explosion, to be blown to pieces, thinking of Lori, of Billy.

Nothing happened, but the vibration continued.

Like a ringing phone.

He moved a trembling hand from the wheel and felt around the vest until he noticed the spot where a phone had been sewn in.

He was still alive. Nothing had happened. The phone kept humming.

Then it stopped.

"Do we have your attention, Dan?"

"Yes."

"That was a little test. The next time you feel that vibration, you'll know your life is about to end. Now, unless you'd like to feel that right away, you're going to do as we say and get your ass north on the Cross Island Parkway to Throgs Neck."

Dan's body was numb as he turned and made his way to Northern Boulevard, merging with the northbound traffic on the expressway. As the parkway hugged the western shore of Little Neck Bay, he searched the expanse of water for answers while praying for his wife and son.

11

Throgs Neck Bridge, New York

Not knowing what had happened to Lori and Billy tore Dan up as his Chevy Impala ascended the approach to Throgs Neck Bridge, which connected Queens with the Bronx. One of the three northbound lanes was under construction, blocked with orange cones. He got into the middle lane and watched his speed.

He looked at New Rochelle's skyline in the distance, then up at the bridge tower rising above him. Sections of the deck clicked under his wheels with regular cadence, like time ticking away on a clock.

Ticking down on us.

Dan dragged the back of his hand across his sweaty face, thinking of Lori and Billy in their vests, feeling the bulk of his own, his fear and anger broiling with a desire to tear it off, to fight back. He looked out at the East River more than one hundred and fifty feet below and begged God to help him, to keep Lori and Billy alive so he could find some way out of this.

He knew Lori would never give up. She'd protect Billy with her life. In his heart he knew that she was a fighter, a survivor, that despite what had happened to her in California, she'd overcome the odds. In the years since they'd moved to New York, Dan had watched over her and stood by her, ready to catch her if she stumbled.

The worst is behind us.

That's what he'd always told her. The worst is behind *us*, not *you*. Because what had happened to Lori, happened to him. It's how he felt about everything in their marriage.

Lean on me. Let me take this on with you.

Lori had done well. She'd had good days and bad days, but mostly good ones.

The worst is behind us.

At least it was. Until this.

Dan felt panic rising to the surface as he took in the sweep of the bridge, the water and the sky.

God, please, keep them alive!

The toll plaza was just ahead, but Dan didn't have a pass. As he slowed and guided his car into a cash lane, his pulse raced with a mixture of dread and hope.

License plate readers!

He remembered a report in the *Daily News* that police had installed license plate recognition technology at most toll plazas. They were using cameras that read license plates and checked them instantly against databases with hot lists of wanted plates.

Dan studied the gates. Did they have plate readers here?

As he crawled ahead in his line, he fumbled in his wallet for money.

"Don't try anything here," Vic said into his ear. "We're watching you, and you know what will happen."

Dan let out a slow breath. The thought of them detonating his vest here sent a chill up his spine. It would end any chance to save Lori and Billy. And innocent people would die.

He was now one car from the booth. Gripping a folded ten-dollar bill in his hand, he prayed that his plates would come up as stolen, alerting police, helping them get closer.

Thud!

Dan's head snapped back. His car had been rear-ended.

After taking a moment to assess that he wasn't hurt, he got out.

"I'm so sorry! Are you okay?" A woman in her twenties came toward him gripping a cell phone, her face reddening. She stared at Dan, then at the area where her Toyota was pressed against the bumper of his Impala.

"Sir," the toll officer said. "I'm going to need you to drive through."

Dan noticed a baby in the rear of the woman's car, strapped in its car seat.

"Get back in your car!" Vic ordered Dan.

"I guess, do you want my insurance and stuff?" The woman was now in tears. "It was my fault. I'm so sorry."

Horns were sounding behind them.

"People—" the toll officer had stepped from his booth "—return to your cars. We need to keep this line moving. You can sort this out after going through the gate. Just move over to the right shoulder."

"Get in your car, Dan!" Vic said. "We'll kill everybody—you, her and her baby!"

"I don't see any damage," Dan said to the woman, wanting to get everyone out of danger as quickly as possible.

"Really? Are you sure? Let me pull my car back a bit, so you can have a better look."

"Ma'am, do not back up," the toll officer interrupted.

"I think we're okay," Dan said.

"Oh, thank you! Thank you! I've been having the worst morning!"

Dan handed the toll officer his cash.

"Keep the change," he said, getting back in his car.

The officer returned to his booth, and the bar lifted for Dan to pass through.

"Good," Vic said. "Now get on the Cross Bronx Expressway to the George Washington Bridge to New Jersey."

Dan accelerated and merged with the traffic, his heart hammering.

"I'm cooperating, okay? You can see I won't

make trouble. Will you please let me talk to my family again?"

Vic didn't respond.

12

Newslead was located in one of the city's largest skyscrapers, a modern glass structure rising over Penn Station in the Hudson Yards area of Manhattan.

Tenants in the recently renovated building included the head offices of a TV network, a cosmetics chain, a fashion house, a brokerage firm and an advertising agency.

Kate swiped her ID through one of the main floor security turnstiles and joined the flow of workers to the banks of elevators. She stepped out at Newslead's world headquarters on the fortieth floor. Each time she walked through reception she was inspired. The walls displayed enlarged news photos captured by Newslead photographers of history's most dramatic moments from the past half century.

Those powerful images stood as testament to the fact that even though Kate's industry faced challenging times, Newslead remained a formidable force as one of the globe's largest news operations.

It operated a bureau in every major US city and some one hundred fifty bureaus in one hundred countries around the world, supplying a continual flow of fast, accurate information to thousands of newspapers, radio, TV, corporate and online subscribers everywhere.

Its track record for reporting excellence had earned it countless awards, including twenty Pulitzers. It was highly regarded by its chief rivals across the country, including the Associated Press, Bloomberg, Reuters, the World Press Alliance and the new Signal Point Newswire. It also competed with those organizations globally, along with Agence France-Presse, Deutsche Presse-Agentur, China's Xinhua News Agency and Russia's Interfax News Agency.

Corporate offices took up half of the fortieth floor, and the newsroom occupied the rest with a grid of low-walled cubicles. Above them were flat-screen monitors tuned to 24/7 news networks around the world.

Kate looked fondly at the glass enclosure tucked in one corner—the scanner room, or what some called "the torture chamber." It was where a news assistant, usually a journalism intern desperate to pay their dues, was assigned to listen to more than a dozen emergency radio scanners.

Kate, like most seasoned reporters, knew that scanners were the lifeblood of any news organization.

Students were trained on how to listen, decipher and translate the stream of coded transmissions and squawking cross talk blaring from the radios of police, fire, paramedic and other emergency services. They knew how to pluck a key piece of data that signaled a breaking story, how to detect the hint of stress in a dispatcher's voice or the significance of a partial transmission, and how to follow it up instantly before alerting the news desk. Scanners were sacred. They alerted you to the first cries for help, pulling you into a story that could stop the heart of a city.

Or break it.

Kate had spent long hours listening to scanners. She smiled at the softened sound of chaos from the torture chamber as she walked through the newsroom, which was bordered by the glass-walled offices of senior editors. On her way to her desk she paid silent respect to those that were still empty, a cruel reminder that staff had been let go in recent years as the business struggled to stem the flow of revenue losses.

The plain truth was that people were now relying on other online sources for information. While much of it was inaccurate and lacked the quality of a credible, professional news organization, it came free, which seemed to be more important these days.

As Kate settled into her desk, she took stock of the newsroom with some apprehension. She'd sensed tension in the air. Some reporters and editors were huddled in small groups. A few people appeared concerned.

Kate did a quick survey of the suspended TVs.

Nothing seemed to be breaking. Then a shadow crossed her computer monitor.

"There you are." Reeka Beck had approached her from behind, head bowed over her phone as she typed.

"Good morning. How are you?"

"Fine." A message popped up in Kate's inbox—it was from Reeka. As discussed earlier, we'd like a story out of the security conference at the Grand Hyatt this afternoon. I suggest you get in touch with Professor Randall Rees-Goodman, who's attending from Georgetown University. Reeka tapped Kate's screen with her pen. "I just sent you his information. He's an expert on current threats in the geopolitical context."

"I know, but like I said before, I really think Hugh's better for this. And besides, Chuck cleared me to enterprise. I need to put in some time following up some leads I'm working on."

Reeka's thumbs move furiously over her keyboard as she dispatched another text from her phone, then she lifted her head. She blinked and smiled her perfect smile at Kate.

"This is the assignment I've given you. Are you refusing it?"

"No."

"I didn't think so. Thank you."

Kate cursed to herself as Reeka pivoted on her heel and walked away. Reeka was a young, rising star of an editor at Newslead, but she was so curt and officious with reporters that it bordered on rudeness. Every conversation with her was nearly a confrontation.

Reeka's boss, Chuck Laneer, the man who'd hired Kate to cover and break crime stories, was a battle-scarred veteran. Chuck was gruff but wise. He could kick your ass while showing you respect. Moreover, where Reeka pathologically adhered to filling a news budget, Chuck believed in the value of letting reporters dig for stories.

"Hey, Kate, you heard about Chuck?"

Thane Dolan, an assistant editor, had emerged at her desk.

"No, I just got in."

"He resigned this morning."

"No way!"

"Rumor is he's gone to head news at Yahoo or Google."

"I don't believe this! That's terrible."

"That means young Reeka likely moves up a notch."

Kate shut her eyes for a long moment.

"Say it ain't so. Thane, what're we gonna do?"

"No idea. It's a big loss."

"Monumental. Chuck hired me, you know."

"Everybody loves the guy."

Kate and Thane were soon joined by Craig Kryzer, the newsroom intern assigned to monitor the scanners.

"Excuse me…" He was gripping a notebook. "Um, something's happening on the scanners, and I'm not sure who to tell. I can't find Chuck."

"Go ahead, Craig," Kate said.

"There was a lot of chatter, and I confirmed much of this with 111th Precinct in Queens."

"Get to it," Thane said.

"They're sending ESU—you know, the SWAT team—to a bank manager's home in Queens. They think there's a hostage situation."

"What, like a domestic?" Kate asked.

"No, there was talk that this guy robbed his own bank this morning, a SkyNational Trust branch."

"Holy crap! You got an address?" Kate said.

"Yep. It's 3222 Forest Trail Drive in Roseoak Park."

"Gabe!" Thane shouted to a news photographer, then pointed to Kate, who was struggling with her bag and jacket and trotting out of the newsroom. "Go with Kate! We've got a story breaking in Queens!"

13

Queens, New York

Sergeant Paul Roman put two crumpled dollar bills on the counter at Spiro's Café, took his takeout coffee outside, lifted the lid and blew gently on the surface.

Today was his last shift before his vacation. Once he punched out, he and his wife would fly to Miami for a one-week Caribbean cruise. He'd hoped to spend most of his day finishing off paperwork at the office.

So far, so good, he thought. Then his phone rang.

"Paulie, its Walsh. We got one in Roseoak Park. Bank manager just robbed his own branch—his family's being held hostage at their home. We need you to get there."

Roman took a second to absorb what his lieutenant had said.

"Where're they setting up?"

"Forest Trail Drive and Maple. I'm sending you details now."

"On my way."

"One thing you should know—the family's possibly rigged with explosives."

Roman's eyes widened.

Explosives.

A hostage negotiator with the NYPD's Emergency Services Unit, Roman was assigned to ESU Squad 10. It covered the territory known as Queens North, out of the 109th Precinct in Flushing. Squad 10 would be rolling to the scene now, he knew. The bomb squad would be on its way, as well. As Roman cut across the borough he took several hits of coffee and began a mental review of his situation checklist.

You only get one shot to do things right.

Some forty-five minutes after the call, Squad 10's big white equipment truck creaked to a halt at a small park at Maple Street and Forest Trail Drive, joining the cluster of other emergency vehicles.

The location was nine doors down the curved street from the Fultons' address. Just out of sight of the house, it served as the tactical command post. A dozen ESU SWAT team members, each wearing helmets, armor, headset walkie-talkies, and equipped with rifles and handguns, huddled at the command post, checking and rechecking gear.

As the commanders developed a strategy, marked units established the outer perimeter. Officers choked off traffic at all access points to Forest Trail Drive. They consulted driver's license photos of Dan and Lori Fulton, recorded plates and checked vehicles leaving, or attempting to enter the hot zone.

Other officers began quietly evacuating neighbors, taking them behind the yellow taped lines, ensuring they were clear of the blast radius and line of fire. Everything was done through back doors and side entrances to ensure nothing was visible from the Fultons' windows.

Without making a sound, four SWAT team members scouted the area surrounding the house and garage. The stillness held an eerie quiet, conveying a false sense of calm. They deployed an extension mirror to peer into the house and they used a stethoscope device placed carefully against the walls and window to pick up voices or activity.

They detected no movement.

They did the same for the garage and detected no activity.

The scouts were ordered to pull back.

Inside the command post truck, hostage negotiator Paul Roman watched Wilfred Walsh, the tactical commander, study a floor plan of the Fultons' home, hastily sketched from memory by a shaken next door neighbor.

"Okay, so here's what we know," Walsh said to the other investigators, huddled in the truck. "Dan Fulton, manager of the SkyNational Trust Branch 487, takes a bag of cash from his bank and drives away after leaving a note that reads, 'Family held hostage at home! Strapped bombs on us!'

"That's all we have, so far. We've been unable to

locate Dan Fulton. His wife, Lori Fulton, has not shown up for work. Billy Fulton's not at school. We've been unable to contact anyone in the house. We've got no movement or visuals of people in the house. But that does not mean we don't have people inside. Until we clear the property, we will regard it as still hot."

"Absolutely," Mac Hirsch, lieutenant for the bomb squad, said. "We regard everything as an explosive, unless my people confirm otherwise."

They reviewed options. Using selective sniper fire was ruled out, for the time being. There were no clear targets. Other options: a blitz assault with flash bangs, or unleashing chemicals into the house.

SWAT commander Kevin Haggerty objected.

"I'm not sending my people in there until we know it's clear of bombs."

"All right, there's one alternative—Kevin, you get your people to breach the door, and we'll send in the robot to search the house and drop a phone, so Roman, here, can start negotiations with whoever's in there. We've got to try to resolve this peacefully."

The bomb squad's robot was controlled remotely and equipped with a camera to transmit live feed to the technician manipulating it. It moved with the speed of a tortoise, its tracks humming and whizzing as it took its position at the front door, waiting like a mechanized alien visitor.

The SWAT team surrounded the entrance, weapons at the ready, as one member used a crowbar to pry the door open. The cracking of the frame echoed in the deserted neighborhood. The robot hummed over the debris, toddled inside and the SWAT team retreated.

The video pictures were sharp and clear.

The detective operating the robot used its speaker system, calling on anyone inside to surrender to the NYPD. Roman watched the video feed over the detective's shoulder and prepared himself.

He glanced at his phone and the photos of Lori, Dan and Billy Fulton intel had provided him. Dan was a good-looking suburban dad, Lori had an attractive smile, and Billy, in his ball cap with Dad at Yankee Stadium, was the all-American kid.

The safety of the hostages was Roman's chief concern. He'd need to find common ground with the hostage taker—*was it Dan, who'd cracked under pressure? Or was someone else involved?* Roman would work fast to establish credibility and trust, then find the cause of the problem. He needed to reduce all the risks. He'd never lie, but he wouldn't be quick to reveal the whole truth. He'd need to keep the hostage taker's mind off harming the hostages or himself. He'd probe the problem, let the hostage taker vent. Roman would use a tone of concern, not authority, to reduce anxieties. Above all, he'd be careful to address any immediate needs and keep hope alive for everyone.

He would never forget Pruitt, a negotiator in the Bronx who badly misread his situation when a distraught father took his wife and four kids hostage. After seven hours, Pruitt was convinced the SWAT team didn't need to go in because he'd resolved it when the father agreed, saying: "There's only one way outta this." Pruitt missed the signal and the standoff ended with the dad killing the family before putting a bullet in his head. Pruitt never forgave himself, and six months later ended his own life.

Roman had been a pallbearer.

The robot had descended into the basement, searched it but found nothing. Now it was moving through the living room and the kitchen, sending back live images of the table, the fridge and the calendar on the corkboard, marked with game dates and a note: *Billy dentist.* Then it lumbered up the stairs to slowly inspect the bedrooms and bathrooms, before returning to the main floor, placing a phone there.

"If you are concealed in this house, the NYPD wants to talk to you. This phone will ring shortly. We advise you to answer."

The robot exited.

The tactical commander nodded to the SWAT commander, who dispatched his team.

They moved silently from behind trees, parked cars, house corners. One sniper was flat on his stomach on the roof of the house next door, a bedroom window filling his rifle scope. Another sharpshooter used the hood of an SUV to take a line on a living room window.

Team members crept up tight to the Fultons'

house, the utility man, the breacher, the gas team and other shooters. The squad had taken positions. Members were prone at the front and rear. Each officer knew that the robot could easily have missed bombs, or people, hiding in closets, appliances, walls and ceilings.

The building was still hot.

The squad leader whispered to the command post.

"We're set."

The tactical commander nodded to Roman, who dialed the cell phone. In the stillness, the SWAT team could hear it ringing. And ringing. Roman let it ring twenty-five times.

No one answered.

He turned to the commanders.

Haggerty green-lighted his squad.

"Go!"

Five seconds later the pop-pop and shattering glass sounds of tear gas canisters echoed down the street. White clouds billowed from the main floor, followed by a deafening *crack-crack* and lightning flashes of stun grenades as the SWAT team rushed into the house from both entrances.

Flashlight beams and red-line laser sights pierced the acrid fog. The Darth Vader breathing of the heavily armed and gas-masked squad filled the home as they swept each floor.

In the basement they found used duct tape, chains, a padlock, a pile of sheets, towels and snow tires heaped oddly next to the washer and dryer. In the kitchen, remnants of pizza in a box and empty soda cans littered the table. Upstairs, the beds were unmade. Bedroom number one: empty. Bedroom number two: empty. Bathroom number one: empty. Bathroom number two: empty. Closets: empty. The ceiling, floors and walls were tapped for body mass.

Empty.

No people.

Nothing.

"Looks like somebody was tied up down here, but there ain't nothing here now, sir," the SWAT squad leader in the basement radioed to the command post.

"Okay," Walsh said. "Get the fans in there, clear out the gas. We need Crime Scene working on what they can find for us ASAP."

14

Roseoak Park, New York

Kate spotted the woman.

She was hugging her cat in the back of a police car, amid the tangle of emergency vehicles just inside the tape.

Why have they isolated her? What does she know?

Kate had noticed her from a vantage point outside the line where she and Gabe Atwater, a Newslead photographer, had watched ESU do its work on the house.

"Got some dramatic images." Gabe's face was clenched behind his camera and he was gently rolling its long lens, shooting the SWAT team in the distance.

"Get one of her. In the back of the car, see? Look tight between the vans," Kate said, nodding to the cat lady. "I want to get to her later." She kept an eye on the woman while talking on her phone to Craig in the newsroom. He'd been monitoring ESU's play-by-play on the scanners.

"Sounds like it's winding down," he said. "No one's in the house."

"Okay, thanks."

Kate hung up and gave Gabe the update.

"So the mystery deepens." He'd resumed shooting the SWAT team after a few shots of the cat lady.

"Do you see a name on a mailbox or anything?"

"Nothing."

Kate bit her bottom lip.

Who is this family? Where are they now? And why would a manager rob his own bank?

Thanks to her years as a crime reporter, Kate knew how to read a scene, knew what to glean from it to give her stories depth and accuracy. She'd studied the same textbooks detectives studied to pass their exams. She'd researched and reported on enough homicides, fires, robberies, kidnappings, trials and a spectrum of other crimes to know the anatomy of an investigation.

Police radios that had been muted began crackling again with dispatches leaking from the emergency crews at the outer perimeter. A few dozen residents and rubberneckers from streets nearby had gathered at the line with about a dozen news types clustered at the row of TV cameras.

Kate anticipated that at any moment the perimeter tape would come down, police would rope off the house and the crime scene techs would begin to process it. While the NYPD was all over this, she knew that bank robberies also fell to the FBI's jurisdiction. Investigators would take statements from witnesses, friends and neighbors, getting their accounts here and at the bank, or any other location that was a factor.

Some of the marked units began moving out to let traffic flow as uniformed officers began pulling down the tape.

"It's all over, folks," an officer said, collecting the tape. "All clear, you're free to go."

"What's going on?" A TV reporter, face encased in makeup, had thrust a microphone into the officer's face. "Can you give me a statement?"

"I don't have any information right now."

"Come on, we need a spokesperson on camera!"

"They'll put out a press release later."

Kate and Gabe walked quickly down the street toward the house. Kate was determined to stay ahead of their competition. They'd already overheard other reporters interviewing people, but getting nothing substantial.

"Police just told us to leave."

"We had to get out."

"We don't know who lives down there."

"Not sure what's going on."

"You know more than us."

Kate needed someone who could give her a sense of the family, an idea of what the real story was. She couldn't get to the cat lady in the back of the squad car, which had now moved to a distant stretch of the street.

Something's going on with her.

Kate noticed two uniformed officers were talking to the woman. She'd have to hold off approaching her. Besides, Kate was certain no other press people had seen her so far.

Kate's phone rang and she answered.

"Who told you to go to Queens?" Reeka asked.

"This story was breaking. Didn't Thane tell you?"

"Thane Dolan's not your supervisor. What you have is a local bank robbery, not a national story. I want you to do what I assigned you to do."

"Reeka, the elements here are significant. A bank manager has robbed his own bank and there're indications his family was taken hostage."

A tense silence passed.

"Do you have it confirmed on the record? Is this just another case of someone passing an exaggerated note at a run-of-the-mill robbery?"

"No, I don't have it confirmed yet, but I have a gut feeling—"

"A gut feeling?"

"Reeka, this one's different. Why don't you let me check this out? Unless you want AP or Reuters to break the story?"

Reeka let another few seconds pass.

"All right, you've got a few hours to nail this down. Otherwise you'll be at the Hyatt covering the conference. Is that clear, Kate?"

"Crystalline."

After hanging up, Kate nudged Gabe.

A man and woman had emerged from the curved end of the street, far down where the command post had been. They looked as though they were in their late sixties or early seventies. They went to the driveway of the house directly across from the one the SWAT team had stormed.

"Excuse me," Kate said before anyone else saw them. "Kate Page and Gabe Atwater, we're with Newslead." Kate held up her press ID. "Will you talk to us a minute about what's happened?"

The two people exchanged looks before the woman, bothered by the faint ammonia-like traces of tear gas lingering in the air, fanned her face and said: "Yes, but let's go in the back."

Their backyard had a glorious flower garden with mature oak trees that shaded the lush manicured lawn. A dog emerged to give Kate and Gabe a friendly greeting.

"May I get your names?" Kate asked, starting her recorder and holding her pen over a clean page in her notebook.

The man looked at the notebook and rubbed his chin, adding to the worry etched deeply in his face. Kate couldn't tell if it was the gas, emotion or both, but the woman was fighting tears.

"Do you really need our names?" he asked. "Things are a little unsettling."

"I understand, but in situations like this, people often accuse reporters of making things up. They don't believe we actually talk to real people, like you."

The man looked at the woman. "I don't suppose giving our names could be any worse than what's going on?"

"That's true. I don't care, it's all so horrible." The

woman turned to Kate. "I'm Violet Selway and this is my husband, Ward."

After Kate got her to spell their names, she asked: "Do you know the people next door?"

"Dan and Lori Fulton," Ward said. "They have a son, Billy."

"Any chance you'd know their ages?"

"Well, Billy's nine," Ward said.

"Dan just turned thirty-six," Violet said. "We went to a backyard party for him, and Lori's thirty-four."

"Thanks. What do you think happened?"

Violet shook her head.

"Police asked us the same thing," Ward said. "We don't know anything. Whatever happened must've happened in the night. We didn't see or hear anything. I woke up this morning, and Sam, here, Billy's dog, was in our backyard. I thought it was strange, that he must've got out in the night. I took him with me and went to ring their bell this morning. No one was home. We'll keep Sam with us until we know what's going on."

"How well do you know the Fultons?"

"They're dear friends." Violet's voice quivered. "I drew the inside of their house for police."

"Where do the Fultons work?"

"Dan's the manager of the SkyNational Trust branch, and Lori's a claims adjuster at Dixon Donlevy Mutual Life Insurance."

"What kind of people are they, how would you characterize them?"

"The salt of the earth," Ward said.

"Dan's a family man," Violet said. "Lori's a devoted mom, and young Billy's just a joy."

"Any idea of trouble, stress? Or if anyone would want to harm them?"

"Absolutely not," Ward said.

"What do you think happened?"

"We wish we knew, so we could help," Violet said. "All we know is what police told us."

Kate's radar locked on that as Ward shot his wife a cautionary glance. But Kate remained casual. She was skilled at extracting information.

"That Dan robbed his own bank this morning," Kate said, "and that there was supposedly a hostage situation at his home," she added, inviting the Selways to elaborate. "It's so troubling, isn't it?"

"It is," Violet said. "Especially since they all had bombs strapped to them."

Kate shot a look to Violet then Ward.

"Really?"

"According to police," Ward said.

"Did they give any indication of who's behind it?"

"No. And now they can't find Dan, or Lori, or Billy!" Violet sobbed into her hands and Ward put his arms around her. "I pray they're okay!"

"I'm sorry," Ward said. "This is too upsetting. We'll have to end it there."

After thanking them, Kate and Gabe returned to the street. Kate exhaled, stopped to check her notes and her recording.

Gabe, who'd stepped back during Kate's interview, angled his camera to her, displaying the pictures he'd taken, favoring one of Violet Selway, anguished face buried in her hands, Ward's arm around her, Sam at their feet looking up at them with big eyes.

"Distraught neighbors and the Fultons' dog," Gabe said.

"It's good," Kate said, noticing that down the block the situation had changed with the cat lady. "Let's talk to her."

The woman was now out of the patrol car, leaning against it, holding her cat. The officers with her had moved off to consult other cops at a van nearby.

Kate approached, smiling once the woman noticed her.

"That's a pretty cat," she said. "What's her name?"

"Lacey Lou."

"Very cute." Kate, bearing in mind the officers were near, kept her voice soft. "I'm Kate Page, and this is Gabe Atwater. We're with Newslead. Some neighbors of the Fultons' have been sharing their thoughts with us. Can we talk to you briefly?"

The woman looked around as if seeking permission.

"It'll only take a second." Kate opened her notebook and shrugged. "You could summarize what you told police, like the other neighbors did."

"Well, I guess it would be all right."

"What's your name?"

"Charlene Biddle."

Kate took down the spelling.

"Charlene, do you know the Fultons?"

"No, I don't. I live around the block."

"What did you tell police?"

"Well, last night Lacey didn't come home at her usual time. I waited and waited until I got worried. So I got up and looked for her around the block because I thought that's where she'd gone."

"What time was this?"

"Oh, about two or two-thirty, I'm not sure."

"You went alone?"

"This is a good neighborhood. I wasn't afraid."

Gabe nudged Kate. Two men in suits had left the Selway house and were heading up the street, staring directly at Kate and Charlene Biddle.

"What happened when you went looking for Lacey?" Kate asked.

"When we got near the house there, Lacey was in the yard beside it. I called her, and she wouldn't come—this stubborn cat has a mind of her own. I tiptoed into the yard to get her. When I did, I saw a van parked in the driveway." Charlene nodded to the Fultons' house. "And people were getting into it. It looked like two men were sort of…pushing a woman and smaller person into the van. It was all quiet and quick and then they drove off."

"Do you recall—" Kate glanced at the approaching men "—do you recall any details, like a license plate?"

"I didn't see anything clearly. It was dark. I know it was odd, but I thought it was people going home from a party, and a few of them were drunk, kidding around. I got Lacey and went home. Then this morning police came knocking on everyone's door to move us out because of something happening, and so I told them what I saw. They wanted me to wait right here so I could talk to the detectives."

"Okay, thanks, Charlene." Kate closed her notebook, turned to leave.

"Hold up there!" A big-chested man, the older of the two, stepped into Kate's space. "Who're you?"

"Kate Page, Newslead." She held up her ID. "This is Gabe Atwater, Newslead." Kate tried to read the badge hanging from the older man's chain. "Who're you guys?"

"Detective Tilden, NYPD."

Kate glanced at the younger man, who had a Brad Pitt thing going.

"Nick Varner, FBI. Over here, please."

The two men took Kate and Gabe aside to talk privately.

"What've you got?" Kate opened her notebook, pen poised.

"We've got a problem," Tilden said.

"What problem?"

"Well, for one, we don't want you talking to our witnesses before we do," Tilden said.

"What'd you mean? I'm exercising my right, freedom of the press."

"Exercise it carefully," Tilden said.

"Excuse me?"

"We've got a very dangerous situation here, Ms. Page," Varner said.

"I kinda figured that, what with the SWAT team and the street sealed."

The grim-faced men said nothing.

"Can you elaborate on *dangerous*?" Kate asked.

"We'll put out a release later," Varner said.

"Can you confirm that bombs were strapped to the Fultons?"

"I told you, we'll put out a press release."

"But you're not denying that bombs were strapped to the family?"

"I didn't say that."

"Agent Varner, can we stop this 'can't confirm or deny' game?"

"Is this a game to you?"

"No, of course not."

"Maybe before you go ahead and print anything, you should run it by us," Tilden said.

"You're kidding, right?"

The two men said nothing.

"Look." Kate stared at both of them. "Why don't you guys do your job, and I'll do mine," she said, closing her notebook.

15

Somewhere in New York

Lori Fulton opened her eyes.

Her ears were pounding in time with her heart.

The van had stopped hours ago and since then sleep had come in tortured snatches. Each time Lori woke, she realized that she was a prisoner in a nightmare.

Billy was asleep, his head on her lap.

They were sitting on the floor of the windowless van, backs against the reinforced wall that divided the cab from the rear. She could feel him trembling. They were still wearing the bomb vests. The tiny red light on each of their battery packs continued to blink.

How much time do we have?

Ever since they'd stopped, she hadn't seen their captors. She had no idea where they were—she heard no sounds of the city. No traffic, no construction, no noise other than a few chirping birds.

Did they abandon us?

She didn't know what time it was. Daylight

seeped in through the van's door frame, so she knew it was no longer night. Tape still sealed their mouths and their hands. Suddenly Lori chided herself—*should've thought of this sooner*—and raised her hands, working her fingers to pull the tape from her mouth. She drank in the cool air, welcomed it on her skin as she stretched her jaw.

Her movements had awakened Billy and he sat up, blinking.

"Shh."

She kissed his forehead, then slowly pulled the tape from his mouth. He took a deep breath.

"Better?" she whispered.

He nodded.

Lori pulled off the tape around his wrists. His hands were still restrained with plastic handcuffs. Lori held out her wrists so Billy could pull off her tape. Plastic cuffs were locked on her, as well.

She began gnawing on the cuffs, but it was futile, the plastic was too thick. She searched the van's metal frame for a sharp edge to cut the plastic, but found none. She was afraid to try anything more—there was no telling what might set off the bomb vest—but she couldn't give up.

She cocked her ears, listening for anyone outside the van, and then very carefully moved to the van's side door, took hold of the handle and pulled. It refused to move. She turned to the cab. The dividing wall was solid, floor to ceiling. Taking great care, Lori crawled to the van's rear and tried that door, pulling on the handle with every ounce of strength she had.

No use.

They were locked inside.

She tried to think of a way to take off the vest. She could slide it over her head. Or over her shoulder, shimmy it down and step out of it. The problem was she couldn't open the front. It was zippered, Velcroed and had wires running across the opening.

It was definitely too risky to start pulling and twisting at it. Besides, she'd overlooked the fact her wrists were locked together.

Then, for a brief moment, she wondered if the vests were real. It was obviously dangerous to drive around in a van with someone wearing a bomb, but maybe they were confident that the vests wouldn't detonate unless they dialed the programmed cell phone. Still…convincing someone you'd strapped a suicide vest on them was a good way to get them to do whatever you wanted—even if the bombs weren't real.

Then Lori remembered how Thorne and the others were careful to place the snow tires near them, creating a makeshift blast mat, and that was enough to convince her the vests were real. She rejected any idea of tampering with them. She wasn't going to gamble with her son's life.

"Mom?" Billy whispered.

"Shh, honey."

"Maybe we should yell and scream for help?"

Lori considered it as she shifted next to him.

"That could bring the men right back to us." Lori brushed his hair.

"Mom, I couldn't see Sam. What happened to Sam?"

"Shh. I bet he got out through his door. I think I forgot to lock it. You know he's a big baby around strangers, so he probably ran over to Ward and Violet's house."

"Do you think Dad's going to bring help?"

"We can pray he does. Don't worry, sweetie. Someone will help us, or we'll help ourselves. We'll think of something."

But what?

A new wave of panic began rippling in the pit of Lori's stomach. As her eyes swept the van's interior, she thought of the man named Thorne and what he'd spat at her.

"You deserve what's going to happen."

Lori didn't understand what he'd meant. She hadn't recognized any of their voices, their mannerisms, their body types. Nothing. So who were they, and why did they talk as if they knew her?

They seemed young, and she wondered if they were military types—experts in explosives, maybe?

But why us?

There were plenty of other, bigger banks in the city they could have chosen. What made them choose Dan's? The thought of Dan had her stomach roiling again—shouldn't he have gotten them their money by now? Lori held back her tears, remembering how they'd been arguing for the past few days. All because she'd had a glass of wine at the Coopers' party because she thought she could handle it.

Dan hadn't said anything; it was just a look that he'd given her. One that had told her she'd let him down. She'd been hurt by it and lashed back at him when they were alone.

"Get off my back! I don't need you to babysit me anymore!"

But the truth of it was, she knew he was watching out for her, taking care of her. After all she'd put him through, after Tim, after everything. Dan always stood by her. Always had her back.

The last thing he'd said to her before they'd been separated: "Lori, did they hurt you?"

Oh, God, Dan, I'm so sorry. What if I never see you again, never have the chance to tell you that I love you?

Lori searched the ceiling, trying not to lose control in front of her son.

What did they do with you, Dan?

Lori brushed Billy's hair, thinking back to having been driven around in the night. They'd been on the road for hours—it must have been hundreds of miles—but how would she know if they'd only gone in circles to confuse her?

She tried to remember if she heard the hum of expressways, the rhythmic clicking of a bridge or the echoing of a tunnel. But it was useless. She had no idea where they might be.

Holding Billy next to her, Lori watched the red lights blinking on the bomb vests. She'd seen videos on news reports of suicide bombers—"We caution you, the images you are about to see are graphic and disturbing"—she'd seen how they obliterated a human being, and those images pushed her back through time to when she was…*sitting in the street covered with Tim's blood, helpless to do anything…*

The memory of that night anguished her.

Lori wanted to pray, but Thorne's words loomed over her.

"You deserve what's going to happen to you."

Billy lifted his head.

"Mom?"

"Yes, sweetie?"

"Listen!"

The sound of someone approaching the van grew louder.

16

Roseoak Park, New York

Like a band of protective angels, the group had encircled two distraught women.

Kate Page counted seven women dressed in jackets, skirt suits and blazers, hugging their two troubled friends and looking around worriedly, as if searching for answers to what had befallen Branch 487 of SkyNational Trust Banking.

Some of them were smoking. It must've been the reason they were now outside, gathered at one end of the parking lot, deep in the corral of emergency vehicles.

Kate heard Gabe's camera clicking as he shot frame after frame.

They'd come directly from the Fulton house to the branch. Kate had to find out what exactly had taken place in the bank this morning.

How does an upstanding man like Dan Fulton come to rob his own branch with bombs strapped to him and his family? What's the driving force behind this?

Kate deduced that the women clustered at the far side of the lot were bank employees. The two upset women they were consoling had to be staff members who'd been present when Fulton took the money.

Little chance I can talk to anybody in that group.

Given their defensive posture and the fact they were enclosed in a fortress of patrol cars and surrounded by an array of police, Kate considered her options as Gabe left her to scout better positions.

Searching the area for any news competitors, Kate saw two TV news trucks at one end of the lot; a car from one of New York's all-news radio stations was next to it, along with cars from the *New York Daily News* and the *Queens Chronicle.*

This isn't going to be easy.

At the front of the bank, customers were trickling up to the sign posted at the door that informed them the branch was closed. After reading it and taking a few minutes to scope out the police presence, they left.

But one man didn't.

He headed down the lot toward the group of distraught women. One staff member broke from the cluster, met him near some parked cars, hugged him and talked for a few moments before returning to her friends. As the man came back through the lot, Kate moved quickly toward him, using the cars to shield her so she wouldn't be seen by the other reporters.

"Sir, excuse me, sir!"

The man went to her.

"I'm Kate Page with Newslead. I understand there was a robbery—do you know much about it?"

The man gave her question some thought. He appeared to be in his sixties. He had a sturdy frame, a handsome, craggy face and white hair with sideburns.

"My daughter called me not too long ago," he said. "I just came down to see that she's all right. She was one of the two tellers on duty when it happened."

"Is she okay, sir?"

"Thank heaven, yes. She's shook-up, though. It's quite a jarring thing."

"Could I get your name?"

"Ernest Beeson."

"Could you spell that for me?"

The man did and Kate asked for his daughter's name.

"Jolleen Ballinger, but she goes by Jo."

Beeson spelled out her name.

"Did she tell you what happened?"

"I guess the manager came in and just walked out with a lot of cash."

"Anything more?"

Beeson shrugged. "That's about it."

Kate glanced at the group in the distance.

"Mr. Beeson, do you think Jo would talk to me for a second?"

He stuck out his bottom lip. "I suppose you could go over there and ask her yourself."

"I think we'd both prefer if she and I talked here, where it's a bit private." Kate touched his arm.

"Would you consider asking her to join us here for a moment? You could tell her I'd be happy to share what I've learned about the Fultons."

Beeson glanced toward his daughter.

"No harm in asking, I suppose. The girls are just waiting there for other investigators."

Beeson went to the group, talked to his daughter and pointed to Kate. Immediately, Jo Ballinger's attention, and that of some of the others, shot to Kate, who was standing seven or eight parked cars away. Several moments passed before Beeson accompanied his daughter to Kate, who introduced herself.

Jo Ballinger was uneasy.

"I don't want my name in the papers. You can't use my name."

"I'll just say a source close to the case."

"Okay, but I really can't tell you much," Jo said. "I shouldn't be talking to you, but Dad said you knew something about what's happened?"

"I know a little, Jo, and I'll help you if you help me, okay?"

"I will if I can. Did they find Dan?"

"Not yet. The SWAT team and bomb squad searched his house."

Jo cupped her hands to her face.

"They found nothing. No sign of Dan, his wife or his son," Kate said.

"Oh, my God!"

"Can you tell me what happened here earlier this morning? You were there when it happened, right?"

"Yes. This is my week to open with Annie,

Annie Trippe, the head teller. I'm not sure what I'm supposed to say."

"Jo, I'm going to get most of the details anyway. You can help me make sure I get it right. I won't use your name at all."

Jo hesitated and bit her bottom lip. "Well, we went through our usual procedure for opening, then Dan came in and told Annie there was an inventory problem at South Branch. He drafted a directive for her to cosign about an emergency interbranch transfer that he was going to deliver himself."

"So he planned to personally take the money himself to the other branch?"

"Yes."

"Is that how transfers are usually done?"

"No, of course not! It's a violation of procedure. Annie refused to sign it." Jo glanced at the group. "I don't know if I should be telling you this… I should get back."

"Wait, Jo, just a few more seconds. Do you know how much money was going to be transferred?"

Jo hesitated before answering in a quiet voice, "A quarter million."

"Two hundred and fifty thousand dollars?"

"Yes. He just walked into the vault, put the cash in a bag and walked out."

"So, what about the bomb he was supposedly wearing? Did he say anything about bombs?"

"He wrote a note on the directive, I guess so Annie would see it. Something about being held hostage, and that they all—him and his family—

had bombs strapped to them. I really should get back."

"Hang on, take these." Kate reached into her pocket and gave Jo several business cards. "Pass them to your coworkers and ask them to call me. I'll share any updates when I get them. Okay?"

Jo nodded and rejoined the group accompanied by her father, who'd decided to wait with her. Kate was glad to see Jo passing out her cards and the others glancing toward her. She was relieved that no other reporters had seen her interview Jo.

Kate used the hood of a car and reviewed her notes, confident that she now had the inside track on the story. She called the newsroom and asked for Reeka. It took a few seconds to transfer the call.

"Reeka Beck."

"It's Kate at the bank."

"What do you have?"

"Dan Fulton, manager of the SkyNational Trust Banking in Roseoak Park, Queens, takes a quarter million dollars from his own branch after scrawling a note that 'they' have placed bombs on him and his family."

"That's solid? You've got it confirmed, Kate?"

"A person who was there when it happened detailed it for me. I don't think anyone has what we have, Reeka. I think this is a national interest case. We don't know where the manager is, or where his wife and nine-year-old son are. They're all believed to be strapped with bombs, and no one seems to have a clue who's behind it all."

"Okay, get this on our news budget and give me a story within the hour. Did we get art with it?"

"Yes. Gabe Atwater's got some dramatic stuff."

"All right."

"There's still a few people I need to talk to."

"I want a story in an hour, Kate. You can update through the day."

"And the conference?"

"We'll send a stringer."

Kate ended her call.

As she turned to look for Gabe, she stepped directly into FBI agent Nick Varner.

"You're something else, Kate, I'll give you that." He was tapping her business card in his hand and shaking his head. "You want to know everything, and you want to know it *now.*"

"I'm a reporter, Agent Varner. It's what I do."

"You're doing a helluva job."

"Well, that's what I'm paid for. What's your problem, anyway?"

"I'm telling you for the last time." Varner jabbed a finger toward Kate. "Do not jeopardize this case."

"And I'm telling you, I'm not going away."

17

Roseoak Park, New York

Gabe Atwater's Jeep Patriot accelerated down Orchard Boulevard. Destination: Dixon Donlevy Mutual Life Insurance, Lori Fulton's employer.

Kate eyed the dashboard clock.

Like all reporters, she worked to a perpetual deadline ticking down on her. Most would be writing their story right now. They would've made a quick phone call to the company, plugged in its response and filed.

Not Kate.

She was old-school and still believed in digging for information face-to-face, abiding by the wisdom a rumpled old police reporter in San Francisco had once passed to her. *Phone somebody, you get one story. Talk to them in person, you'll get more than one story.*

"Almost there," Gabe said, glancing at his GPS.

Kate would make her deadline. She was a fast writer. She reviewed her notes, mentally shaping her story, still vexed by Tilden and Varner for jamming her at the Fultons' house. Why were they in her face? Especially Varner, the good-looking FBI agent. Why was he being a hard-ass when she was only doing her job?

Maybe I'm getting close to something...

"Here we go." Gabe stopped in front of a six-story rectangle of blue-tinted glass that reflected the small plaza across the street. "You're on your own, Kate. I've got to get to another job in Brooklyn. Call the photo desk if anything breaks. We got plenty of freelancers in Queens."

"That's fine. I'll write in the coffee shop in there—" Kate nodded to the plaza across the street "—then cab it back to the office. Thanks, Gabe."

Dixon Donlevy was on the fifth floor of the glass building.

As the elevator rose, Kate weighed the pros and cons of making a cold visit. Sure, showing up without an appointment wasn't ideal, but her competitors may have already called—even been here in person. She had to keep moving.

She stepped from the elevator, went down a polished hallway and passed through the brass-plated doors of Dixon Donlevy Mutual Life Insurance.

The lobby floor gleamed against the dark wood desk where the receptionist sat. A huge shield encircling a mountain range against a blue sky and the company's name graced the wall behind her.

"Can I help you?"

"Hi, I'm Kate Page. I'm a reporter with Newslead." She placed her card on the counter. "I'd like to speak with Lori Fulton's supervisor. It'll only take a moment."

"Do you have an appointment?"

"No. Sorry, but I'm facing a tight deadline."

The receptionist took Kate's card and examined it.

"Please, have a seat," she said, nodding to the waiting area.

The cushioned chairs were inviting, but Kate chose to stand by the gurgling water of a hanging wall fountain.

"Excuse me?" The receptionist called to Kate a few minutes later, her hand over the phone's mouth-piece. "I'm told we're not making any statements to the press at this time."

"I understand, but it's important I speak with someone while I'm here, to ensure my story is accurate concerning this company. Someone could talk to me now, or explain to their boss why they didn't after the story is published."

"One moment."

Kate couldn't hear what the receptionist said into the phone, so she turned back to the fountain until she ended her call.

"Someone will be out shortly."

"Thank you."

Kate moved from the fountain, admiring the landscape paintings, the palms in the floor plant-ers, all the while shaping her story and checking the time. She was glancing at a glossy travel magazine featuring treks across Iceland on the cover when a tall woman in a well-cut navy skirt suit arrived.

"You're Kate Page?"

"Yes."

"Denise Marigold, with Corporate Communications."

"Thank you for seeing me. In the wake of what's happened, I just had a few questions about Lori Fulton, an employee of yours."

"We've only just been informed about what's happened by police and really can't comment at this time."

"I just need to confirm how long Lori Fulton's been employed here."

"Unfortunately, given the gravity of the situation, we really can't discuss her employment here or her previous employment, the whole situation. We have to refer all questions to the authorities. Okay?"

"I understand. Can you offer any statement at all?"

Marigold's face creased in thought. "We can say this—we're deeply concerned for Lori and her family, and we're cooperating fully with police in every way possible."

Kate wrote down every word.

Denise Marigold didn't give her much, but it was something, Kate thought as she hurried across the street to Fredrico's Coffee Shop. She got a coffee and an apple muffin, found an empty table and began writing. Shutting out the noise of the busy shop, Kate entered her zone, concentrating as she wrote on her phone. Her story came together quickly as she firmed up the structure, inserting the quotes and details she'd managed to gather.

She proofread it twice, then sent it to Reeka Beck.

Kate checked the time. She'd made her deadline. She reached for her coffee and muffin to savor a small celebration. As she ate, something Denise Marigold had said niggled at her. She looked at her notebook, rereading the words she'd underlined, *previous employment*. Kate replayed Marigold's comment on her recorder: "…can't comment on her employment here or her previous employment…"

That's an odd thing to say. Is Lori's previous employment somehow a factor?

Kate gave it consideration before growing cognizant of the conversation people were having at a table behind her.

"…he robbed his own bank…they can't find Lori…"

Kate withdrew her compact mirror from her bag and made as if to check her hair. Tilting it, she saw the two women and a man who were talking about the case. They had to be Lori Fulton's coworkers, she thought, as one of the women continued.

"…my sister lives on the same street. I was talking to her this morning, she told me Lori didn't show up for work…"

Kate put her mirror away and sat a little straighter, eavesdropping until they prepared to leave. Keeping her back to them, she cleared her table, put her garbage in the trash and left ahead of the group. She waited in the street, and when the group exited, she went toward them.

"Excuse me. But by any chance, do you happen to work in that building?" Kate indicated the glass office complex across the street.

"Yeah," the man said.

"I'm looking for people who work at Dixon Donlevy Insurance."

"Why?"

"Do you guys work there?"

"Maybe. Who are you?" the man asked.

"Kate Page. I'm a reporter with Newslead." She took her Newslead ID from her bag and showed it to them. "I'm covering the robbery at the SkyNational bank. I've been to the bank, the Fulton home and I've spoken with Denise Marigold. I'm looking for people who know Lori Fulton. Do any of you work with her? Maybe you know her and her husband, Dan? He's the manager of the bank that was robbed."

The man and women exchanged silent looks as if waiting to decide who among them would answer.

"We don't know her that well," one of the women said. "She works in another department—insurance fraud."

"I worked with her for a short time when I was in fraud," the second woman said.

"Could I talk to you folks for a minute?" Kate took out her notebook. "I'd be happy to tell you what we know."

"Did the police find them?" the second woman asked.

"Not yet."

"Dear Lord," the woman said. "We'd heard that Dan was forced to rob his bank, that someone took Lori and Billy hostage. Is that true?"

"From what I've heard, it's true," Kate said. "What can you tell me about Lori?"

"She's a good person. They love her here. I think she's involved at her son's school and never misses a ball game."

"How long has she been with the company?"

The woman looked to her friends. "Five years, maybe?"

The others nodded and shrugged. "Around that, I think," offered the man.

"You say she worked in fraud. Did she ever receive any threats from one of her cases?"

The group exchanged concerned looks.

"We haven't heard anything like that," the women said.

"Do you know where she worked before coming to Dixon Donlevy?"

"No idea," the woman said.

"I think they lived in Nevada, or Arizona or someplace around there," the man said.

"Do you know what Lori did when she lived there?"

"No," the second woman interjected, "but I heard from someone in our section that the family had some tragedy out there."

"Really? What kind of tragedy?"

The three of them shook their heads and shrugged.

"And it was in Nevada or Arizona?"

"Not sure," the second woman said. "I did hear that Lori didn't like to talk about it."

It wasn't much, but office gossip counted for something. As Kate made notes, the man looked at his phone.

"We should be getting back," he said.

"Can I get your names before you go?" Kate asked.

"Not mine," the man said. "I don't want to be quoted."

The women declined to give their names, as well, and started to cross the street with the man.

"Wait, please," Kate said. "Let me give you my card. I'd be happy to share any information we have on the case as it develops. Please, call me if you hear anything more. Please. Thanks."

18

Roseoak Park, New York

A few miles from Dixon Donlevy where Kate Page had questioned people on Lori Fulton's history, investigators at the bank were probing Dan Fulton's background.

In one of the empty offices, Ted Shummard, SkyNational's regional security director, had loosened his tie and was tapping his pen on the desk as he read Dan Fulton's personnel file on the computer monitor. Human Resources at headquarters had emailed it ten minutes earlier, in response to his demand. "Send me every damned thing we have on Fulton and send it now!"

Shummard had put in twenty-five years with the US Secret Service, working in financial crimes and diplomatic security before punching out and taking a job with SkyNational.

Nick Varner and Marv Tilden sat across the desk from him, studying printouts of the file with some urgency.

"Okay." Shummard scrolled to the end of the last

page. "You asked if Fulton had money problems. This is everything we've got."

"I see a lot of numbers here," Varner said. "You wanna tell me what they all mean?"

"He's in good standing. He's received performance compensation, bonuses, awards, no black marks on his record."

"He's got a lot of debt, though." Varner had circled various figures. "He's carrying a mortgage, line of credit, car loans, large credit card balances. The works."

"As an executive he gets a discount on all financial services," Shummard said, "including his mortgage and preferred rates on his line and loans. He's taken advantage of them. He's making his payments on time. So far, I see no red flags here."

"By my quick count, he owes about two hundred and…forty thousand," Varner said.

"Two forty-six," Shummard corrected.

"And what did your people estimate he walked out of here with today?" Varner asked.

"Two hundred and fifty-nine thousand."

"He owes two forty-six and takes two fifty-nine," Tilden said.

Shummard shot Tilden then Varner a surprised glance.

"What? You think Fulton's involved? That maybe he planned this?"

"It's been known to happen," Tilden said.

Shummard shook his head. "It doesn't fit. Not with a record this clean."

"We can't rule anything out," Tilden said before

he and Shummard were distracted by Varner standing at the office window.

"Who's that?" Varner asked, pointing through the glass to a middle-aged man smoking and pacing in front of the bank near the other employees.

Shummard flipped open his notebook. "Charles McGarridge, he's a loan officer with the branch."

"Looks like he's got a lot on his mind," Varner said. "We'll want to talk to him when we're done here."

"All right," Shummard said.

Varner shifted back to the file.

"Marv's right, we can't rule anything out. Any security incidents we should know about, Ted?"

"Nothing. This branch has never been hit. Three years ago there was an argument in the parking lot. Didn't amount to anything. So, nothing. Zip."

Tilden turned back to an earlier page in the file.

"I see Fulton had served with the National Guard in California," Tilden said. "We'll need to find out if he was deployed overseas. See if he experienced any posttraumatic stress. It could be a factor."

"I don't think he saw any action," Shummard said.

"Do we know if he has any gambling debts?" Tilden asked. "If he uses drugs, has any problem with alcohol?"

"What about marital stress?" Varner asked. "Any stress in the family?"

"If we were aware, or if he'd sought help through us at any point, it would've come to my desk." Shummard removed his glasses. "From my read here, and what I know, Fulton's a clean-living law abider. He volunteers at a homeless shelter in Rego Park. He helps organize a fund-raiser for kids with terminal conditions. Fulton's a solid guy."

A knock sounded at the door and a detective stuck his head in.

"Marv, got a teller out here you guys should talk to."

"Send her in."

The detective pushed the door open and indicated a chair. "This is Dolores Spivak, been with the branch for nearly twenty years," he said. The woman was in her early sixties and held a crumpled tissue in her hand. Her attempted smile at the grim-faced investigators was underscored with anxiety.

"Do you have some information for us?" Shummard said.

"Well, I don't know if this is relevant, but when I told the other girls, they said I should tell you. I... I saw something that looked sort of strange to me."

"Go ahead," Varner said.

"Well, I live over on Cedar, you know, close enough to walk to work. I come down the boulevard and pass the Roseview Plaza." She pointed out the window toward a small building. "The little strip mall that's kitty-cornered over there to the bank."

"Okay," Varner said.

"Well, about two weeks ago, for three, maybe four days, I saw a young man sitting in a parked car."

"What's strange about that?" Tilden asked.

"He was looking through binoculars."

"At what?"

"I don't know for sure."

"At the bank?"

"Maybe, I don't know. But one time he caught me looking at him, and he put the binoculars down quickly, moved them out of sight."

"Did you tell anyone about it?"

"No."

"Didn't you think it was suspicious?"

"Well, not then because…" Dolores stared at the tissue in her hand. "I didn't think much of it at the time, to be honest. I mean, he could've been watching the birds in the trees, I don't know. This is such a quiet neighborhood—it's always been safe. So when you see something like that, you just assume there's a perfectly normal explanation for it. But now, after what's happened, I feel so stupid. I should've reported him."

"Any chance you got a license plate?" Tilden asked.

Dolores shook her head.

"What about the kind of car it was—anything about it you can remember?"

"No."

"Was the man white, black?"

"White. In his twenties, maybe? I'm sorry."

"It's all right, Dolores," Varner said. "Thank you. This is still helpful. You can go home now, though. We'll talk to you again later if we have any more questions."

After she left, Tilden turned to Varner and said, "They had to be casing the place."

"Yup. We'll need the plaza to volunteer its security video." Varner nodded to the loan officer pacing out front. "And we need to talk to him."

19

As Dan drove through Washington Heights, the lattice towers of the George Washington Bridge soared above the building tops.

He'd cleared the stretch of gridlock caused by a tractor trailer breakdown earlier. Now he guided his car along an on-ramp to the bridge.

He prayed Port Authority security cameras would record him traveling into New Jersey as he merged into one of the four lanes of westbound traffic on the upper deck.

Will I ever see my family again?

Looking out at the Hudson River some two hundred feet below, he remembered the first time he'd set eyes on Lori.

It was at Cal State.

He'd been in a food court, and when he'd looked up from his book… She was at a table nearby, alone, on her phone crying and he'd thought, *Who would be stupid enough to make a girl like that cry?*

He'd stolen glimpses of her composing herself.

When she'd gotten up to leave, he'd noticed that she'd forgotten a book at her table. Dan had grabbed it and run after her. He'd made a little joke when he caught up to her, which made her laugh. She had the most beautiful smile, the most beautiful eyes, he'd ever seen.

And she'd agreed to go out with him.

They'd walked along the beach at Santa Monica, and she'd told him that she'd been crying because her boyfriend had found someone else.

"His loss," Dan had said.

Soon after that, Dan and Lori had begun dating more seriously. She'd been studying criminology, he'd been studying business. They were happy together. They had chemistry. It was clear from the start that Lori was the right one for him. She owned his heart.

Three years after they graduated and were well into their careers, they'd gotten married. A few years later they'd had Billy. Dan had been there with Lori every step of the pregnancy, attending all the birthing classes, doing all the breathing exercises, shopping for clothes and furniture.

When he'd witnessed the birth of their son, Dan had felt a degree of love he'd never known existed. Soon, he'd grappled with his own mortality. It had frightened him, overwhelmed him, along with the realization that he was a father. He feared he would fail at fatherhood, so he compensated the only way he could: by striving to be a good husband, a good provider and a good protector.

But it was Lori who was more adept at handling

life's crises, a point made clear the night they'd gone to a movie and come upon two intimidating young men testing the doors on their car in the lot. Dan had stopped a distance away, kept his voice low and reached for his phone.

"I think we should call nine-one-one."

But Lori had strode right by him and confronted the men.

"Excuse me, can we help you? That's our car."

They two men had eyed Lori coldly, then glanced at Dan as if he was pathetic and it amused them.

"We was just checkin'," one of them had said. "Ya know, so's to make sure everything's locked up safe, like mall security."

"That so? How about you show me ID?"

They'd flashed their empty palms and backed away.

"Not necessary, baby. All cool."

As they'd backed off, the two shared a loud joke about "the bitch and the scared-ass pussy," and their laughter had painfully underlined the truth: Dan was weak, while Lori was the rock of the family.

At least, that's how it was until it all went wrong and nearly destroyed her.

But Dan had been there for her. When she'd thought she could no longer endure, he'd hung on for both of them, finally getting the chance to prove himself—to show that he could take care of them, too.

"We'll get through this together, Lori," he'd said a hundred times. "I'll do whatever it takes."

He'd sought the new job with the bank in New

York not long after. Not for himself but for Lori, since it provided a chance for her to start over. It wasn't easy at first, but eventually it worked out. Things got better. Ever since the move five years ago, she'd been healing. The worst time of their lives was behind them, convincing Dan that they'd never face anything as horrible again.

Until now.

Now, when Lori needed him most. And he'd failed her.

He'd done nothing to protect her and Billy.

He descended the bridge, his heart heavy with the shame of having failed them. As he rolled by the toll plaza, he had to face the fact that he was a coward, afraid to take action, to fight back.

"Take the Four to Hackensack," Vic said.

Dan eyed his fuel gauge. "I'm getting low on gas," he said. "I'll need to stop."

Vic did not respond.

As Dan drove ahead, he signaled and got into the lane for Hackensack, dreading what was coming as they took him farther and farther away from Roseoak and the happy life he, Lori and Billy had known there.

20

Charles McGarridge's small eyes were taut with worry behind his dark-framed glasses.

He was a short, balding man in his late forties with a thin moustache and a tailored suit—the bank's senior loan officer. Tilden and Varner were interviewing him in his office.

"What time did I get here?" McGarridge said, repeating the detectives' question. He smelled of cigarettes, and he rotated the small bowl of peppermints on his desk. The two investigators had declined his offer to share them. "I got here a little before ten, maybe around nine-thirty. It was after it happened. The police were already here talking to Annie and Jo."

"You've worked with Dan Fulton for five years?" Varner asked.

"That's correct."

"Was he under any stress that you knew of, maybe acting strangely in the time leading up to this incident?"

"No, nothing like that."

"So you would consider this behavior out of character?"

"Absolutely. Managers don't usually rob their own banks." McGarridge shook his head. "I can't believe this is happening. I mean, bomb vests! This is crazy."

Tilden leaned forward.

"Mr. McGarridge, we need to move fast on this and we need your help."

"Of course, of course."

"Has anything happened recently that might indicate who could be behind this? Anything suspicious? Anything unusual?"

McGarridge's jaw muscle pulsated and he licked his lips, suggesting to both Tilden and Varner that something was troubling the loan officer.

"Anything at all that you can recall?" Tilden nudged him.

"Well, there's one client…" McGarridge stopped as if to ask himself if he should proceed.

"Mr. McGarridge, we don't have a lot of time," Tilden said.

"There's one client whose past behavior disturbs me—you know, in light of what's happened." McGarridge realigned his stapler and penholder, then rubbed his chin. "I, uh…don't want them to know this came from me."

"It'll stay confidential. Now, who's the client?" Tilden asked.

"Vitori Bazerinni."

"And what exactly has you disturbed?"

"He owns Bazerinni Trucking and it's the loan he's taken out that concerns me—an eight-hundred-thousand-dollar business loan."

"What about it?" Tilden asked.

McGarridge hesitated, then rubbed his lips.

"About five or six months ago his son, Luca Bazerinni, a vice president of the company, stormed into the branch, claiming we'd misled Bazerinni Trucking on the terms of the loan."

"Was that the case?" Varner asked.

"Absolutely not. Mr. Bazerinni and his family had misunderstood the terms of the loan."

"How's this relevant to what's happening now?" Tilden asked.

"Bazerinni Trucking was losing income. Several business accounts were consistently overdrawn. They were having difficulties with suppliers and subcontractors. They wanted loan modifications. In fact, they said they'd been guaranteed a loan modification, which was absolutely not the case for the type of loan and interest rates they'd secured. The terms were very strict for that type of loan."

"So, what happened?" Tilden asked.

"We explained this to Luca Bazerinni and he got very upset."

"Upset how?" Tilden asked.

"He threatened the bank."

"With what?"

"When he left I remember exactly what he said. It was, 'Do you know who you're talking to? You mothers better watch your back, 'cause one day you're gonna regret this!'"

Tilden and Varner exchanged looks.

"Was Dan Fulton party to this?"

"No, Dan never knew. I was handling this with Martin Green, a junior loan officer, who's since moved to Seattle."

"Why didn't you tell Dan?"

McGarridge blinked several times and stared off.

"Mr. McGarridge, that's a serious threat you received. Why didn't you report it?"

McGarridge pulled off his glasses and rubbed his eyes. "I was Martin's supervisor. I knew Martin had a penchant for 'overselling' the loan terms, implying the bank could, or would, do better than what was on paper, and I'd cautioned him many times on that. There are regulations and laws. But in this case, I'd convinced myself that this was just a matter of Luca Bazerinni blowing off steam because the company was losing money."

Tilden and Varner let a moment pass. They knew there was more.

"What's the truth, here?" Tilden asked.

McGarridge's hands started shaking.

"Nothing happened after that with Bazerinni, so I thought everything was okay. All water under the bridge." His chin trembled. "But the truth? The truth was I was due to be reviewed for a bonus, and this case would've ruined that. And now— now after what's happened… If Dan and his family are… This could all be my fault! I'm—they've got a nine-year-old son… Please, you have to find them! Please."

21

Meredith DeSalvo had braced for what was coming.

Wearing a lab coat, white latex gloves and a hair and face covering, she was hunched over her microscope in the Latent Print Development Unit of the NYPD crime lab.

The lab was in a drab, five-story complex that was once part of the City University of New York. Meredith, a Level 2 criminalist with the unit, was setting aside her analysis on a cold rape case, clearing her workload.

Earlier that morning she'd been alerted to an ongoing hostage-abduction situation involving a bank manager and his family. Meredith was assigned to lead the small team that would process the evidence for prints. The material would also be examined by the hair-and-fiber unit.

This case was the NYPD's top priority—beyond urgent.

Investigators needed evidence to point them to the people behind the crime and they needed it now.

"Heads up, here it is," said Rita Chow, Meredith's manager.

Rita was accompanied by two Crime Scene Unit detectives carrying several brown paper bags containing evidence collected from Dan and Lori Fulton's home. They'd placed the bags on Meredith's workbench. After everyone signed off on chain-of-evidence documentation, Meredith and the other criminalists in the unit began processing the material. If a suspect had left something behind at the scene, Meredith's team would find it.

They opened the bags and logged and recorded the items inside, which included towels, swatches collected from sofa cushions, armrests, soda cans, pizza boxes, used napkins, used forks, spoons, knives, balled-up duct tape, crystal figurines and take-out containers for Chinese food.

Meredith and her team began by making visual inspections of the items under high-powered magnifying lamps.

They searched for patent prints, those that are visible when fingers touch a clean surface after they'd been contaminated with substances like blood, dirt, ink, paint, grease, powders or oils.

Next, they collected possible DNA by using moistened cotton swabs to rub the items over the areas where the suspect would have touched them, particularly around the lid of soda cans. The swabs were documented and shipped immediately to the

Office of the Chief Medical Examiner for DNA analysis.

The criminalists then switched off the lab's lights to examine the material under ultraviolet and infrared lights for naturally fluorescent prints.

Once that was done, they moved into a process known as superglue fuming. They placed items in the chamber with a volume of superglue, watching as the fumes that vaporized from the glue adhered to residue left from the prints, leaving a white coating that could be photographed.

After twenty minutes they used a plastic bottle of fluorescent water-based dye and submerged the evidence with it. Then let it dry for another twenty minutes.

Meredith was pleased.

So far her team had collected a number of clear prints.

But her highest hope was with the duct tape.

She knew the probability of getting usable prints from the tape was high, since criminals often bound their victims with it. She also knew that in most cases the tape was impossible to manipulate while wearing gloves. At some point, a suspect would leave a print—either on the smooth side or the sticky side.

The challenge was in unbinding the tape so as not to damage any prints captured on it. First, a liquid release agent was applied where two pieces of tape met. Meredith and a coworker did this stage together, using tweezers to separate the tape sections while generously applying the release agent. Once that was done, they flattened the salvaged pieces.

It used to require twenty-four hours before they could move on to the next stage, but scientists in Japan had developed a new, rapid adhesive-side developer to apply to the sticky side of the duct tape. After letting it dry for several minutes, they rinsed off the powder, and prints emerged.

"Fantastic," Meredith said.

She photographed them, protected them with clear tape. Then she viewed them on her computer monitor, along with the other prints her team had collected. After entering all the appropriate evidentiary data, Meredith submitted the prints with a few clicks to fingerprint detectives, who were standing by at One Police Plaza to identify them.

Staring hard at the images on her screen, Meredith was convinced.

One of these has to belong to a suspect.

22

"It's always something in this town."

Kate couldn't tell if her taxicab driver—Nazir, according to the license displayed over the back of the front seat—was complaining to her or himself.

The cab had come to a gently sloping segment of the Long Island Expressway where westbound traffic had slowed near the Midtown Tunnel.

"See?" Exasperated, Nazir lifted his hands from the wheel. "It's backed up more than normal. It's always something."

Kate looked out at the apartment buildings, warehouses, factories and billboards. Taking stock of the Empire State and Manhattan's skyline rising above the clogged lanes, Kate surmised that the delay might be linked to the robbery and hostage situation.

They must've issued lookouts, maybe set up a dragnet at toll plazas and bridges by now.

As Kate's mind raced with thoughts of Lori, Billy, Dan and the horror they must be experiencing, she looked at the screen of her phone, at the image of Grace and Vanessa.

They'd faced terrible events, too, but they'd prevailed.

Kate traced her finger lightly over Grace's and Vanessa's smiles. At this very moment, Grace would be at school, happy and playing with her friends. Vanessa would be working at the diner, rebuilding her life, getting stronger every day.

Both of them were safe.

Kate then called up the pictures she'd taken of Dan Fulton's bank in Roseoak.

What happened? Who forced Dan to rob his own bank?

Kate tapped her screen, scrolling to photos of the Fultons' house on Forest Trail Drive.

What went on in that home? Who would strap a bomb on a nine-year-old boy?

Kate suddenly realized Billy Fulton was only one year older than her daughter, Grace, and her heart went out to their family once again.

When she lifted her head, the cab was approaching the toll plaza at the entrance to the Midtown Tunnel. Emergency lights flashed on the NYPD patrol cars that lined the shoulders. Uniformed officers stood at the traffic cones leading to the toll gates, halting traffic, eyeballing each vehicle and driver.

Kate dropped her window and told her driver to slow down when they were next to one of the cops.

"Excuse me, Officer!" Kate called. "Is this related to the robbery situation in Roseoak, Queens?"

"Yes, do you have information?"

"No. I'm a reporter, just checking. Thanks."

"Move it along."

The cab rolled through the toll gate, the tunnel gleaming in brilliant orange-and-yellow light as it curved under the East River to Manhattan.

As traffic rushed along, Kate resumed thinking of the Fultons.

They've got to be somewhere in this city.

23

With sirens wailing and lights flashing, NYPD units from the 115th Precinct blocked the north, south and east entrances to Bazerinni Trucking on Astoria Boulevard.

The depot stood at the edge of a commercial strip lined with tired-looking one- and two-story buildings just beyond. The company was not far from La Guardia Airport and other busy freight and cargo operations. But today, Bazerinni's business had ground to a halt as heavily armed officers, a K-9 unit and a group of detectives descended on the yard.

"What the hell's this?" A man rushed out from the garage, angry and perplexed, searching amid the loading bays and grind of diesel engines for someone to provide an answer. His shirtsleeves were rolled up, his tie was loosened. He gripped a tablet in one hand.

"We're looking for Luca Bazerinni," said one of the suited men.

"I'm Luca. Mind telling me who you are and what you're doing on my property?"

"I'm Detective Tilden, NYPD, and this is Agent Varner, FBI. We're investigating the robbery of a SkyNational Trust branch in Roseoak Park."

"What about it?"

"You're aware of it?"

"Yeah, heard it on the news."

"You have business dealings with the branch."

"A loan, sure. So what? I didn't rob the freakin' place." The yelp of the German shepherd diverted Bazerinni, who took quick inventory of the armed officers and detectives searching his property. "What the hell's this? Do you have a warrant?"

"We do, Mr. Bazerinni," Varner said. "It authorizes us to search the premises and all records relevant to our investigation."

The stress lines on Bazerinni's face deepened and he pulled his cell phone from his pocket. "I want my lawyer here." He scrolled through his contact numbers.

"That's your right," Tilden said, "but you're not under arrest and things would go quicker for us to clear you if you'd cooperate by answering a few questions."

"Clear me? Clear me from what?"

"Let's talk over there." Varner nodded to a rest area with lockers and wooden tables and chairs.

Bazerinni hesitated, taking another look around before returning his phone to his pocket and leading the two men to the tables.

Tilden and Varner took out notebooks.

"You acknowledge your company took out a loan for the amount of eight hundred thousand dollars with Branch 487 for SkyNational Trust Banking Corp.?"

"That's what this is about?"

"Just answer the question," Tilden said.

"If you know the amount, then you know it's true."

"But you took issue with the terms of that loan and some five or six months ago went to the branch to discuss it."

"I sure as hell did. Back then we were facing a helluva time. We were getting squeezed on all fronts, contracts were low. We weren't getting paid on time and we had issues with insurance, suppliers and subcontractors."

"So you went to the bank to seek relief on the terms of the loan?"

"Exactly. We were told when we negotiated the loan that it was geared to income and that we had the option to relax the payments, should we face hard times. The rates and terms were good. That's why we went out to Roseoak. They gave us a good deal."

"Tell us what happened when you visited the branch to discuss those terms."

"I'll tell you exactly what happened. The loan officer there started singing a different tune, said we couldn't modify the original terms. He said I'd misunderstood what he'd told me before, that it was all clear in the fine print. I was pissed off and I left."

"You were pissed off?"

"You're damned right. That prick, Green, lied to me."

"Did you tell him, and I quote, 'Do you know who you're talking to? You mothers better watch your back 'cause one day you're gonna regret this!'"

Bazerinni shrugged. "Sounds right."

"You understand that's considered a threat, Mr. Bazerinni."

"Give me a freakin' break. This is Queens! I run a trucking operation, and the asshole in the suit lied to me. I wanted to beat him to a pulp. I was losing sleep, going crazy with worry over my company. What do you think I'm gonna say to that prick—thanks and have a nice day?"

"In light of what's happened at the bank today, you understand why we're forced to see your comment in a different light," Varner said.

"A different light?"

"Luca—" Tilden looked him in the eye "—are you involved in any way with the robbery of Branch 487 for SkyNational Trust Banking Corp., and the disappearance of Dan Fulton, Lori Fulton and their son, Billy?"

"Are you crazy? No, no way!"

The investigators let his response hang in the air amid the idling diesels and ongoing search of his property.

Bazerinni sat forward, pointing his finger at Tilden.

"Let me tell you something. Me and my dad started this company with a beat-up Ford F-150 pickup twenty years ago. Now we got a fleet of twenty units and fifty people on the payroll. We cooperate with every vehicle inspection, every driver inspection, every license and bond review, every audit. We pay our bills and our taxes. On time! I had to sell some equipment to deal with our rough patch six months ago but we never missed a payment. We're back on solid ground now. We're strong and we're clean. There's no reason for us to be involved in this robbery—and there never would be."

"Luca!" A woman held up her hands as she shouted down from the railing outside the office on the second level.

Bazerinni saw detectives carrying out computers. He turned to Varner and Tilden. "What the hell're you doing?"

"Unfortunately, we're going to have to shut you down for a while before we can clear you," Tilden said. "We've got to review all your records, including your computers, phones and employee files."

Bazerinni dragged both hands over his face.

"All because I shot off my mouth to that lying prick at the bank."

Varner nudged Tilden, then nodded toward a few rolls of duct tape stacked on a nearby bench, along with a few other packing supplies. Varner knew the techs would need to collect a sample for comparison with the tape used at the Fulton home.

24

Manhattan, New York

The headlines streaked along the news ribbon that wrapped around the old *New York Times* building in Times Square.

… Manager Robs Own Bank… Vanishes with Wife and Son…

The Fulton story was heating up.

As Kate's cab threaded through Midtown traffic, her focus returned to the question of Varner and Tilden's ultrasensitivity over this case. It was a red flag and suggested there might be more to the story than what she knew so far.

Did Fulton have secret drug or gambling debts? What about the supposed tragedy the family had had when they lived in the West?

As the cab got closer to Newslead, Kate received another text from Reeka Beck.

Everybody's all over the story. What's your ETA?

Fifteen minutes.

We've got a problem to discuss.

What problem?

Tell you when you get here.

By the time her cab halted in front of the News-lead building, tension had knotted in Kate's neck and shoulders. In the lobby she checked coverage online. Her story was out there, it had been issued about an hour ago, shortly after she'd filed it. She'd met her deadline. In the elevator she searched and scanned stories by the Associated Press, Reuters and the others. They were all similar straight-up accounts—but nobody had what she had—the exact amount Dan Fulton had taken from the bank.

Kate had broken the fact that it was a quarter-million-dollar heist, making it a Newslead exclusive.

Hold on. What's this?

She came upon an item by the new Signal Point Newswire. Citing an unnamed source, they had reported that the amount taken was two million dollars, and that Fulton had left note, "warning employees that a bomb had been placed in the bank."

What? No. That's dead wrong.

The doors opened on the fortieth floor and Kate stepped into the newsroom.

She glanced at one of the TV monitors and caught the end of a report on the heist in Queens. Then she looked to the glass walls of the editors' offices. Reeka was on her phone, texting. Her door was open, so Kate tapped on it. Reeka nodded for her to sit in the chair in front of her desk. When Reeka finished, she put her phone down and let out a long breath.

"You have an error in your story."

"An error?"

"The amount taken in the robbery. Signal Point's reporting that it's two million—our story says a quarter million."

"Signal Point has the error. Not us."

"There's also the aspect of Fulton's note. Signal Point says—"

"I know what their story says and it's wrong on both counts, Reeka."

"You need to verify your facts."

"Verify my facts? What do you think I've been doing in Queens?"

Reeka shot Kate an icy look.

"I want you to check your facts. And, if we need to, we'll issue a correction with the next story update."

Kate didn't move.

She burned at Reeka's insulting regard for her work. All morning she'd pinballed across Queens, talking to the Fultons' neighbors, coworkers and confronting investigators.

Reeka had no concept of street-level journalism. She'd never covered a murder, a fire or a disaster, never stared into the eyes of an inconsolable parent and asked for a picture of their dead child. She was young, pretty and had degrees from Harvard and Yale. They were up there on the wall.

And she'd been on the desk at Newslead's Boston bureau at a time when the entire staff's collective work on a breaking story was a Pulitzer finalist. Reeka's uncle, a legend in the news business, sat on Newslead's board of directors. Word was he'd pushed for his niece to be moved to headquarters in Manhattan.

"Reeka, why do you automatically assume my story's wrong?"

"Look, you just need to verify your information, to ensure your source is valid."

"Valid?"

Kate seized her phone from her bag and began swiping through photos she'd taken, finding the images she was searching for and thrusting them at Reeka.

"This is Jolleen Ballinger, one of the tellers. She's my source. She spoke with me on the condition of anonymity. She was there when Dan Fulton robbed their branch. I verified the quarter-million-dollar figure with her. She's *valid*. I know how to do my job and I did it."

Reeka looked at the photo, then picked up her pen, rotating it for several seconds.

"Let's put her name in your story, give it unchallengeable credibility."

"Did you hear what I just said? This woman trusted me. I gave her my word that Newslead would protect her identity. She was afraid. If I follow your instructions and burn her, we *lose* credibility."

"Then call her and request permission to use her name."

"No! She's wasn't at a Yankees' game, Reeka. Her bank was robbed. This woman's already traumatized. Pressing her to use her name in a national news story won't help. In talking to me she took a risk with her employer and the investigation. We need to respect that."

Reeka remained deep in thought, rocking in her chair until her phone vibrated. Before picking it up, she dismissed Kate with a parting order.

"All right. I want you to stay on this story, keep us out front. But first, you need to verify the two outstanding aspects with your police source. Do it as soon as possible."

Biting back on her anger, Kate strode down the hall. She passed Chuck Laneer's empty office, mourning his departure. This crap with Reeka wouldn't be happening if Chuck were here. Kate took several deep breaths, chiding herself.

You've got to watch your mouth and be smart about this. Use Reeka's request strategically.

At her desk she fished out the cards Nick Varner and Marv Tilden had given her. She'd planned to call them anyway to try to squeeze more information from them. As icy as they'd been to her, Kate had to admit there was something about Varner that she liked. He had nice eyes, but there seemed to be sadness behind them. She reached for her phone and hit the numbers on her keypad.

The line rang twice.

"Varner."

"Agent Varner with the FBI?"

"Yes."

"Kate Page, with Newslead—we met earlier. Do you have a quick second to talk?"

A moment passed.

"Kate, you really should call the FBI or NYPD press office."

"But your press people aren't investigating, you are. And as I recall, Detective Tilden requested I run my information by you. I believe you were present when he made that request."

Another silence.

"All I'm asking for is a little professional courtesy," Kate said.

"What've you got?"

"We've reported the amount Fulton took was a quarter million and that he left a note saying bombs had been strapped to him and his family, who were being held hostage. But Signal Point Newswire has the figure at two million and says Fulton's note warned that a bomb had been placed in the bank. Which version is correct?"

Varner muttered something under his breath.

"Listen," he said, "like I told you before, this is an extremely active investigation. The release of too much information is dangerous."

"The story's already been flashing around the zippers in Times Square. I know you guys don't like releasing information, but you don't want misleading stuff out there, that could be dangerous, too."

She heard his irritation as he exhaled, but sensed him warming to her.

"This is not for attribution to me, not even to the Bureau. You got that?"

"Of course."

"I'm not confirming anything."

"Okay."

"You'd be correct to disregard the information reported by Signal Point."

"Thank you. Do you have any suspects, or possible motives? What about the family's history?"

"That's it, Kate. I've got to go. There might be a press conference at One Police Plaza later today."

After the call, Kate immediately wrote Reeka an email.

Our story's correct. Signal Point's is wrong. This has been verified by police sources close to the investigation.

She jabbed the enter key hard, sending it with a vengeance.

Getting up to get a fresh coffee from the lunchroom, Kate reconsidered her initial impression of Varner. He'd impressed her just now. Sure, he'd played the surly investigator at the crime scene, but he'd just demonstrated that he was willing to work with her, which put matters in a different light. What she really liked was how he'd used her first name. *That was nice,* she thought, adding milk to her coffee when her phone rang.

The caller's number was blocked.

"Kate Page, Newslead."

"You're the reporter who's asking questions about the Fulton family in Queens?"

The woman on the phone sounded a little shaky, as if she'd had trouble deciding to call.

"Yes."

"I have information that might help you."

"That's great. Who's this?"

"I… We can't talk over the phone. Are you in Manhattan? I understand that's where your office is."

"Yes, I'm at the office now."

"Can you meet me in thirty minutes?"

"I'm sorry, but I can't meet with you unless you give me some sense of what you want to talk about."

The woman hesitated. When she spoke again, her voice quavered.

"I know the truth about Lori Fulton."

25

Across the city, near the Manhattan side of the Brooklyn Bridge at NYPD Headquarters, Mae Clarke downed the last of her tepid coffee, fighting the urge to get a fresh cup.

She was trying to cut down. Besides, she couldn't leave her desk because at any moment she was expecting prints on the red ball out of Queens, the bank robbery abduction case. The lab had called her supervisor to say the file was on its way.

Mae shoved a stick of Juicy Fruit in her mouth.

She was one of the NYPD's best fingerprint techs and she was ready. Investigators had already obtained a set of elimination prints for each of the family members—from the parents' workplaces, and through a child ID safety program for the son.

That was good.

Although Mae didn't have prints for their relatives, or for friends or neighbors who may have been invited into the family's home, she knew that having prints for the key players was a big advantage.

Mae's computer chimed.

Here we go.

Chewing faster on her gum, she opened the file—a clear set of unidentified impressions from the right hand: one from the right thumb and one from the right forefinger. They'd been collected from balled duct tape.

Mae began studying the loops, whorls and arches, analyzing and comparing them against the elimination set. It didn't take long to confirm that the prints on the tape did not come from any member of the family.

With a few keystrokes she submitted the unidentified prints to the New York State Criminal History Record Database—the state's primary system for fingerprint identification. The database stored prints belonging to anyone arrested for a fingerprintable offense.

It allowed for rapid searching through a range of state fingerprint files—those taken from crime scenes, from gun permit holders, from various professional license applications and also from unsolved cases.

After some thirty seconds, her submission came back with two hits.

That's a start.

Her keyboard clacked as she submitted the prints to the mother of all databases, the FBI's Integrated Automated Fingerprint Identification System, or IAFIS. The system held the criminal histories and fingerprints for more than seventy million people in every state across the country, drawn from every local, regional, state and national network.

This search would take a bit longer, so she returned to the lunchroom where she talked herself into a bottle of water instead of the coffee she was really craving. By the time she'd returned to her desk, her search was done.

IAFIS offered a list of five "possibles" who closely matched her unidentified submission. With the two from the New York system, she now had seven candidates.

She unwrapped a fresh stick of gum, enjoying its sweetness as she began making a visual point-by-point comparison between the duct tape prints and her seven samples. This was when she was at her best, zeroing in on the critical minutiae points, like the trail of ridges near the tip of the forefinger where she'd found dissimilarities. That eliminated the first two candidates right off.

For the next set she enlarged the sample to the point where she could count the number of ridges on the thumb. Definite differences emerged.

That eliminated all of the others but one.

Mae sat up, narrowing her eyes as she compared her submission from the duct tape with the computer's remaining sample. She concentrated on cluster details, spots, hooks, bifurcations and tented arches.

All the minutiae points matched.

The branching of the ridges matched.

Her breathing quickened as she began counting up the clear points of comparison where the two samples aligned. Some courts required ten to fifteen clear point matches. She had twenty-three and was still counting, knowing that one divergent point would instantly eliminate a print. By the time she'd compared the left slanting patterns from the thumb, she had twenty-eight clear points of comparison and was thinking ahead to what it would be like when she was testifying in court.

These prints are consistent with those collected at the crime scene.

She confirmed the identification number of her new subject and submitted a query to several databanks, including the FBI's National Crime Information Center.

Who are you?

While waiting, forever-thorough Mae submitted the elimination prints—those that belonged to Dan, Lori and Billy Fulton—to the New York State and FBI databases, as well.

It was a routine check.

After a few more minutes she got a response to her query for her unidentified mystery print lifted from the duct tape.

The print was out of California.

The query had been run through an array of California's systems, the California Law Enforcement Telecommunication System, California's DMV, the Department of Corrections, including the Parole Law Enforcement Automated Data System, and the Automated Criminal History System, which could verify parolee history, offender identification, arrest records, convictions, holds and commitments for all California law enforcement agencies, even create All Points Bulletins and drop warrants.

The single hit identified the prints from the duct tape. The face of a white male appeared on her monitor, and Mae read the accompanying information, then hurriedly went to the subject's central file summary to search for offenses.

It was blank.

His prints were on record because he'd once been charged for a misdemeanor drunk driving offense, but the charge had been dropped because the blood test results were lost.

Mae's supervisor had cleared her to call the primary detective immediately once she had a hit, so she reached for her telephone. The line was answered on the second ring.

"Tilden."

"Detective Marv Tilden?"

"That's me."

"Mae Clarke with the latent print section. We got a match on a print from the duct tape in your case. Ready to copy?"

"Go."

"Jerricko Titus Blaine. I'll send you the spelling."

"Got it."

"Age, twenty-three. Last known address, Dallas, Texas."

"His sheet?"

"He's clean. A misdemeanor drunk driving charge that was dropped. I'll send you everything I've got, DOB, height, weight, et cetera."

"Thanks, Mae."

After sending Jerricko Blaine's file to Tilden, Mae finished her water, then let out a long breath.

Now we've got a lead, something to work with.

She was preparing to return to her other cases when her computer pinged.

Another hit?

She wondered if Jerricko Blaine popped up in another jurisdiction, but instead it was a new hit— one from Lori Fulton's prints.

Mae's brow creased when she read the notice.

She reached for her phone to call Detective Tilden again.

26

New York Thruway

Dan's grip tightened on the wheel.

"I need gas," he said.

"No, you don't," Vic said. "You started with a full tank."

"I'm telling you, I need gas!" Dan stared at the gauge, so Vic could see through the camera that the needle had dropped into the red zone. "Look!"

No response from Vic.

Dan had just left New Jersey. He was heading northbound on the New York Thruway, and was somewhere between Suffern and Sloatsburg, an hour out of New York City's frenzy. Here, the metropolis had conceded to rivers, rock formations and undulating oceans of trees. The highway wound through the rolling hills, further isolating him and deepening his fear that he'd never see Lori and Billy again.

Are they alive?

He felt dwarfed by the vastness of the region, the Catskills rising around him.

Where're they sending me? What're they going to do?

His heart pounded against the sweaty confines of the bomb vest, and all he had to pass the time were his own terrified thoughts. While he couldn't make any sense of who these guys were or why they'd chosen him. Could it be about someone his branch had dealings with? Maybe tied to an insurance cheat, someone Lori dealt with? One thing he did know was that Vic and his gang were planning something beyond the robbery.

Why would they make me drive across New Jersey and back into New York with the money? Why not just take it and let us go?

Dan dragged the back of his trembling hand over his mouth.

It's as if they know I don't have the guts to fight back. That I'm a coward. These people are going to kill us all, and I'm just going to let it happen. God help me.

His eyes strayed to the bag on the passenger floor, bulging with the cash.

At some point they were going to take the money from him. That's when Dan would have to make a decision—to give up or to fight for his family's life.

He studied the traffic in his side and rearview mirrors, eyeing an SUV, a delivery truck and two late-model sedans that trailed behind him.

Is Vic in one of them?

He didn't know their vehicle or how close they were. He didn't even know if they were keeping Lori and Billy with them.

"I want to talk to my family," he said.

"Shut up and keep driving," Vic said.

"I need to know they're alive, or… I'll go to police, I swear! If they're already dead I've got nothing to lose."

A long silence passed. Then he heard a commotion in his ear and his heart swelled.

"Dad?"

The connection was filled with static as if patched from a radio to a cell phone.

"Billy! Son, are you hurt?"

"Dad, you gotta just do what they say!"

Dan's head swiveled to look at the traffic around him, desperate to catch some glimpse of his son in a nearby car.

"Billy, where are you?"

Another bleat of confusion, then over the scratchy air he heard his wife's voice.

"Dan, just listen to them. Do what they say!"

A disturbance filled his ear. Then nothing.

"Lori? Lori!" Blinking quickly, Dan took a deep breath and adjusted his hold on the wheel and himself.

"They're alive, Dan," Vic said calmly. "Now just keep doing what we tell you to do and you'll see them soon. The next exit comes up in two miles. Take it. Go east to the gas station called Weldon's."

A quarter mile from the exit, down a forlorn rural road that cut through fields with horses and cows on one side and a few rusting cars on the other, Dan came to Weldon's Gas and Grocery.

Four pumps stood out front of the building's weathered wooden walls. A faded metal awning stretched over the Coke and ice machines. Tires were neatly stacked next to a pyramid of motor oil. A neon sign over the door said Open, while one above the pumps said Self-Serv.

Two vehicles were parked at the edge of the paved lot. A pickup with a dented fender and a van with a small banner reading: Dereck's Electric. Several cars and trucks whizzed by the station. Dan scrutinized them. Before getting out he was stopped by Vic's orders.

"Pay with cash," he said. "I saw a ball cap in the car—put it on, play it smart and everything will go smoothly."

The Stars and Stripes flapped as Dan fueled the Ford's tank.

He went inside to pay, walking up to a man with a full white beard who stood behind the counter.

"All I'm saying, Roy, is I won't use that type for bluegill or smallmouth," said a man in overalls, who was leaning against the counter, sipping from a take-out coffeecup.

"Just the gas today, friend?" the bearded man behind the counter said to Dan.

Dan nodded, placed the cash on the counter. "May I use your restroom?"

"Just around the corner."

As Dan started for the room, a man wearing a flannel work shirt rushed from the area, muttering to himself. As he passed Dan, he called out:

"I know I got that part in my truck, Roy, be right back."

"Well, it's not like I'm going anywhere."

"Hey, Hank." The man in the overalls winked. "Alice have the baby yet?"

"Doctor said anytime, I tell you—" Hank continued talking while outside, something about no sleep.

Dan rounded the corner to see that Hank had been working on an outlet between the entrances to the men's and women's restrooms. A large open tool box was on a shelf between the two rooms.

Dan knew Vic could see whatever he saw.

Dan looked away from the toolbox, keeping his eyes ahead on the bathroom door as he made his way down the hall. As he passed close to the shelf, he reached out and took two small items from the tool tray, shoving them in his pocket while still keeping his eyes—and Vic's view—straight ahead. In the restroom, while standing alone at the urinal, Dan used one hand to reach into his pocket and uncap the felt-tipped marker he'd stolen from the box. His heart rate was galloping, but he kept his eyes forward as he began scrawling on the metal wall of the stall. The ongoing rush of flushing water drowned out any sound from the pen as he wrote as fast as he could—hoping it would be legible since he wouldn't be able to check it.

After finishing, Dan washed his hands, feeling the bulk of the vest. Then he dried them and returned to his car and resumed driving northbound on the Thruway.

After he'd gone several miles, he was careful to keep his eyes on the road while he retrieved the second item from his pocket, lowered his left hand and slowly pulled up the trouser cuff of his left leg. Keeping the rest of his body still, he positioned the item he'd stolen from the tool box and tucked it into his left sock.

His heart was pounding as he replaced his hand on the wheel, confident Vic hadn't seen the actions he'd taken, now or back at the gas station.

As he drove farther upstate, he tightened his grip on the wheel.

I'm not going down without a fight.

27

Kate's cab moved along West 40th Street.

Her mystery caller had provided no details on Lori Fulton over the phone but was willing to meet in Bryant Park, only a short cab ride from Newslead.

Kate didn't know what to make of the woman's call. Over the years she'd encountered all sorts of "tipsters"—people who were lonely, people demanding money, conspiracy nuts, mystics, weirdoes and creeps. Kate had seen all kinds.

Most were a waste of time.

In every case, when callers insisted on meeting, Kate weighed the circumstances carefully. Tips were the lifeblood of any news operation. No reporter, if they were any good, dismissed them. You never knew which tip, no matter how it came to you, could break a story wide-open.

And time was ticking on the Fulton story.

It had been several hours since the robbery that morning, and they still hadn't found a trace of the family or the money. Kate needed to take readers deeper into the story, but while she had some threads on the Fultons, she had no firm leads.

Trusting her instincts, she decided to meet this woman who claimed to know the "truth" about Lori Fulton. Other than wasting her time, the risk was low. They would be at a public place and it was midday. Still, she remained a bit wary when she got out of the cab on Sixth Avenue.

Bryant Park sat in the heart of Midtown behind the New York Public Library's main branch, on ten acres of beautiful green lawn. It was bordered with gardens and trees sheltering tables and chairs, offering a tranquil outdoor café setting, an urban oasis amid glass and steel skyscrapers. People dotted the great lawn, reading or napping; some were picnicking.

Kate searched the tables near the carousel. Her caller had said that she'd be alone there, with a white bag on the table and reading a hardcover copy of *Great Expectations*.

After scanning a few families at tables near the carousel, Kate approached an older woman who was wearing casual white pants and a mint-colored top. She was at a table with a white bag on it and—as promised—was reading *Great Expectations*. Kate stood at the table until the book was lowered and the woman removed her sunglasses.

"Kate Page?" she asked.

"Yes."

"Please, sit down."

The woman closed her book and placed her sunglasses on it.

"I don't want you to use my name or take my picture. Will you give me that assurance?"

"I'll see how this goes. Remember, you called me, and I don't even know your name. Look, I don't have much time. What do you know about Lori Fulton?"

The woman repositioned herself in her chair.

"The news reports portray the Fultons as the epitome of a wholesome, all-American family—pillars of the community."

"And you think they're not?"

"I didn't say that. Don't get me wrong. I'm sympathetic to what's happening to them. I hope they're safe, of course—they have a little boy! But I think—I mean, I *know* there's more to the story and I believe people should know about it."

Kate put her recorder on the table and her notebook.

The woman hesitated.

"You have nothing to worry about," Kate said, "if you're telling me the truth."

The woman considered the situation.

"And I don't have much time," Kate added.

"Before he died, my husband worked for Dixon Donlevy Mutual Life Insurance as a claims adjuster. He was due for a promotion to be a senior investigator of fraudulent claims out of the office in Queens, where we were living at the time."

Kate made notes.

"But the job went to Lori Fulton. My husband

was crushed. He'd been with the company over twenty years. To make room for Lori, he was given a lateral position, which meant a grinding commute into Manhattan."

"Okay." Kate stopped. "I'm sorry, but I'm not sure this is the information I'm looking for. What's this got to do with what's happening now?"

"My husband's boss had a connection with the bank and Lori's husband, so when they were moving from California, he'd arranged for Lori to get the job that should've gone to my husband."

"All right, so he was passed over for a promotion. I still don't think this has any relevance to the current situation." Kate checked the time. This was a mistake. This was a case of a woman who'd held a grudge and was looking to vent, and it all seemed rather petty.

"Sorry, I'm complicating this. I still get a bit emotional. The reason Lori got the job as a fraud investigator is because in California she'd been a police officer."

"A police officer?" Kate sat up and made a note underlining it.

"Yes, and… I think that may be connected to what's happened now."

"That's quite a leap," Kate said. "How does her being a police officer have anything to do with her husband robbing his bank—or with her and her son being held hostage?"

"Well, I don't know. That's for the police to figure out."

"And did you contact them with your suspicion?"

"No, but I'm sure they must know that she was a cop. Police have access to these things. My husband's boss was an ex-cop and favored hiring ex-cops for investigations." The woman pulled a tissue from her bag. "It's understandable, I know. But my Jackie had put in twenty-two years and had an exemplary record with the company. Then this Lori, who'd done nothing for Dixon Donlevy, aside from showing up, is handed his job on a platter. Jack never complained. He was loyal to the company. He made the commute every day…until his heart attack."

"Do you know where in California Lori Fulton was a cop?"

The woman shrugged. "I don't know. But one night, Jack told me that he'd heard that Lori Fulton was involved in something terrible. Something happened when she was a cop that forced her to quit, to leave the force—and that was the reason the Fultons had moved to New York."

"I need something that proves you have a connection to this. How can I be sure you're not making this up?"

The woman reached into her bag.

"I knew you might ask." She pulled out a small stack of papers and photos and put them on the table. "This is me and my husband, Jack, on our last vacation in South Carolina," she said, pointing to the photo at the top of the pile.

It was a photo of the woman and man smiling on a beach.

"And here's a photo of our last Dixon Donlevy

Christmas party. That's me with Jack, and there… you see? Lori and Dan Fulton."

Kate saw the faces of several smiling people, including the Fultons.

"And here," the woman continued, pulling a piece of paper from the bottom of the stack, "is the staff notice Dixon Donlevy put out when Lori got the job and Jack got his transfer. Jack brought it home and showed me—he was so disappointed. We kept it in our files."

"May I take pictures of this material to show my editors that it supports what you've told me?"

"As long as you swear to me you won't publish them."

"I wouldn't—not without your permission."

"And you won't use my name or Jack's name, either? You'll find them on some of these papers."

"Not without permission."

The woman touched her tissue to her eyes.

"I know in my heart that had my husband got the job he earned instead of Lori Fulton, he'd be alive today."

"What about your husband's boss at the company, the ex-cop. What's his name? I could talk to him?" Kate asked, after snapping a few photos of the items on the table.

"Angelo Korda. But you won't be able to talk to him. He drowned two years ago, fishing in Maine."

"Did your husband ever hint at what went wrong for Lori?"

"No. I have no idea of what she was up to in California. But if it was bad enough that she had to quit her job and leave the state, then maybe it could be linked to what's happened to her family."

Kate got a number and email address from the woman in case she needed to contact her again. Then Kate promised once more to protect her identity, thanked her and left. She wove around the dozens of families surrounding the carousel. Amid the huffing pipe organ and squeals of happy children, she realized one thing.

She was getting closer to a bigger story.

28

Manhattan, New York

The subject was a white male with large, soft eyes that hinted at innocence, a stubbled chin and tousled hair framing the face of a man barely out of his teens.

His photo filled the large monitor in the boardroom at the FBI's office at 26 Federal Plaza in Lower Manhattan.

"This is our prime suspect. Jerricko Titus Blaine," Nick Varner told the investigators at the table and those who'd dialed in from across the country for the emergency case-status meeting on the robbery. "Based on the evidence, which we've outlined in the case summary notes we've provided you, we don't believe Blaine acted alone."

The FBI, the NYPD, New York State Police, Homeland Security and a range of local, state and federal law enforcement agencies had joined the ongoing investigation, which grew with every passing hour.

After summarizing key facts known so far,

Varner's top agenda item was to find their primary suspect: Jerricko Titus Blaine.

"Blaine's prints were left on duct tape found in the Fulton home that we believe was used to bind the family," Varner said. "You've all been provided with our status sheet on this case—Blaine's height, weight, DOB and any other information we currently have. Blaine's last known address was in Dallas, Texas, so that's where we're headed. Doyle, what do you have?"

The voice of Trent Doyle, an agent with the FBI's Dallas division, came through loud and clear over the conference phone speaker.

"We've got our people heading to Blaine's last address with warrants, and we've got detectives from DPD initiating a canvass and scouring all local and state records. We're pursuing any employers, relatives, friends and associates."

"Good," Varner said, as he took notes. He noticed how one detective hadn't stopped staring at Blaine's photo. Almost as though he recognized him. Varner kept his eye on him as he continued. "Blaine's Social Security Number shows he was born in Torrance, California, and attended school there. Over to you, LA. What can you tell us?"

Bill Kendrick with the FBI's Los Angeles division gave an update.

"We're working with the LAPD and Los Angeles County. We've dispatched teams to all addresses associated with Blaine."

"Schools?" Varner said.

"Yes, we're going to schools, looking into any

jobs he held, searching for relatives and any associates."

"Marv, you want to jump in here?"

"Marv Tilden, NYPD. We're circulating Blaine's photo to all confidential informants, we're going door-to-door in the Fultons' neighborhood in Queens. We're also chasing down family, friends, social circles. We're going through the family's computer and phone records for any leads."

"Where are we on Dan Fulton?" an FBI agent at the table asked.

"We haven't located him or his car," Varner said. "There's been no activity on any of the Fultons' credit or bank cards. We're obtaining camera footage from the bank and neighboring businesses, and we're looking at all security footage we can secure from the Fultons' neighbors."

"What about the BOLO for Dan Fulton's Taurus?" the agent asked. "Anything from Real Time Crime Center?"

"Nothing so far," the NYPD commander for the center said. "They could've switched vehicles or changed Fulton's plate. The BOLO remains active."

"What about Fulton as a suspect?" an NYPD detective asked.

Varner flipped pages of his case notes.

"Unlikely, based on everything we know to be true at this stage—including the note he wrote before he left the bank. You've got all the details in the summary."

Varner clicked a button, and Dan Fulton's note appeared on the monitor next to Blaine's photo.

"What's Fulton's personal situation?" the detective asked. "Could he have set this up?"

"It's unlikely. We have no indication of him having any overwhelming debts, gambling or drug problems. Nothing that would require immediate access to a large sum of money, nothing that would make him this desperate. Right now we think the Fulton family was targeted."

"What about this threat from Luca Bazerinni?"

"We've not ruled that out. We've spoken to Bazerinni and executed search warrants on his company and home. So far we've found no grounds to show that Bazerinni acted on his threat. No connection between Blaine and Bazerinni. But we've not ruled him out. We're still processing material seized from his trucking operation and home."

"What about terrorism?" asked Henry Collins, an NYPD detective.

"It hasn't been ruled out," Varner said.

"Well, did Homeland run down Blaine's passport? Is he on any watch lists, or no-fly lists?"

Varner turned to the woman from the Department of Homeland Security, who cleared her throat.

"Our records show that a US passport has not been issued to Jerricko Titus Blaine."

"Maybe he used a fake one, or bought a foreign one?"

"DHS is investigating all possibilities," she said.

"Nick, what makes you think Blaine didn't act alone?" another investigator asked.

"The nature of the crime and the content of Dan Fulton's note."

Varner pointed to the note on the monitor: *Family held hostage at home! Strapped bombs on us!*

"If Dan is at the bank and his family is being held hostage at home, we don't think one person could pull this off alone."

"What about the wife, Lori Fulton?" another detective asked.

"We've got people talking to her employer at the insurance company," Tilden said. "We're looking into the cases where she investigated people involved in fraudulent insurance claims—anyone who might have held a grudge and who could be involved. So far nothing has surfaced. But there's a new aspect concerning Lori Fulton's previous job."

Tilden raised his eyebrows at Varner.

"Right," Varner said. "Now, this may have no bearing on the case here, but we've learned that Lori was with the Santa Ana Police Department in California, but we'll go to our RA in Santa Ana for the details. Wade?"

Wade Darden, with the FBI's resident agency in Orange County, California, gave a report.

"What we know is that she was using her maiden name at the time, Lori Wallace, and was a police officer with SAPD until she resigned after several months of disability leave for psychological trauma. It's believed the trauma resulted from an incident that occurred while she was on duty some six years ago. I'll be meeting with the Santa Ana PD after this call and should get full details as soon as possible."

Varner and Tilden then discussed theories and

other aspects with the group to ensure nothing was overlooked or no investigative threads were left unchecked.

"What about security incidents at the branch?" one detective asked.

"Nothing of consequence on record," Tilden said. "However, one teller told us she'd seen a man in a car using binoculars in the strip mall parking lot across the street from the bank. This happened within a few weeks of the incident. We believe he was casing the branch and we're going to be reviewing security footage from the mall."

"Okay," Varner said. "We'll be holding a press conference later today to share the basics with the public and make an appeal for information. If there are no other questions, that's all we have. Thanks, everyone."

As the investigators were leaving, Varner noticed that Henry Collins remained at the table, fixated on the notes he'd made.

"Henry," Varner said, "what're you thinking?"

"Nick, you're still with the Joint Terrorism Task Force, right?"

"Yes."

"Given that groups have been known to raise funds using drugs, kidnappings, ransoms, robberies and such, I'm thinking…maybe you really have to look at a terrorist connection."

"We are, Henry. We're looking at everything."

29

Near Harrogate, England

Huge white spheres stood against the rolling green hills and farms of North Yorkshire's moorland like a futuristic Stonehenge.

In a chamber deep below the complex, a US intelligence specialist listened to a fragment of an intercepted satellite phone exchange in Arabic.

"...is preparing to bring gifts to the wedding..."

The specialist reexamined the alert and summaries from the traffic operator, the linguist and the cryptologist, then he replayed the recording.

"...is preparing to bring gifts to the wedding... many, many guests...will be a big celebration..."

He sat up in his chair and began entering key notes from his analysis into his computer. His workstation was in a corner of the control room of the military installation known as Menwith Hill.

The base was owned by the British Ministry of Defence but was chiefly operated by the US National Security Agency. It was one of the most secretive intelligence-gathering systems in the world and the most secure. Food and supplies for the two thousand US military personnel and US contractors posted there were either delivered by ship or flown in from the United States.

The nearly three-dozen giant, white golf-ball-like structures rising from the base housed state-of-the-art satellite receivers and transmitters with an unparalleled ability to intercept every sort of communication anywhere on the planet. Operations had emerged from ECHELON, a communications network of listening posts around the world operated by Australia, Canada, New Zealand, the United Kingdom and the United States, to eavesdrop on the Soviet Union and the Eastern Bloc during the Cold War.

Menwith Hill now served as a critical missile warning line as part of the Ballistic Missile Defense System. The site was the European Relay Ground Station for the web of Space Based Infrared Satellites built to provide data on missile launches and trajectories.

But since September 11, 2001, terrorism had grown into the leading threat against the United States, its allies and other countries. Menwith Hill afforded its satellite imagery and surveillance capability to coordinate live, precise, military drone strikes and attacks by Special Forces against hostile elements. And intelligence units at the base ran operations intercepting and analyzing the communications of terror groups. Menwith's supercomputers were capable of making millions of intercepts an hour. In nearly each case, targets used coded internet communication, encrypted satellite phones or disposable phones. Advanced technology helped process the encrypted data at unimaginable speed using data-mining software that could quickly pluck and lock on to key words or phrases.

Then it came down to the human factor, because the information still needed further analysis.

Intelligence officers had to understand and make sense of the complex signals, determining what they meant and where they fit in. To help, they also used information extracted from captured suspects or recovered by technicians from seized equipment. Menwith also relied on the work of agents and sub-contractors in the field, whose sources and informants provided key but ever-changing data and positions.

In addition to the challenge of encrypted, coded exchanges, linguists had to contend with hundreds of languages. While they were the best translators in the world, they inevitably faced hurdles trying to comprehend everything they'd heard. A great deal could get by if you misunderstood slang, dialects or cultural contexts. The fear of missing critical information ran deep among all operators, no matter how long they'd been monitoring their target.

The intelligence specialist, who was fluent in Arabic, concentrated harder as he replayed the fragment of captured communications several more times.

"...is preparing to bring gifts to the wedding... many, many guests...will be a big celebration..."

The exchange was between two senior members

of an active jihadist group. He resumed typing on his keyboard, submitting a few lines of characters. The dialects were Levantine, the kind heard in Syria or Lebanon and the Arabian Peninsula, perhaps. San'ani or Ta'izzi-Adeni, which were known to parts of Yemen.

"...the most beautiful gift will be from the clock maker..."

The specialist continually replayed the conversation. For the past six months he'd been tracking a case that involved intercepts of individuals from Iraq, Afghanistan, Turkey, Athens and London. However, this most recent series of calls had bounced from Syria and Yemen to individuals somewhere in the United States.

The specialist let more of the intercept play out as he continued analyzing it and making notes.

"...will present it...overseas...it will be a celebration gloriously remembered..."

The specialist stopped to focus on what he had so far. He clicked on to the map he'd been maintaining, which included dates, time lines and notations based on the intercepts of this network. For months he'd been finding small connections that always seemed to dead-end. But today, with this intercepted fragment, he'd mined what he believed was a key puzzle piece in an unfolding plot.

An attack against the US is coming.

He called his supervisor to his desk.

"Ma'am, please listen to this. I think we have something here that builds on previous developments. Something big."

The supervisor slipped on the headset and listened.

"...will present it...overseas...it will be a celebration gloriously remembered..."

She listened two more times, consulted the specialist's notes and drew upon all the alerts she'd been privy to from the last forty-eight hours. She nodded.

"Write it up ASAP. We need to get this to our people at home."

30

Back at her desk in the newsroom, Kate took a hit of her take-out coffee.

Upon her return she'd received a text from Varner advising her about the upcoming FBI-NYPD press conference on the Fulton case. She glanced at the clock.

I've got a little time before it starts.

As Kate worked on following the lead from the woman she'd just met in Bryant Park, she continued to question the veracity of her source. The information she'd gotten was intriguing, but so far, Kate had found nothing to support the woman's claim.

Is she just another whack job?

Kate searched databases Newslead subscribed to and requested their news library, one of the best in the business, to help search for anything on a California police officer named Lori Fulton. She went back ten years to ensure everything was covered, but nothing had surfaced. Not one iota of information identifying Lori Fulton as a cop in California.

It made Kate skeptical of the woman's information. It was clear she'd held a grudge against Lori, steeping her account in bitterness. But she seemed certain Fulton had been a cop, and the internal notice by Dixon Donlevy hinted at it. The notice was brief, announcing that Lori Fulton would be the senior investigator of fraudulent claims in the Queens region; that she'd graduated from California State University with a degree in criminology and had many years of investigative experience. There were no details, no elaboration. When Kate called, Cal State couldn't confirm that Lori Fulton had ever attended.

Kate bit her lip to think, then picked up her phone again and dialed a number in Los Angeles belonging to a guy she'd dated a few times.

"*LA Times*, Benjamin Keller."

"Hi, Ben. Kate Page in New York."

"Kate! Hey, superstar, how's things in the Apple?"

"All good, and you?"

"Oh, you know, taking it day by day. What's up?"

"I need a little confidential help, Ben. It's urgent."

"If I can help you, I will. I owe you a few favors. Shoot."

"I need you to check with your sources on the name Lori Fulton. She was supposed to have been a cop in California when something went wrong and caused her to leave the force."

"What force?"

"That's what I need to know."

"How far back?"

"Say five to ten years." Kate gave him the spelling of Lori's name and her age.

"Sure, I can check this out pretty quickly. But promise you won't kill me with a story in my backyard, Kate. You have to share anything relevant for *LA Times*, all right?"

"Promise."

Kate hung up, took a breath, then called a number for San Francisco.

"Betty Yang, *Chronicle*."

"Hi, Betty. It's Kate in New York."

"Oh, my God, Kate! Great to hear from you. How are you?"

"I'm doing fine. It's been a while, though! How are things with you?"

"Mike and I just got a house in Daly City—he says I'm nesting. And I'm sending my love to your sister. My God, Kate, that was a hell of a thing. How's Vanessa doing?"

"Good, she's doing real good."

"And Grace?"

"She loves New York."

"Thanks for sending me the pictures. She's so pretty, just like her mom. So, what's going on?"

Kate, as she'd done with Ben in LA, asked Betty to help her look into Lori Fulton's supposed police background, and Betty agreed to check with her Bay Area police sources.

Then Kate glanced at the time and went to the restroom to check her face in preparation for the press conference. Her calls to Ben and Betty pulled her back to when they'd all worked at the *San Francisco Star.*

It was the best of times and the worst of times.

Kate had still been something of a wide-eyed rookie on the crime desk when, after a short fling with Ben, she'd met another guy—a fantastic guy. He was a cop. He was caring, charming and oh-so-easy on the eyes. She'd fallen hard for him, and after a few months of an intense, wildly physical relationship, Kate had become pregnant. She'd gone through a maelstrom of emotions at the news, but eventually decided to tell him about the baby.

That's when she'd learned that he'd been lying about being divorced. That he was still married, and that he had two little boys she'd had no idea about. He'd admitted that his marriage had gone through a rocky stage, but that he wasn't going to leave his wife. He'd blamed the pregnancy on Kate, offered to pay for an abortion, and, when she'd refused, he wrote her off completely.

They never spoke again.

Kate had been determined to keep her baby. She'd left San Francisco and gotten a job with the Repository in Canton, Ohio, where she'd had Grace at age twenty-three and decided to raise her on her own.

We survived.

For an instant, Kate thought of calling him to ask for help tracking down her lead on Lori Fulton.

An icy shiver coiled up her spine.

No. No way. I've never needed him for anything, and I won't start now.

Back at her desk Kate checked all the other news outlets for their latest on the Fulton story. Nobody had an edge. The *New York Times* noted and credited Newslead as reporting the amount stolen by Dan Fulton was a quarter million dollars. Kate smiled when she came upon a clarification issued by Signal Point Newswire, noting that it had erroneously reported the amount taken in the heist and would update the correct figure when it was available.

Kate's phone chimed with a text from Betty Yang at the *San Francisco Chronicle.* Checked Sacramento + Bay Area sources. Nothing on LF as a Calif cop—still checking.

Kate exhaled. Her tip was fizzling, as suspected. She'd have to look for another angle. Maybe something would come out of the press conference. Or she could pump Varner afterward, she thought, collecting her bag to leave just as her desk phone rang.

"Kate Page, Newslead."

"Hey, it's Ben. So far zip on any cop named Lori Fulton. Checked with LAPD, LA County, Orange, Riverside, San Bernardino, but I'm still looking."

Kate was disappointed but not surprised. "Thanks, Ben."

"I checked with the associations and had our researchers go through municipal employee lists. Nothing there, either."

"That's what I thought you'd say."

"Well, we did find something with Santa Ana PD that might be relevant. However, it's about a Lori Wallace, not Fulton. But the situation seems to fit what you described, and the date falls in the right time frame. Check it out—just emailed you the first clip from our Orange County edition."

Kate opened the file and read the headline: Police Officer and Suspect Killed in Shoot-out.

31

Somewhere in New York State

Lori and Billy watched the van door roll open.

Two men with military assault rifles stood before them.

Cutty and Thorne.

Both were still in coveralls, but they'd removed their masks, revealing two white men in their early twenties. Thorne had tousled hair, large eyes and a stubbled chin; Cutty, the big one, had a shaved head, a beard and a scar high on his left cheek.

She didn't recognize either of the men, but a new realization dawned on her as she looked at them, fear twisting deep in the pit of her stomach.

They can't let us live if we can identify them!

"Get out!" Cutty said.

Lori blinked as she adjusted to the sunlight after hours in the dark van.

They were somewhere in the mountains, atop a ridge overlooking vast sweeping forests stretching to the horizon in every direction. The air had cooled, now carrying the sweet scent of spruce and red cedar, woods so dense they looked impassable.

Where's Dan? Have they brought him here?

Not another vehicle or person in sight.

"Get moving!"

The ridge was crowned with a natural path of twigs and leaves that meandered for some forty to fifty yards up a gentle rise to a cabin. Cutty and Thorne walked behind them, unconcerned that they'd removed the tape from their mouths and wrists. Only the plastic handcuffs bound their hands in front of them. The small red lights on the battery packs of their suicide vests continued blinking.

Lori couldn't stop trembling, couldn't stop the adrenaline coursing through her as she battled to stay ahead of her fear.

Use it. Use it to fight back. Use it to protect Billy.

She swallowed hard and tried to find the strength to not give up.

On her left she'd noticed a small outbuilding that was at the end of a path that led into the woods some distance from the cabin.

Are we in the Catskills or the Adirondacks?

They climbed the stairs of the cabin's covered front deck, entering through the screen door. The interior was one large open area. One corner contained the kitchen, and there was a picnic table and a few Adirondack chairs set up near the middle.

Two large bunk beds occupied another corner.

An opened laptop and a backpack with a large

half-eaten bag of potato chips and bottles of water were on the picnic table. Clothes spilled from duffel bags near the bunk beds. In the far empty corner, a camera mounted on a tripod was pointed to a blank wall.

Lori grew uneasy.

What's that for?

Across from the bunk beds were two mattresses set side by side on the floor with sleeping bags and pillows. Two long, fine dog chains extended from steel hardware bolted to a wooden stud.

"Over there." Cutty pointed his gun to the mattresses.

Lori and Billy took a few steps to their corner before she turned.

"We haven't eaten and we need to go to the bathroom," she said.

Cutty looked at Thorne, who nodded.

"The boy first. Let's go." Cutty pointed to the cabin's rear screen door, which Lori could see opened to the path she'd noticed on her way in. He took Billy and she moved to go with him.

"Sit your ass down." Cutty pointed his gun at Lori and she froze midstep. He kept the gun aimed at her for a moment before heading out alone with Billy.

Lori hesitated at the screen door, watching them.

"Sit down—" Thorne held up his phone "—or I dial a number and he's gone."

Lori sat.

When it was her turn, Cutty took her to the outhouse at the end of the path, about thirty yards from the cabin. He forced her to leave the door open, as he'd done with Billy, and relieve herself at gunpoint with her hands cuffed in plastic.

Necessity helped her endure the humiliation.

When they'd returned to the cabin, Lori saw that they'd locked a metal handcuff on Billy's ankle, fastening him to the chain that hung from the wall. With several quick snaps, they did the same to her. The metal cuff was cold on her skin as she crawled to sit next to Billy on his mattress.

Cutty tossed the handcuff keys onto the table next to Thorne.

"You take them next time," he said, then pulled out store-bought egg salad sandwiches and water from the backpack on the picnic table and handed them to Lori.

Their chains jingled softly as they ate.

Cutty stripped off his coveralls. Now he was wearing jeans and a black Led Zeppelin T-shirt with the words Hammer of the Gods on it. He dragged one of the chairs closer, placing it in front of the back door. He sat with his gun on his lap, watching them over his phone while he played a video game. Thorne had removed his coveralls, too. He was wearing khaki cargo pants and a military green T-shirt. He faced them from the picnic table where he watched them over his laptop as he worked with his gun next to him.

Soft beeping and clicking mingled with birdsong, breezes and the occasional swish of water as Billy drank from his bottle.

After they were done eating, Billy fell asleep.

In that surreal moment, as Lori struggled to understand what had befallen them, she wished Dan was by her side.

"Can I please talk to my husband again?"

Cutty ignored her. Thorne continued working on his laptop. The silence grew ominous.

"Why are you doing this to us?"

Thorne stopped his work and looked at her.

"Because you deserve it."

She was baffled—what could she possibly have done to deserve this? "I don't understand."

"You will. You were chosen because of your crimes as nonbelievers."

"Nonbelievers?"

"Let me show you what happens to nonbelievers."

Thorne got up from the table with his laptop, holding it so Lori could see the video he played for her.

A woman in her thirties was on her knees in the desert. Her hands were tied behind her back.

Lori gasped. The familiar footage was from a recent news report she'd seen on TV. She remembered that the woman was an aid worker from England working in the Middle East before she'd been taken hostage by extremists. Lori had never seen the video in its entirety. It was too graphic for news networks to broadcast. Standing next to the woman was a man, clad head to toe in black. A black balaclava concealed his face. He held a large knife in one hand and was ranting to the camera before he yanked the woman's hair back, exposing her throat and—the knife flashed—Lori turned away.

She knew what followed.

The woman had been beheaded.

32

Music hammered in the hallway.

Empty pizza boxes, beer cans and used napkins were strewn along the floor. Vulgar graffiti bled on the cracked walls near Unit 506 of the apartment complex in South Dallas.

This was Jerricko Titus Blaine's most recent address.

From the command post across the street, Dallas FBI agent Trent Doyle trained his binoculars on Blaine's unit. Colors and shadows flashed as someone inside moved from room to room.

One of Blaine's associates?

Doyle rolled the focus wheel.

The Dallas Police Department had set up the outer perimeter and helped evacuate the building's residents. Children clutched stuffed toys, and a white-haired woman grabbed her Bible as anxious tenants were escorted out of harm's way to a park just beyond the perimeter set up with police tape.

The SWAT team, which had already studied the

building's floor plan, moved swiftly and quietly into position, forming the inner perimeter.

The music still pulsed from behind the door of apartment 506.

This part of Dallas generated a large number of police calls to the neighborhood every day. Over the past six years, five officers had been shot while executing warrants, as the FBI, backed by Dallas PD, was doing today. The five officers had survived, but it was just another reason why Doyle, like all others at the command post, was wearing body armor.

Slowly, he swung his binoculars toward the snipers on the adjacent building's roof. There were others behind Dumpsters, cars, and in apartment units facing the target.

Inside the building, SWAT members had taken positions on the stairs leading up to Unit 506, and on the landing, the fire escape and the roof. Everyone was in place, whispering reports over their headsets above the thunder of the music.

Given that Blaine was suspected in an ongoing robbery-hostage-taking, the team poised for a no-knock, forced rapid entry. After a final round of radio checks, the commander gave the green light to his squad sergeant. A signal was relayed to the electricity company. Power was suddenly cut. The building became eerily silent, save for the distant yelp of a dog.

Within seconds, deafening flash-bang grenades smashed through windows and heavily armed SWAT members charged through the apartment door and the windows from the balcony, shouting orders to the man on the sofa.

"FBI! Get on the floor, now!"

SWAT members, guns drawn, forced him to the floor amid the smoke and chaos.

"Hey, what the hell's this!" the man protested while on his stomach as his hands were cuffed behind him.

He was in his twenties. He wore a tie-dye T-shirt and torn jeans.

His wallet was yanked from his back pocket.

He was Eldon Luna, age 24, of Arlington, according to his Texas driver's license.

"Hey, what the hell? You hurt my ears, assholes!"

The bathroom was checked, closets were checked; special equipment was used to scan the walls and ceiling for body mass. As the smoke from the grenades dissipated, the apartment was inspected two more times. The sound of metal against glass sounded as one agent tapped his weapon against a large rectangular tank in one corner.

"Damn! That a python?"

"It's an Asiatic rock python."

"You got a permit for it, Eldon?"

"It's not mine."

The squad leader radioed his commander, who alerted Doyle and the other agents that the apartment was cleared and declared safe.

By the time they'd entered, Eldon Luna had been placed back on the sofa where he remained handcuffed and under guard. While the other agents tugged on latex gloves and searched the unit, Doyle sat on the coffee table and faced Luna.

"Man, I think you dicks got the wrong place. I'm going to call a lawyer and I'm going to sue your asses off," Luna said.

"Yes, you could do that from jail, Eldon, where we're going to hold you for seventy-two hours. A lot can happen to you in jail in that time. Or...you can cooperate with us."

"Cooperate? Why? I didn't do anything."

"Do you know Jerricko Titus Blaine?"

Luna said nothing.

Doyle leaned into his space.

"Do you want to sleep in a cell tonight?"

"No."

"Answer the question."

"Jerricko rents this place."

"Where is Mr. Blaine?"

"What's this about? Is he in some sort of trouble?"

"Answer the question."

"He's out of town on business."

"Where?"

"I don't know."

"Think again."

"I really don't know. He's been away for a few weeks."

"What're you doing in his apartment, Eldon?"

"He's letting me stay here because my old lady kicked me out."

"How do you know him?"

"I met him at a computer science conference in Fort Worth."

"Eldon, tell me what you know about the robbery."

"What robbery?"

Doyle indicated the cell phone and laptop on the coffee table next to him.

"These yours?"

"Yes."

"We've got warrants to search everything on the premises. I'm sure we'll find all kinds of enlightening evidence once our people probe every aspect of your life."

Luna looked fearfully at Doyle then the other agents.

"I really don't know what you're talking about."

"You think fast and you think hard. Things will go much better for you if you cooperate with us now. Later will be too late."

"Think hard about what? I don't even know what this is about!"

"Are you involved in the robbery in any way?"

"I don't know anything about a robbery."

"Did you help plot it?"

"What? Plot what?"

"How long have you lived here?"

"About a month."

"Can you prove it?"

"Ask my ex-girlfriend, Karen. Karen McWhinney. She kicked me out a month ago. I'll give you her number."

"How did you come to live here?"

"After the conference, Jerricko and I hung out. He liked to talk about politics and we agreed that America had made some bad policy choices in the Middle East. We had some good talks, became friends. Then when Karen kicked me out, Jerricko invited me to live with him and Rose."

"Rose?"

"His python."

Doyle rubbed his hand over his face. This kid was running him in circles. "Tell me about Jerricko."

"Easy to live with. He's quiet, doesn't like rock music. I respected that. He was always in his room on his computer. I could hear him talking to people online or over the phone."

"Do you know who he talked to?"

"No. I'm not nosy—why should I know who he talks to?"

"What did they talk about?"

"I only heard parts. I wasn't listening because it was none of my business. And usually I'm just listening to music on my headphones since he doesn't like it, or watching a movie or something. His TV's awesome."

"Can you recall anything about the conversations you overheard?"

"Not much…"

"Did you ever hear Jerricko mention someone named Dan Fulton? Or anything about New York? Anything about a bank?"

Eldon shook his head.

"Anything about bombs?"

"Bombs? Hell, no. What's going on?"

"Eldon, I need you to focus and tell me anything you did hear."

"I heard some stuff about politics, the news, oppression and…stuff about nonbelievers, or something. But I wasn't listening."

Doyle was making notes.

"Anything else that sticks out? Anything that sounded strange?"

Luna shook his head, then stopped and bit his lip.

"Wait. There was one thing that was weird. The last time he called here to check in, he said that if anything happened to him he wanted me to take care of Rose."

33

Lieutenant Sean Baylor came around his desk and greeted FBI agent Wade Darden with a crushing handshake.

"Have a seat, Wade. Got everything right here."

Darden, the Bureau's resident agent for Orange County, was handling the FBI's urgent request for the Santa Ana PD to share the personnel records of Lori Wallace, a former officer with the force.

Several file folders waited on the small table where Darden and Baylor pored over them.

"Okay, from the top. We've got her application—she was married to Dan Fulton at the time but kept her family name, Wallace. There's her education file. She's got a degree in criminology from Cal State," Baylor said.

Turning over file pages, Darden took his time, reading carefully through Lori Wallace's background investigation, her personal history statement and her psychological evaluation, which included a written exam and an interview with a psychologist.

"She passed her medical and excelled on physical agility, the wall, the long pursuit and the body drag. High scores at the range, too," Baylor said.

They continued flipping pages that reflected an exemplary career.

"In the four years she was on the job she was mostly on patrol. She'd received several commendations. Letters of thanks from the community," Baylor said. "She took a little time off when she had her baby, came back to more commendations."

They turned to pages documenting new assignments.

"She did outstanding investigative work and was on track to become a detective," Baylor said. "Then it all turned to crap. It's the next folder, Wade."

Darden opened the red folder of reports, pages of statements, maps, drawings, photographs and a list of other items relating to one homicide and a police-involved shooting.

"Wallace and her partner, Tim Rowland, a seven-year veteran, are on overnight patrol," Baylor said. "They roll up to a corner store for a coffee and come upon an armed robbery in progress. As they step out of their patrol car, the suspect, who had just robbed the clerk of one hundred and sixty-one dollars, is exiting and firing a handgun into the store, hitting a pregnant woman in the arm. Rowland reacts, reaches for his sidearm but the shooter beats him, getting off three rounds, hitting Rowland in the jaw, neck and shoulder above his vest. Rowland stumbles back, collapsing into Wallace, who manages to catch him while drawing her weapon and firing at the suspect.

"The suspect fires more rounds at Rowland, who is now a shield for Wallace, enabling her to fire repeatedly at the suspect, hitting him in the head and heart, killing him while Rowland dies on top of her in her arms. That's what happened. Much of it was caught on the store's security cameras. I'll get you a copy of the videos."

Darden stared at the photos, shaking his head in awe.

"That's one hell of a firefight, Sean."

"The investigators say it all went down in four or five seconds. It's all there in the report."

Darden turned to the next folder and Baylor continued his story.

"She surrendered her weapon, homicide took over and all procedures were followed to the letter with regard to a police-involved shooting."

The next reports showed that Wallace took leave with pay and underwent counseling.

"The district attorney's office called it a righteous shooting and Wallace was cleared of any wrongdoing," Baylor said.

Reports showed that five months later, Wallace returned to patrol with a new partner but had trouble concentrating on the job.

"One day, they were backing up other units, pursuing a suspect reportedly armed with a gun after a domestic. Wallace had taken a point at the side of the house. When they called on her to move, she didn't respond. She just froze. They found her on her knees, sobbing and calling out Rowland's name. She took another leave from duty after that."

Wallace underwent more intense therapy, according to the files. The next reports showed that her posttraumatic stress after Rowland's murder was more severe than first thought. The final document showed that she'd resigned from the department.

"It was a shame because she was about to make detective," Baylor said. "To help get her life back together, her husband sought a transfer and accepted a post with the branch in Roseoak Park in Queens. They wanted a fresh start. He helped Lori get a job investigating fraudulent claims at Dixon Donlevy Mutual Life Insurance."

Darden read the glowing letter of recommendation Santa Ana's police chief had written to the company on her behalf.

Flipping back through the files he shook his head, stopping to reread her psychological reports detailing how she was grappling with survivor's guilt and guilt over the killing of the twenty-five-year-old suspect, Malcolm Jordan Samadyh.

"Do you have anything on the shooter?" he asked.

"Blue folder," Baylor said.

Darden studied Samadyh's file. He had a long criminal record. When he was twenty, he was sentenced to three years for robbery at Tehachapi, the state prison in Southern California's Cummings Valley.

His mother, an English teacher, had been born in

a war-torn tribal region of Afghanistan where she'd met Malcolm's father, an American aid worker from Los Angeles. They'd moved to California, gotten married and she became a US citizen. She'd given birth to Malcolm soon after and then his younger brother.

According to his file, Malcolm had been fourteen when his dad was killed in a traffic accident. Apparently he'd never gotten over it—instead he'd gotten into trouble, joining a gang, which led to crime, prison and, eventually, his death.

Just as he was closing the binder, Darden stopped cold. He'd almost missed it.

Flipping back through the shooter's file, he found the records showing that, while in prison, Malcolm had taken his mother's family name. Malcolm's father's name was Andrew Blaine.

Malcolm's little brother was Jerricko Titus Blaine.

Darden reached for his phone.

34

Manhattan, New York

Dan Fulton's in the vault, opening his briefcase, unfolding a duffel bag, filling it with bricks of cash then leaving the bank. Now he's walking hurriedly to his Ford Taurus in the near-empty parking lot, driving out of the west exit.

"Run it again, Steph," Varner said.

Agent Stephanie Transki, the New York FBI's forensic video expert, clicked her mouse, replaying the security video taken inside SkyNational Trust Branch 487. They'd received it at the FBI's New York division some thirty minutes earlier from the bank's security team. The recording was packaged with footage from exterior cameras monitoring the building.

The contrast was good, the images clean and sharp. The exterior recording had captured two parked cars in the lot belonging to the tellers who'd opened the bank, but no other movement or individuals.

No new leads here, Varner thought.

"Okay, thanks, Steph. We're still working on getting you video from the businesses nearby." Varner checked his watch. "We don't have much time for you to get this segment ready for the media at the press conference."

"Don't worry, Nick, I'll have it ready."

Varner headed for his floor. He stopped off at the cafeteria for a coffee. He'd missed lunch and grabbed an apple, biting into it in the elevator on his way to the twenty-eighth floor. Leaving the elevator, Varner went down the main reception hall, past the framed photos of executive agents. He glanced at the display nearby honoring agents killed in the line of duty as the result of a direct adversarial force, the "Service Martyrs."

Entering his section, he saw that most members of his squad were at their desks, working the phones and studying data. As he began making notes to prepare for the press conference, he found a story in the online edition of the *New York Post*.

Mob Link to Queens Bank Heist Investigated:
Source

The story alleged that the robbery of a bank in Queens had to do with "bad blood" between the branch manager and a businessman with ties to the mob. It reported that bank manager Dan Fulton robbed his own branch after telling "shocked bank staff" his family had been taken hostage, according to an "inside source."

Varner cursed to himself after digesting the story.

What a load of BS.

Maybe the source was from the NYPD's 115th Precinct, or maybe a disgruntled employee, or one of Luca Bazerinni's competitors was spreading this bull.

It doesn't matter who it is. This kind of crap hurts us.

Varner didn't have time to dwell on it. He had to focus on the facts.

Jerricko Titus Blaine was their suspect.

His were the only prints tied to the crime. But he couldn't have acted alone. The FBI and NYPD were working their confidential informants for any intel from the street as to who was behind the robbery. So far, nothing had surfaced. It could've had something to do with the fact that Blaine was in his early twenties, had no criminal record.

And, he'd left a print, suggesting he was not an experienced criminal.

Something's out of place here.

Varner opened Blaine's photo.

Looking at it, he recalled how one NYPD detective had raised the suspicion of a terrorist connection. Varner, being a member of the New York's Joint Terrorism Task Force, the JTTF, had not ruled that out. There were JTTFs in over one hundred cities in the US, made up of an array of local, state and federal agencies, all monitoring possible threats in their jurisdictions. New York City had the largest

JTTF, and as a member, Varner had access to many resources that were shared nationwide.

One of them was Guardian, a database holding information about threat reports, questionable incidents and other intelligence information. Members entered suspicious activity reports, which could be viewed or searched immediately by all of Guardian's authorized system users. Once Blaine's name had surfaced, Varner took the precaution of submitting it and a summary of the case to Guardian.

He logged in to check for any results.

Nothing.

He logged out.

Apart from Guardian, Blaine's name had also been submitted to a spectrum of national security databases, watch lists and no-fly lists.

Nothing had emerged. He was clear.

Something's up with this one. What am I missing?

He repeated the question to the framed photo of his wife, Jennifer.

Help me here, Jenn, what am I missing?

Varner's heart softened. As he took in her smile he could almost smell her, feel her and hear her laugh. It'd been three years since he'd lost her to brain cancer, just when they'd started talking about having children. His life was never the same. Every year since, he'd run in the charity marathons with her photo tucked into his participant badge, so it faced his heart. Not a day passed that he didn't ache for her.

Next to the photo, he noticed a reporter's business card tucked in with some papers. Pulling it out, a different woman's face came to mind.

Kate Page.

She haunted him because her eyes held the same spark, the same intensity as Jenn's. She was a firebrand, one of the best reporters he'd encountered. She frustrated him, yet he was drawn to her.

Varner shifted his attention to preparing for the press conference and continued working until his phone rang.

"Varner."

"Nick, Bill Kendrick in Los Angeles. Sounds like Wade Darden, our RA in Orange County, got something out of Santa Ana."

"Better give it to me fast, Bill. I'm heading into a news conference."

"When Lori Fulton was with the Santa Ana PD, she used her maiden name, Wallace. She was involved in a shooting where her partner was killed, and she killed his shooter. The shooter was Malcolm Jordan Samadyh, but—get this—his little brother is Jerricko Titus Blaine."

Varner was stunned. "Damn."

"I know. We'll send you everything."

"All right. I've gotta go, but, thanks, Bill. And thank Wade and Santa Ana."

Varner had less than ten minutes before the press conference but first he had to alert his boss...

He hurried from his desk to brief his supervisor face-to-face.

35

Dan, Lori and Billy Fulton stared from enlarged photos posted to the tripod beside the podium with the FBI seal.

On the opposite side of the podium stood another tripod bearing an enlarged head-and-shoulder shot of Jerricko Titus Blaine and a picture of a Ford Taurus identical to the color and year of Dan Fulton's car.

Kate Page estimated some seventy newspeople had gathered for the FBI's press conference at Federal Plaza. Intense light washed over the room's front as news crews adjusted lenses and microphones. Reporters tested recorders, texted, scribbled notes, gossiped or made last-minute calls while FBI, NYPD and other officials took their places, lining up abreast behind the podium.

Standing at the back, Kate tapped her notebook gently against her leg, searching the line of investigators until she found Varner and Tilden. She needed to talk with them privately later about what she'd discovered.

Prior to the press conference she'd contacted one of the legal research agencies Newslead used. After conducting an urgent documents search, they'd obtained records showing Wallace was Lori Fulton's maiden name. Her marriage license showed that she'd kept it after marrying Dan. Later, around the time they'd moved from California to New York, she'd changed her name to Lori Fulton.

In the cab to Federal Plaza, Kate had devoured several more archived articles on the shooting from the *Los Angeles Times* and *Orange County Register.* No other news organization had reported that Lori Fulton had shot and killed Malcolm Jordan Samadyh.

That was all Kate had, and, so far, it appeared that no one else had this information. Her competitors' news reports never went beyond portraying Lori as an insurance fraud investigator with Dixon Donlevy. The shooting was Kate's lead and it could be a significant exclusive.

Kate was doing all she could to keep her friend Ben Keller at the *LA Times* from jumping on the California angle to the New York robbery. She continued promising she would share information once she'd unearthed more about whether Lori's past was tied to the robbery.

"Let's get started," FBI special agent Leo Hurwitz said from the podium.

After introducing the sober-faced men and women in suits and uniforms who were flanking him, Hurwitz gave a summary of the case, which echoed the handout every journalist had received upon arrival. Then he moved on to their latest findings.

"Security video from the branch shows Dan Fulton in the bank's vault removing the cash and departing the parking lot in his blue 2015 Ford Taurus SEL, which has not yet been recovered," Hurwitz said as the FBI then showed about twenty seconds of footage on the large monitors at the front of the room.

"Our investigation has identified Jerricko Titus Blaine as a person of interest."

Kate wrote down the name in her notebook. *Another piece of the puzzle,* she thought as the agent continued.

"We're currently attempting to locate Mr. Blaine. We're appealing to the public, to anyone with any information about this crime, to contact us right away. We'll take a few questions now," Hurwitz said, opening the floodgates.

"If there're bombs involved, have you ruled out a link to terrorists?" a reporter shouted over the cacophony of voices.

"Nothing's been ruled out."

"What about reports that the robbery's connected to someone with mob ties—is this true?"

"While not all reporting on the case has been accurate thus far, nothing can be ruled out at this time."

"Have you dismissed the possibility that Fulton himself is involved, that this is an inside job?"

"We are prepared to say that that scenario is also being investigated."

"What can you tell us about Jerricko Blaine?"

"His last known address is in Dallas, Texas."

"Why are you interested in him? Is he a suspect?"

"We're not prepared to go into that sort of detail."

"Does he know the family?"

"Again, we're not going into that kind of information."

"Is anyone else involved?"

"All part of the investigation."

For the next twenty minutes the press was unrelenting with questions.

Kate watched Varner and Tilden, who remained poker-faced, betraying no reaction to the questions or responses. When many of the questions became repetitive, Hurwitz moved to conclude matters, stating, "Before we wrap this up, we want to stress that this case only became known to law enforcement earlier today. The investigation is ongoing on several fronts. More information will be released when we have it. Again we're asking for anyone with any information about this crime to contact us. Thank you all for coming."

Kate was relieved that no one else had raised questions about Lori Fulton's time as an ex-cop in California. She texted Varner.

Need to speak with you now. Have information on the case.

Kate saw Varner reach for his phone, read her message, lift his head and nod to a corner. She worked her way through the departing press and police pack toward an alcove where Varner and Tilden waited.

"What is it?" Varner kept his voice low.

"There's more to this case than you guys are telling us."

"Is that so?" Tilden said. "Why don't you enlighten us?"

"I know Lori Fulton used to be a cop in California with Santa Ana PD and that she killed the perp who killed her partner. Why did none of that come up here?"

Varner and Tilden shared a look but said nothing.

"How did you come about this information?" Varner asked.

"Journalistic investigation. Some of us still do that sort of thing rather than just swallow what you guys shovel out."

"So why are you telling us your theories?" Tilden said.

"These aren't theories. They're cold, hard facts, Detective Tilden, and I'm going to report them. Now, here's my theory—I think there's way more to this case than you're releasing. I think this could be about somebody settling an old score."

The muscles in Varner's jaw were pulsating.

"Let's cut the bull, Page. I've told you before, this case is complicated. Lives are at stake, and revealing those details at this stage could jeopardize the safety of innocent victims." Varner nodded to the faces of the Fulton family on the tripod. "You want to risk their lives for your story."

Kate glanced toward the photos.

"Are you asking me not to publish what I've learned?"

"I'm asking you to use your head and not rush into anything."

"Let me be clear. I would never, *ever*, want my reporting to be the cause of people getting hurt, but at the same time I'm not going to suppress valid news that I've obtained. Sooner or later, someone else will discover Lori's past life and report it. You both know that's the way it works."

"Look, what do you want, Page?" Tilden asked.

"A deal."

"A deal? We look like we're selling cars?"

"I'll hold off reporting on Lori Fulton's past, and you give me exclusivity to any breaks on the investigation. It's win-win. I get the story, but I only publish it when you give me the green light."

Tilden looked at Varner, who glared at Kate, letting a long, tense moment pass before blinking.

"All right, I'll consider it."

"You'll consider it?"

"No guarantees. That's the best you're going to get right now, Kate. Take it or leave it."

"I'll take it."

"And, Kate? Don't ever pull this again."

36

Manhattan, New York

Reeka swooped upon Kate the instant she'd returned to the newsroom from the press conference.

"How was it? Anything there that will get us ahead on this story?" She walked alongside Kate to her desk while checking her phone.

Kate couldn't reveal what she had on Lori Fulton. Not yet. She needed more time to dig, she thought, as she sat down and logged into her computer.

"I'm working on it."

"What've you got?"

In the tense air of Reeka's question, Kate stuck to her rules.

Never tell an editor what you've got until you've nailed it. And never tell an editor what thorny deals you've arranged with sources. Reeka wouldn't understand or support Kate's agreement with the FBI—she'd want to take the lead and run with it as soon as possible. But this angle had the potential to be huge and she needed her deal with Varner to pay off—if it went sideways, it would be disastrous.

In frustration, Reeka tapped Kate's desk with her phone. "Kate, what've you got?"

"Sorry—nothing concrete at the moment. I'm just following a few loose ends."

"Okay, here we go." Reeka was suddenly distracted by a message on her phone. "Here's a development. FBI agents have just raided Jerricko Blaine's apartment in Texas. Our Dallas bureau has sent us raw copy. I'm flipping it to you now. I want you to weave it into your update story."

"Okay, got it."

"Kate, we have to go deep on Jerricko Blaine. Work with our Dallas people to find out who he is. Let's craft a biography."

After Reeka left, Kate quickly read through the copy sent by Tasha Krause from Newslead's Dallas bureau. It was solid stuff on the SWAT team at Jerricko Blaine's apartment and the reaction from residents. Kate called Tasha for more details.

When Tasha answered, Kate could hear a honking horn and laughing children in the background. Tasha was outside on the street.

"Hi, Tasha? It's Kate Page in New York. Got your copy on Blaine—looks good. Anything new on Jerricko Blaine to add?"

"Bits and pieces. I'm still talking to residents."

"Do we know much more about him?"

"A little. The FBI took a roommate in for questioning. Neighbors say Blaine was pretty quiet, kept to himself. That's what they always say, isn't it? One weird thing—he had a pet snake, a python or boa. Anyway, it's illegal and the animal control people took it away. They needed four guys to carry it. We got pictures."

"You find any relatives or friends?"

"Not yet. I'll try to get the roommate."

"What about Blaine? Does he work? Is he a student?"

"He works. Hold on… I've got something here from a neighbor." Tasha was quiet and Kate could hear as she paged through her notes. "Here it is— he works, or worked, at the Fire and Steel Truck Emporium, washing big rigs. It's a truck stop on the LBJ Freeway."

Kate wrote it down.

"You talk to anybody there, Tasha?"

"Not yet."

"Okay, leave the truck stop to me. Keep us posted if you get anything from the roommate."

Kate went online and found the website for Fire and Steel Truck Emporium. She combed through several pages until she found a number for the truck wash and called it.

"Truck wash, J. T. Flores."

"Hi, J.T. I'm Kate Page, a reporter with Newslead in New York."

"You don't say."

"Do you have a second?"

"That's about all I got. I got units waiting."

"Do you know Jerricko Blaine?"

Kate heard a two-way radio then heard Flores yell to someone.

"You're done, buddy, take it! Go! Jerricko, yeah. He used to work here. Quit a while back. What's this all about, anyway? I got a business card here from some FBI agent who dropped by asking about Jerricko when I was at the dentist today. I'm supposed to call him. You wanna tell me what the hell's going on?"

"You haven't seen the news?"

"Ma'am, I'm a busy workin' man." Another crackle on the radio, and Flores shouted, "Roll it ahead, to the left. No! Left!"

"Blaine's wanted by the FBI for a bank robbery in Queens, New York."

"What? A bank robbery? In New York? Jerricko—no way. Hell, that's gotta be wrong. I *do not* believe it. Not one bit."

"Why's that?"

"He was just such a quiet kid and a good worker. I can't see him doing something like this."

"Did you ever talk with him much?"

"Not much. Like I said, he was mostly pretty quiet. When he did talk, though, it was usually about the same thing—he was worried about all the suffering in the Middle East. I never understood why he got so intense about that stuff. It's not like he was from there, at least as far as I knew. It just seemed odd to me."

"When you say he got intense, can you give me an example?"

"Well if it wasn't trouble in the Middle East that got him going, it would be some music video that would come on the TV in the break room and he'd get going about how it was immoral or something. I guess he didn't approve of the behavior of some young people—he seemed pretty conservative, you know? But, hey, this is Texas."

"How did you come to hire him?"

"I got him through an online job posting. I had an opening for a truck washer, he applied. We liked him, hired him, and it all worked out for a while. About ten months, I guess. Then he told me he had to quit for another job he'd got in Kentucky or Ohio, someplace like that."

"Do you remember where he worked before he started with your company?"

"Huh… I think it was… Oh, at the airport, that's right. He was cleaning rental cars."

"Did you know much about his background, check his references?"

"Naw, he did fine in the interview and I needed him that day."

"Do you know if he has any family or friends in Dallas?"

"He never said much about that stuff. But, come to think of it, one time we were working late together and during our break he talked about where he grew up and how he sometimes missed it."

"Where's that?"

"California."

Kate caught her breath.

"California?"

"Somewhere around LA, I think."

37

Varner clawed at his collar button and yanked his tie loose as he stepped into his office after his exchange with Kate at the news conference.

He dropped into his chair, jabbed the keys of his keyboard looking for the data Bill Kendrick in Los Angeles had promised to send him on Lori Fulton's connection to Jerricko Titus Blaine.

This was a critical lead, and Varner was sickened that it could be handed directly to the suspects by a reporter, which could lead Blaine and the other subjects to destroy evidence and jeopardize prosecution of the case, ruining any element of surprise that might work in their favor when it came time to close in.

How did Page get on to this? Is she that good? Or is someone leaking to her?

Varner's monitor came to life with the report from LA and he raced through it twice, devouring Lori's history with the Santa Ana PD—including the shootings, the fallout and the toll.

There's a strong motive here for Blaine, he thought.

Blaine must have targeted the Fultons in revenge for Lori killing his brother, Malcolm. It still left Varner with many unanswered questions. He was certain Blaine wasn't acting alone, so who were his associates—and why didn't they just go after Lori directly? Why escalate to such an extreme, taking hostages, using bombs and robbing a bank? There had to be a reason, but the deeper they dug, the more questions they had. Why did Malcolm take his mother's name? What about Malcolm's time in prison and the family's connection to Afghanistan—was any of that related to what was happening now? Varner had submitted the name Malcolm Jordan Samadyh to Guardian and other national security databases, but nothing had come back yet.

Meanwhile, investigators analyzed and assessed the physical, factual and theoretical aspects of the Blaine/Samadyh link to Fulton: Blaine's fingerprints on the duct tape, Blaine's blood tie to Samadyh and Samadyh's connection to Lori Fulton. It was often a matter of degrees of separation, but all it took was one key piece of information to bring everything together and Varner was certain that piece would surface soon.

Still, the fact that Kate Page had the inside track didn't sit well with him.

38

Dan drove for miles enveloped by gloom.

Eventually mountains began to ascend over the highway, and he recognized Mount Tremper dominating the skyline as he continued winding west. The scenery was beautiful, but he sensed menace in every shadow and every blind curve. He studied a stretch of road by a creek then a ramshackle outbuilding tucked in a dense stand of woods, as if he could somehow identify the final destination.

Sooner or later, everything was going to be decided. Whether he'd live or die, if he'd ever see his family again—it would all end. He could feel it. Everything that he valued became crystalline to him. It was not his job, not the house, not the bag of cash beside him or his reputation in Roseoak Park.

There were only two things he cherished in his life.

Lori and Billy.

They were all that counted in his world, and as he drove he vowed that no matter what happened—

no matter what the assholes were planning—he would not make it easy for them.

"Turn right at that large boulder," Vic said.

Dan pulled off the highway on to a paved, narrow course that cut into forest for a mile or two before devolving into a serpentine gravel road, the stones popcorning against the car's undercarriage.

"Turn left at that big rock," Vic said.

Dan slowed the car when he reached the jutting granite rock formation.

The turn's entrance was all but concealed by shrubs that swallowed his vehicle as he rolled on to the earthen pathway. He inched his way delicately along the dirt strip, awakening branches that slapped and scraped against the wheels, the doors, the windows.

He traveled about fifty yards, coming to a small grassy clearing where Vic ordered him to stop and kill the engine.

Less than a minute later, Dan heard the distant crunch of gravel and the slap of branches against metal as an SUV lumbered into the clearing behind him.

Two men got out and approached the Chevy— Vic and Percy. He recognized them by their coveralls, but this time they were carrying what he thought were AK-47s.

They're not wearing masks.

"Get out!" Vic called to him from outside the car.

Both men were white and in their early twenties. Vic's long dark hair and an unkempt beard only added to his imposing height. Percy looked about the same age, with thick brown hair and a wispy beard.

Dan got out of the car while Percy opened the passenger door, seized the bag of cash, unzipped and checked it. Satisfied, he rezipped the bag.

"Where…where are Lori and Billy?" Dan asked.

Ignoring Dan, Vic watched Percy put the bag in the SUV.

"I did everything you wanted," Dan said. "You said no one would get hurt. It's done now…you can let us—"

"Shut up!"

Vic used his gun to march Dan to the rear of the SUV. Percy secured Dan's wrists with plastic handcuffs then wrapped them with duct tape. He shoved him into the back of the SUV and covered him with a tarp.

Doors slammed. The SUV wheeled in a circle and returned to the road.

It hadn't gone far when Dan was suddenly pitched to one side amid the roar and rumble of churning gravel as the SUV swayed violently. A horn blasted, and a faint stream of cursing and clanking passed, but the SUV corrected itself and continued.

As they gathered speed Dan felt hope fading like a dying star.

39

Officer Rocco Campisi downed the last of his coffee as he turned into the Empire Coastal Mall.

Tonight was going to be sweet.

His brother-in-law had scored tickets to the Mets' game behind home plate. It was all Campisi could think of as he neared the end of his tour on patrol in the 111th Precinct. He'd swing through the mall and scope the lot for cars on his hot sheet. That would take him to the end of his shift.

Campisi guided his blue-and-white patrol car into the north entrance where the lot was pretty much at capacity.

Two cars topped his list.

The first was a red 2013 Toyota Corolla, wanted in the hit-and-run of a three-year-old boy in Brooklyn this morning. The boy was in critical condition, and Campisi was eager to grab the asshole who'd taken off and left him for dead. The second was the car from the bank heist. They'd been screaming for that one all day—a 2015 blue Ford Taurus.

Campisi and other patrol units had already searched this lot earlier, but he wasn't confident the other unit had been as thorough as he'd like, which was why he'd decided to swing back and double-check.

Campisi crawled through every zone in the lot, concentrating on red Corollas and blue Tauruses. Shoppers pushing carts to their cars cleared the way for him, while people walking to the mall gave him a cursory glance.

He drove slowly up and down rows of sedans, vans, compacts, hybrids, SUVs and pickup trucks, working his way from one section to the next.

In Zone 11, he came across two red Corollas that were candidates, but the year and partial plate didn't match. Rolling through Zone 12, he discovered a blue Taurus, but the year was way off.

He got zilch in Zone 13.

Zone 14 was farthest from the others and held fewer vehicles. It would be a fast search, Campisi thought, threading around shopping carts and vehicles dotting the area.

What's this?

His focus shifted to a sedan in the back corner. It was a blue Ford, a Taurus, and his breath quickened as he approached.

It was a 2015 blue Ford Taurus SEL.

His eyes widened as he read the plate.

"Bingo!"

Campisi reached for his radio.

* * *

Varner was alerted to the discovery of Dan Fulton's car, which had set off a chain reaction of fast-moving investigative events.

Instructions for the Taurus were sent with an extreme caution—*explosives may be present*—and Varner was glad to see the officer had cordoned off a large area around it using yellow tape tied to shopping carts. Soon sirens wailed as police, fire and paramedics arrived.

As the NYPD bomb squad examined the car, Varner and Tilden made their way inside to obtain the mall security video.

"I'll bet my pension they used a switch car, or took Fulton with them in their vehicle," Tilden said as they hustled to the security office.

Empire Coastal's security chief took Tilden and Varner into the dimly lit security control room where they viewed footage taken of Zone 14 in the time after the robbery.

"And there it is," Tilden said.

Cameras had captured crisp images of Fulton leaving his Taurus with a duffel bag and getting into a green Chevy Impala.

"Go back even earlier," Varner said. "We need to see how the Impala got there."

The security chief reversed, then slowed the footage, showing the Chevy as it emerged in the lot. It was parked there about an hour before the heist and would not have drawn suspicion. The driver was wearing dark clothing with a hoodie and ball cap, making identification a challenge. It appeared he was wearing gloves. The cameras recorded the driver walking off the lot after leaving the Impala.

"Pull in on the car," Tilden said.

The mall's security cameras were first-rate and easily captured the Chevy's plate, a New York tag, which Tilden and Varner noted. A few quick calls resulted in Empire Coastal volunteering the security video and sending it electronically to the NYPD's forensic experts for further analysis.

Several hundred yards from the mall control room, bomb squad techs cleared Fulton's Ford. They'd found no explosive devices in the vehicle and the forensic team moved in to process it for evidence.

After the latest information was assessed, a new lookout with key details was blasted to law enforcement agencies, urging them to locate a white male in a green 2014 Chevy Impala, possibly wearing a suicide vest.

The Impala was registered to Roxanne Butler, age sixty-four, of 28 Rugged Shore Drive, Alexandria Bay, New York.

There was no response when a New York State Trooper checked on the residence, but a neighbor said that Roxanne and her husband, Jeff Butler, had left five days earlier for Florida for a ten-day Caribbean cruise. They'd driven to Ogdensburg, where they'd flown out of Ogdensburg International Airport.

Homeland Security confirmed the Butlers' flights and the Ogdensburg Police Department determined that the Butlers' Chevy Impala had been taken from the long-term parking lot at the local airport.

They had no GPS on the vehicle.

A lot of planning had gone into the heist, Varner thought while driving back to Federal Plaza. Blaine and his associates had made a few mistakes—the fingerprint on the tape was practically rookie— but they'd thought this through. Taking the Impala from long-term parking had given them time, and who knew what they planned to do with it?

Varner was nearing the Brooklyn Bridge when his phone rang. He took the call using hands-free.

"Varner."

"Nick, its Marv. Port Authority and the Real Time Center tracked the Impala crossing the Throgs Neck Bridge into the Bronx, then taking the George Washington Bridge into New Jersey. Then New Jersey has him on the Four north, where we lose him for a bit, but we pick him up again heading north on the New York Thruway." Varner could hear the excitement in Tilden's voice. "This is a huge break, pal."

"We're gaining on them, Marv."

"Damn straight. Talk to you soon."

The break was encouraging, but Varner couldn't shake off his underlying fear arising from Jerricko Blaine's connection to Lori Fulton.

This case gets darker at every turn and we just don't know where it's going to lead.

40

Manhattan, New York

Kate looked at the notes she'd written after ending her call with J. T. Flores at the truck wash in Dallas where Jerricko Blaine had worked.

She'd underlined *California* twice.

What were the odds that Jerricko and Lori would both be from California?

Whatever they were, it made the possibility of a connection between them even stronger.

But what could it be?

Again, she searched through the clippings of Lori's shooting tragedy in Santa Ana. No mention of anyone named Blaine, but she was betting the key lay somewhere in that case and she was determined to dig deeper. There had to have been an investigation and an inquiry, but she couldn't go back to Ben for more help. He was already impatient about holding back the California angle on this story, and Kate didn't want to lose the edge she had ahead of the other news outlets. She'd have to keep digging on her own.

Checking the time, she was hit with another reality—her daughter would be getting out of school soon.

Kate would have to make arrangements for someone to pick up Grace, but first she needed to do more work on the Santa Ana shooting. Citing the case, she called Santa Ana PD, then she called the Orange County DA's office and then the California Justice Department. She also called the legal research agency that Newslead used to search for records on the case.

In each instance, Kate was told someone would get back to her.

In each instance, she took names and contact information.

"I'm on a deadline, if I don't hear back in twenty minutes, I'll call again."

Moving on to the news reports that said Malcolm Jordan Samadyh was from Torrance, California, Kate searched for listings of Samadyhs in Torrance, then in all of California and then in all the US. She did the same for Blaines. She'd use the lists she compiled to start making cold calls, hoping that one of these names led to a relative and more information.

Before starting, she checked the time again and called Nancy Clark, her neighbor.

"Hi, Nancy, it's Kate. Can I ask you for a huge favor?"

"You name it, kiddo."

"Vanessa's got classes and I'm going to be working late and—"

"Want me to get Grace at school and keep her with me?"

"Could you?"

"I'd love to, dear."

"Thank you, Nancy. You're a lifesaver! I'll send a message to the school."

"No thanks needed. You know I love Grace. Are you working on that bank robbery story in Queens?"

"That's the one."

"It's on the news."

"Yeah, I know. It's been going on all day."

"No, I mean it's live on the news right now. They found the banker's car."

"What? Thanks, Nancy. Gotta go!"

Just as Kate turned to check the TV monitors in the newsroom, she found Reeka and Thane standing at her desk.

"How did we not know about this, Kate?" Reeka asked.

"I—I don't know."

"This is supposed to be your story. You have sources, don't you? Why don't we have this?"

Reeka was right, and the TV footage was proof Kate was getting beaten badly.

"Look, I'll make some calls and I'll get out there right now."

"You'll never make it through the traffic at this time," Thane said, sending a message on his phone. "We've got a stringer and freelance shooter in Queens. They're five minutes away. I just sent you their numbers."

Reeka was frosty as she instructed Kate. "You're staying here. Focus on the Dallas angle and work with the stringer on the new development in Queens. We need to know what they found in the banker's car. Any bodies, any money, any bombs—whatever. Do not drop the ball again, Kate."

"I'm on it."

Once Reeka and Thane were out of earshot, Kate called Nick Varner.

"Varner."

"What the hell is going on with the car in Queens? I thought we had a deal!"

The line crackled in the silence.

"Come on, Varner. I sat on a lead for you, but I'm not going to do it much longer."

"We found his car."

"Yeah, no kidding! Everybody knows that now. So what else? Did you find Fulton?"

"There's not much more I can tell you."

"Come on, the whole country's seeing this live. Did you find him? Or the money? A note? A bomb? Anything?"

"Listen to me, I can't jeopardize the case and give you information that will aid the suspects."

"Given what's already gone public, I think they know you're on to them. Did you find Fulton?"

"No, but…" Varner seemed hesitant to continue but eventually added, "We're looking for a second car."

"So they dumped his at the mall and switched?" Kate asked, reading the news ticker that ran across the bottom of the TV screen as it showed Dan Fulton's blue Taurus surrounded by police tape and a gathering crowd.

"It appears that way. We'll put out details on the second car shortly."

"Can you tell me now? I need something to report here, Varner—and it's either this or the details about Lori's past. We had a deal."

Varner sighed. "It's a 2014 green Chevy Impala with New York plates, registered out of Alexandria Bay."

"Anything else?"

"It was stolen from the airport lot in Ogdensburg. That's all I can give you for now."

41

Not long after Dan Fulton had stopped at Weldon's Gas and Grocery, the little station was overrun.

A big yellow Blue Bird school bus carrying "The Fighting Wildcats," a New Jersey high school football team, had stopped to refuel, emptying close to forty players and coaching staff into the store.

Boisterous teenage boys formed a long, winding line to the restroom. Given that no girls were present, Roy Weldon, the proprietor, told them to use the women's room, too, prompting shoving and teasing.

"You have to do it sitting down, DeFoozie!"

"That line's for wusses and wimps!"

"This line's for men! Get your candy ass over there, Wilson!"

Roy didn't mind the chaos because of the business it brought. The players grabbed sodas, chips, snack cakes, candy bars, gum, magazines, juices, milk and cookies. With the gas for the bus, Roy did a couple of hundred dollars' worth of business in less than half an hour.

But there was a price to pay.

In the calm that followed the departure of the Wildcats, Roy shook open a big orange plastic garbage bag, got his cleaning bucket holding his brushes, cloths and bottle of cleaner, tugged on rubber gloves and waded into the aftermath.

He was a stickler for cleanliness. Ever since his days as a hotel manager in Boston he had a thing about spotless bathrooms. It was a dirty job but Roy insisted his operation be a clean one at all times.

He started with the women's room, bracing for the worst and was pleasantly surprised.

Some water had been splashed on the mirror over the sink, the trash can overflowed with damp, crumpled napkins. A few sheets of toilet tissue covered the floor in the women's stall.

Not too bad.

He tidied up, emptied the trash into the plastic bag, opened the window and moved on to the men's room.

He nearly slipped and fell when he entered.

As he'd expected, the floor was soaked—likely from a water fight. Crumpled napkins were strewn everywhere, torn shards of toilet paper were dissolving on the floor of the stall. Cleaning this mess would take a bit longer. Roy got his mop and broom and set to work establishing order.

He stopped when he saw what else the boys had done.

Fresh, dark graffiti shouted at him from the stall

wall next to the urinal. What foul thing was it this time? He drew his face up to the scrawl.

"DAN FULTON GREEN IMPALA HH47H490 CALL POLICE!"

Roy drew back, shaking his head.

Kids.

Still shaking his head, he ran his damp cloth over it. It was just as he thought. They'd used a permanent felt-tip pen.

Roy read it again. He'd have to repaint the wall to cover it up, but he was pretty sure he had some extra paint in the storage room.

He froze when he got to the door.

Wait. Just hold everything for one damned minute.

Something about the message made him turn around once again.

Dan Fulton.

That's the guy in the news!

42

Los Angeles, California

Everyone Is Welcome.

The sun-faded sign rattled above the doors of the mission in downtown LA. Old men, women, teenage boys and young mothers with children were leaving the building after the last meal.

Inside, twenty long tables topped with vinyl tablecloths filled the dining hall. The rules were written on laminated pages and displayed everywhere: *All meals are to be eaten in this room. No swearing, no fighting, no drugs, no booze, no weapons. We offer food, love and respect.*

The walls were papered with optimism in the form of children's art, finger-paintings and crayon-colored presentations of flowers, rainbows and happy people. They were clustered around passages of Scripture, some of the pages fluttering in the wake of two FBI agents who'd rushed passed them.

They'd pinpointed their subject to this location. He was a retired accountant who'd volunteered seven days a week at the mission. When the agents found him, he was wiping tables.

"Ted Irwin?"

The man glanced at the IDs the agents held up. "Yes."

"Bill Kendrick and Wade Darden, FBI. We'd like to talk to you about your nephew Jerricko Titus Blaine. It's urgent."

Sadness washed across Irwin's face and he took them to a private corner table where he wiped his hands with a dish towel.

"I expected this when I saw the news report earlier today, only not this fast. It's been weighing on my mind. In fact, I was going to call police when I finished up here, but I—"

"Mr. Irwin, do you know your nephew's whereabouts?" Kendrick asked.

"No, I'm sorry, I don't."

"What about an address, phone number, an email?"

"No."

"You understand that lying or holding back information could be construed as obstruction of justice, sir?"

"I'm telling you, I have no idea where he is. I haven't seen him in years—not until I noticed his face and name flashing on the news about those hostages in New York. It's terrible," the man said. "Just like it was with his older brother."

"When exactly was the last time you had contact with Jerricko?"

"Oh, ages ago. Years. We just lost touch with Naz and the boys after Andrew died."

"Who's Naz?"

"Nazihah. Andrew's wife and Jerricko's mother. We all called her Naz."

"Do you know where can we locate her?"

"I believe she's in Afghanistan, last I heard. She went back a long time ago."

Kendrick and Wade exchanged quick glances before Kendrick continued.

"Tell us what you can about the family's history."

"My wife, Michelle, and her older brother, Andrew, were true Good Samaritans who wanted to make this world better. Years ago, Andrew took a leave of absence from his job as an electrical engineer and volunteered with a church group as an aid worker in Afghanistan."

"What were Andrew Blaine's politics?"

"He had none, really. He just wanted to help people. He was working in a volatile area of Kandahar. I think it was Zhari, where he'd met Naz. She was born in the region. She was an aid worker, too, a teacher, and quite striking. They fell in love, and he brought her home to Los Angeles. They got married, she became a citizen, and they had two boys, Malcolm and Jerricko."

"Were you and your wife close to them?"

"We were at that time, yes. They seemed to be a happy family. We had no children of our own and we thought the world of the boys. Then Andrew told Michelle that, even after several years, Naz was not settling in. I guess she was having a hard time adjusting to life in America."

"In what way?"

"Just with accepting American behavior, attitudes, values, that sort of thing. Naz had an ultraconservative religious upbringing—it's very different from life in the States. She couldn't adapt—didn't want to. She wanted to return to Afghanistan with her sons. Andrew didn't want to leave the US, but she kept insisting that she couldn't raise the boys properly as long as they stayed here."

"What happened?"

"It was around then, when she became determined to move back, that Andrew was killed in a traffic accident on the Hollywood Freeway. It was horrible. A tanker truck jackknifed and exploded. They said Andrew died instantly." Irwin paused, staring at nothing, lost in a memory. After a few moments, he continued. "That really hit us hard. By this time, the boys were older and Malcolm began running with gangs, just as his mother had feared. He got into trouble so often, and eventually he was convicted of a robbery and sent to prison in Tehachapi."

"Was his mother still in the country at that time?"

"Yes, she and Jerricko would visit Malcolm in prison. Michelle still kept in touch, then. She worried about them all and talked often on the phone with Naz."

Kendrick glanced at the clock on the wall. Time was ticking by, but he didn't want to rush this man as he opened up.

"Prison had hardened Malcolm, changed him. He came out a cold, embittered man. He took his mom's name, calling himself Malcolm Jordan Samadyh. He seemed…disdainful of his American heritage and he continued with his criminal ways until—" Ted paused again, shaking his head. "He was killed during a robbery in Santa Ana."

"What happened to his family after that?"

"Naz was devastated, out of her mind with grief. During one call with Michelle, Naz blamed America for the deaths of her husband and son. She really believed everything would have been different if they'd gone back to Afghanistan when she'd asked."

"Malcolm murdered a police officer and shot a pregnant woman while robbing a convenience store. And she blamed America for his actions?" Kendrick asked.

"I know, it was her *son*. Naz refused to accept reality. She claimed there was some sort of conspiracy against her family, that they were being punished by the US because Andrew had helped people in Afghanistan. It wasn't long after Malcolm's death that she returned home."

"What about Jerricko?"

"He idolized his big brother and was never the same after Malcolm's death. He was lost. My wife heard that he drifted across the country doing odd jobs, but we couldn't find a way to contact him."

"He didn't go to Afghanistan with his mother?"

"Not initially, but we'd heard that he did a few years later—stayed a few years and then returned to America a very angry young man."

"Who told you this?"

"My wife. She'd tried so hard to stay in touch with Naz after she'd left. They both had something important in common—they loved Andrew. And Michelle felt like she owed it to her brother to keep Naz close, to remember they were family, despite everything else."

"We'll need to talk with your wife," Kendrick said.

Ted stared hard at them, something dark and painful behind his eyes.

"Michelle died a year ago. Heart failure. That's why I'm down here doing what I do. It's what she would've wanted."

"I'm sorry about your loss, Ted," Kendrick said. "I'm sure you'll understand, we'll need contact information of everyone in the family. Can you provide it to us as soon as possible?"

"Yes, anything to help. There's only a few people—a cousin in New York, one in Texas." Irwin reached for his cell phone, shaking his head while scrolling through contacts. "It's a sad irony, isn't it?"

"What is?"

"Andrew went to Afghanistan to help people in need, a wonderful legacy. But that legacy also includes a son who killed a police officer, another involved in a terrible robbery and hostage situation, and their mother, who blames America for it all."

43

Deer Kill River, New York

"What the f— Watch where you're going, jerk!"

Bruce Grover battled to control his Jeep Wrangler after a white SUV barreling around a blind turn had forced him off the dirt road.

The Jeep bucked, gravel peppered the undercarriage and broiling dust clouds swirled as Grover slid to a stop on the shoulder. His blood thumping, he looked hard in his rearview mirror until the clouds dissipated and the SUV was long gone.

Where did that idiot come from? Nobody ever uses this road.

He let out a long breath, shoving the incident out of his mind and his Jeep into gear, as he continued. Although wary, he strained to reclaim the serenity he had been enjoying before his encounter with stupidity.

After all, this was his vacation, his first real break in two years since he took over as editor-in-chief of the *Weekly Highlands Sun-Bulletin*.

Running a small paper had taken over his life.

It meant that every complaint like, *"My paper was left in the rain again, I'm going to cancel."*

"Your website sucks. It freezes my computer."

"You're obviously on the payroll of corporations."

"Why are you covering up what's really going on at that military base?"

"I want you to write about my neighbor's barking dog"—came to him 24/7.

Still, Bruce loved it because he was also part owner of a paper that, surprisingly, even in these dismal times for the industry, was turning a profit. And he loved it because he was a news junkie who craved panning every call for the gold that would lead to a real story.

He'd gotten that from sixteen years as a reporter, then editor, at the *New York Post*. His appetite for news was impossible to satisfy. It's why the whole time he was on the Thruway he'd followed radio news reports of that bank robbery in Queens.

Manager takes a quarter million from his own bank. Bombs strapped to him and his own family, and maybe a mob tie? It's one helluva story. Wish I was on it.

But he'd made a promise to his wife when he'd kissed her goodbye this morning—he would turn off the news, forget about the business and go fishing. It was just what the doctor ordered, and she never failed to remind him of that.

"Don't forget what the doctor said about your blood pressure, Bruce."

So he'd shut off the radio when he'd left the freeway and took in the scenery instead, embracing memories of the "Nick Adams, Big Two-Hearted River" period of his life when he'd come up here alone to fish. Over the years he'd still driven through the area to keep a vigil on all the secret places he knew.

Like this one.

The jagged rock formation jutted from the forest up ahead.

The dense growth hid the entrance he knew was there and he slowly guided his Jeep on to the rugged path. As he tottered along the earthen trail, branches smacked and scraped at the Wrangler, as if he was driving through a woodland car wash.

Bruce loved how the light had dimmed, slivers of sunshine piercing the forest canopy in brilliant shafts as if through the stained-glass windows of a great cathedral.

His fishing tackle and camping gear rattled in the back. The Deer Kill River was a mile ahead. It was one of the best regions in the country for brook and brown trout and this long-forgotten logger's trail led to pockets of deep pools and frigid springs that were heaven for fly-fishing.

Then Bruce's reverie was suddenly interrupted by a flash of chrome.

So much for my undiscovered trail, he thought with disappointment.

As he reached a clearing he saw the trespasser's car. A little ticked, though admittedly selfish, Grover stopped beside it to make an assessment of the interloper. No one else was around, but the green Chevy had a New York plate.

Hope I don't see you upstream.

Bruce tightened his grip on the gearshift to move on when a twinge of concern stopped him. From his vantage on the car's right side, he noticed something odd.

The keys were still in the ignition.

Who does that?

He looked around again. No one in sight.

Hold on. That's a green Chevy Impala—a late model green Chevy Impala! Damn, that's—that could be the one from the robbery!

He seized his phone and took several pictures. Checking his bars, he saw cell phone service here was spotty.

Sorry, honey, he thought, knowing his relaxing fishing weekend just got canceled.

The Wrangler's motor roared as he wheeled back down the pathway to the road and the New York Thruway where he could call police.

44

McLean, Virginia

The National Counterterrorism Center, one of the country's most vital security facilities, was located at the edge of Washington, DC.

The fortified glass and stone complex rose several stories in a hilly wooded Virginia suburb northwest of the capital. In this building, analysts and agents from government branches such as the Central Intelligence Agency, the Federal Bureau of Investigation, the National Security Agency and the Defense Intelligence Agency used the most sophisticated intelligence gathering systems in the world to analyze threats to national security.

The point of control was the Operations Center, a cavernous room whose far wall was dominated by huge screens listing known terror threats and incidents. All were coded by priority and analysis. Other large screens displayed every major US news network and those in countries around the globe.

Below the screens, on the tiered floor, there were twenty workstations where intelligence officers worked together 24/7 to break down the constant flow of information received by the center. They examined data that might otherwise seem unrelated to pursue leads.

It was challenging work; more than seven thousand reports poured into the center every twenty-four hours. They came in from intelligence sources, embassies, police departments and the general public.

On any given day, those reports could include a suspicious package at a mall, an anonymous 911 call promising "something's going to happen," or an airline reporting strange comments or behavior of a passenger. And the nonstop flow of reports was merely in addition to analysis already being done with ongoing files.

Operations officer Shane Hudson took a drink from his bottled water and resumed work at his desk. Hudson, the son of a US diplomat, had grown up in the Gulf States. He was fluent in several languages and had a degree in Middle Eastern Studies from Harvard. He sat before three computer monitors. On one, he'd cued up a video to replay.

He'd been analyzing a report submitted by FBI agent Nick Varner through the Guardian database. Varner was overseeing the live investigation of a quarter-million-robbery-abduction case out of New York. He'd requested further analysis of the names Jerricko Blaine and Malcolm Jordan Samadyh, two American-born men, and their mother, Nazihah Bilaal Samadyh, born in Afghanistan and married to now-deceased American Andrew Blaine.

After Hudson submitted the names to the highly classified Terrorist Identities Datamart Environment, the central database on known or suspected international terrorists, he made other inquiries.

While awaiting responses, he replayed the video, which opened tight on a placard: America Murdered My Son! Death to America!

The sign was written in English. The woman in the video was waving it during a large-scale anti-American protest that had taken place in Kabul, Afghanistan, a year ago. The demonstration raised a number of issues, but this one was a concern and flagged for assessment.

The woman holding the placard was Nazihah Bilaal Samadyh.

Suddenly, one of his monitors began to flash with urgent NSA intercepts from the US base in Menwith, England—apparently there was concern about the potential for a planned attack. The summary showed communication originating from an active jihadist group. The conversations were disguised to focus on "a wedding with many gifts from many guests resulting in a glorious celebration." Decrypted, that stood to mean an attack with many victims. The intercepts had been tracked for the past six months out of Iraq, Afghanistan, Turkey, Athens and London. But they'd grown more active with the most recent series of calls, bouncing from Syria and Yemen to individuals somewhere in the United States.

Hudson needed to assess the intercepts against other data.

He took another swig of water as a new alert flashed with information coming in from the California Department of Corrections and Rehabilitation. It concerned Malcolm Jordan Samadyh and his activities while an inmate at the California Correctional Institution at Tehachapi.

While serving three years for robbery at the prison, he'd converted to Islam but soon gravitated to a rogue prisoner group of extremists that called on Muslims to violently attack nonbelievers and infidels who were the enemies of Islam.

The CDCR and the California Justice Department were moving fast to provide more background on all known members of the fringe group and their affiliations.

Hudson let out a long breath. There was a lot of information in front of him but no clear proof that any of it was connected.

He glanced to one of his monitors and the latest news reports on the Queens case. Every minute that passed put the hostages at greater risk.

It's time to get to work.

45

Sweat webbed along Dan's brow, stinging when it hit his eyes.

Under the tarp in the back of the SUV, the drone and hum of the wheels vibrated against his rib cage like a dark opera. The ride was smooth now. They were on the freeway, rolling to the next step.

The final step, Dan thought.

In the darkness, his fears assailed him. He'd seen his captors' faces and knew what that meant.

It's over.

Even if they reunited him with his family, it would only be so they could die together, or force him to watch Lori and Billy die.

If they're not already dead.

Dan struggled to push the thought from his head but it was futile.

They win. No police are coming. No one can help us. We were dead from the moment they invaded our home.

He swallowed and the image of shallow graves in a wooded area flashed before him.

Please, let Lori and Billy be alive. Let me talk to them one last time.

Suddenly the SUV thudded over a bump and Dan felt a weighty, hard knock on his ankle. His breath caught as he remembered.

The knife!

At the gas station near the restroom he'd stolen a small utility knife from the electrician's toolbox and tucked it in his sock.

He shifted his body slowly so he wouldn't disturb the vest or alert his captors. Carefully he drew up his knees while reaching with his bound hands for the edge of his sock. It was a difficult movement. It took several agonizing moments before he was touching the knife and even longer until he got the fingers of his right hand around the handle.

He held it tight.

His heart lifted and he breathed deeply. Now he had hope.

He estimated the knife was five inches long, with a button to extend the retractable blade. By the feel of the padded non-slip handle, the contour and weight, he could tell it was a professional-quality knife.

Something solid.

It felt good in his hand.

In the darkness, he took great pains to move the knife around until he had it where he could get his thumb on the spring button and extend the steel blade. He brushed his finger over the edge, testing its sharpness.

Like a razor. Good.

Holding the knife between his fingertips and positioning it just so, he began cutting at the tape around his wrists, forcing them apart just a little so he could get at the plastic handcuffs underneath.

As he worked, the tape and cuffs began to give way but still held.

He took surgical care to ensure his bindings remained connected and in place, but weakened enough so that he could free his hands at will in an instant.

Each small rip, each tiny twist, was a victory.

It's working.

Satisfied he'd gone as far as he could, he stopped.

He had a plan now and he reached deep down inside of himself, using his fear and anger to forge the courage he needed to act.

Dan slid the knife under the cuff of his sleeve, wedging the blade under his watchband.

He was ready.

46

Deer Kill River, New York

Less than an hour after leaving Manhattan, Kate glimpsed the hills flowing by as news photographer Stan Strobic pushed his pickup beyond the speed limit north on the New York Thruway.

A TV station in Kingston, New York, had reported that a car sought in the bank robbery in Queens was just discovered by a fisherman near the Deer Kill River. The Associated Press had picked up the story, and within minutes Kate and Strobic were driving to the scene.

Strobic's truck was his prized possession, a Chevrolet Silverado 2014, regular cab with a long box cargo bed with cap, all in Victory Red, baby.

He loved to play his country music and was prone to peculiar behavior. Strobic never, ever cleaned out the bed of his truck. "As messy as a disorganized serial killer," one of their coworkers had said. That's why people were reluctant to work with him.

Kate had learned that Strobic's assignments in

Iraq and Afghanistan had changed him, but one thing was certain: no one could touch him when it came to shooting news. He was the best.

It was late in the day and Strobic bemoaned the growing shadows as they drove.

"We're not going to have a lot of light left when we get there."

Kate was on her phone watching for developments. She'd put out a lot of calls while digging for links between Lori Fulton and Blaine. Nothing had surfaced so far, doubling her disappointment because Varner had failed to alert her to the car at Deer Kill River.

Nick Varner.

Though his reluctance to help her had been frustrating, something about him seemed to fill her mind whenever she had a spare moment to think.

God, it's been so long since I've been with someone.

Kate indulged herself with thoughts of Varner. She'd learned from a few police sources that he was widowed. His wife had died a few years ago, but they'd had no children and he wasn't married or seeing anyone.

But why was she drawn to him? He'd done nothing but block her at every turn so far and yet…

He's easy on the eyes. But it was more than that. She sensed that he had a good heart, even though he played the role of the hard-ass exceptionally well. But she had to be careful here. She couldn't let emotion cloud her work and she sure as hell couldn't depend on Varner to help her.

She was capable of doing her own investigating.

At that moment, Kate caught something on her Twitter feed.

"Whoa, what's this?"

Help note left at gas station may be from fugitive banker.

She clicked on the link and read aloud a short news story from a local radio station identifying Weldon's Gas and Grocery as the location. Kate Googled the store, got an address, and Strobic keyed it into his GPS.

"That's Exit 16B, only a few miles up ahead," he said.

"Let's check it out."

Several state police and Rockland County Sheriff's Office emergency vehicles were parked in Weldon's small lot when Kate and Strobic arrived.

A patrol officer stood at the door, blocking the entrance.

"I want to talk with the owner. We're press."

Kate and Strobic held up their Newslead IDs. Behind the officer, she saw crime scene technicians working deep inside the store.

"He's over there." The officer nodded to a corner of the parking lot behind a van where a couple of local news types were talking to a tall man with a thick, white beard.

Kate set her phone to record, Strobic got his

camera ready and they joined a woman with a note-book and a man holding a microphone.

"Hi, Kate Page and Stan Strobic with Newslead. Are you the owner?" she asked the older man.

"That's me, Roy Weldon, like it says on the sign."

"You found a note related to the bank robbery in Queens?"

"Sure looks that way."

"Sorry to interrupt," Kate said, giving an apologetic smile to the other reporters, who didn't seem to mind. From the look of them, she guessed they were news rookies. She turned back to Roy. "Can you tell us how you discovered it?"

"Like I was saying to these good folks, this customer came in a few hours ago, just a few minutes before a bus full of high school football players. After everyone left, I went to clean up and found the note in the restroom. I thought it was a prank at first, but when I remembered the news, I put two and two together and figured this was the real deal. I mean, the man was driving a green Chevy Impala and looked kind of tense. Wouldn't you, if you were wearing a bomb?"

"What does the note say?"

"That he's involved in the robbery, there were bombs and to call police."

"Can you show us the note?"

"He wrote it on the stall. I let Robbie here take a picture. He got here before police—listens to police radios. You reporters are crafty that way."

"Sorry," Kate said, turning to the male reporter

who looked like he was still in high school. "You're Robbie?"

"Rob Cantly, Hilltop Radio News."

"Can you show us the note, Rob?"

"Sure." He cued up a clear image on his phone for Kate and Strobic, who both took a photo of it.

DAN FULTON GREEN IMPALA HH47H490 CALL POLICE!

"Did you show this to anyone or post it anywhere?" Strobic asked.

"Not yet. I was just going to put it on the station's Facebook page."

"Don't. Listen, can Newslead buy it for exclusive use from you? It'll go across the country—along with your photo credit."

Cantly swelled and looked at Weldon, who winked.

"I'm just a freelancer at the station…"

"Then freelance it to us. You took the photo, which means you own it," Strobic said. "We're a wire service, this will go global. Just send it to me right now with your contact information, and we'll take it from there." Strobic tilted his phone, Cantly copied his info, and within seconds Strobic had Cantly's original image. "Perfect. Now, you can't show it or share it with anyone else," Strobic said. "Our photo rights guy will get in touch shortly. You'll get a photo credit and a few hundred bucks."

After Kate asked Weldon a few more questions, she and Strobic returned to the Thruway and continued north. Kate worked on the story on her phone in between calls to Nick Varner that went unanswered. She wrote fast and clean, knowing that it was a red-hot exclusive for Newslead. Reeka loved it, but without missing a beat she continued pressing Kate to get to the car scene at Deer Kill River, which was another fifty miles away.

"Not much is coming out of there," Reeka said. "We have to know if that is where this story ends."

As Strobic drove faster, Kate stared into the forests.

Are we following the Fultons' final trail? Will we find corpses in that car at Deer Kill River?

After leaving the paved highway, Strobic's Silverado raced along a twisting gravel road.

He braked hard when they came to some two dozen media and police vehicles lining each shoulder. A group of people stood near a large rock formation where Kate saw a flash of plastic yellow tape that appeared to seal the mouth of a forest back road. New York state troopers and county patrol officers protected the way to the scene where the car was found.

Kate and Strobic trotted to the gathering, passing emergency vehicles, news vans and cars from Albany, Newark, Patterson and New York City. Two helicopters thudded overhead and dogs yipped from inside the forest.

TV cameras and newspeople encircled a man who was gesturing as he spoke. He was not in uniform and didn't look like a cop to Kate. She approached the group, standing next to a woman who was taking notes while recording.

"Kate Page, Newslead."

"Alicia Walker, *Newark Star-Ledger.* I read your stuff. It's good."

"Thanks. Who's this guy?"

"Bruce Grover—he found the car. You won't get into the scene and they're not saying much. They're waiting for the FBI to take control here."

Kate listened as Grover repeated his story for the benefit of other reporters as they continued arriving.

"...a white SUV, it forced me off the road. Then, on my way along the trail—" Grover pointed to the woods "—I found the car... No, there was no sign of anyone inside, or near it and no sign of any money."

Strobic nudged Kate after taking several frames of Grover.

"There's no picture here. I have to get an aerial. I'm heading out with a TV crew—they chartered a plane at a small strip. I won't be long. I'll pick you up here afterward."

Kate nodded as she got an alert on her phone and saw a story just posted by the *New York Post* with photos of the abandoned Impala taken by Grover, who, it turned out, was a former editor with the paper. No indication of a body, or money, or bombs found. When she looked up from her phone, Strobic was gone, but she glimpsed a car arriving in the distance.

She recognized Tilden and Varner stepping out of it and made her way over to them, careful to walk on the other side of parked vehicles so other reporters wouldn't see her.

She caught up to them before they headed to the scene.

"Agent Varner, Detective Tilden, wait! Please, just give me a second."

They stopped, though neither looked happy to see her.

"Can you tell me what you have here?"

"You tell us, Kate," Tilden said. "You were here first."

"Come on."

"You know what we know," Tilden said.

"Is there anything more than a car in there?"

"Maybe deer, rabbits," Tilden teased, sticking out his bottom lip. "A bear or two."

"Really, Marv? You want to play it like this?" Kate turned to Varner. "What's the connection between Lori and your suspect, Blaine?"

"That's still under investigation," Varner said.

"They knew each other in California, didn't they?"

"That's under investigation," Varner repeated.

"Well, I can't guarantee I'm going to hold off reporting on your investigation. Seems like there's a lot going on here, and if you can't help me out…"

"We got work to do." Tilden walked away.

"Dammit, Varner, give me something I can use. I've been keeping up my end of the deal. I think you owe me something."

He spun around and gave her a long, hard look that softened, acknowledging that she was right.

"I'll tell you one thing, and it's not for attribution. You got that?"

"Got it."

"You're further ahead on this case than any other press people. Our problem is we don't want you tipping off the suspects to details that would help them."

"I get that, so what can you tell me?"

"We believe that the motive in this case is more than a financial one, that it's connected to crimes in the past and possibly other conspiracies."

"What other conspiracies?"

"That's all you're getting."

"Okay, thanks." Kate wrote it down.

47

Somewhere in New York State

Lori Fulton stared hard through the cabin window and into the forest, refusing to look any longer at the computer screen Thorne held in front of her.

She looked at the treetops swaying in the late-day breezes until something inside her cracked.

She groped for answers, begging to be wrong about what she now knew to be true. What was happening to her family went beyond a robbery, beyond a hostage-taking.

Thorne pulled the computer away and returned to the table.

Lori's mind swirled at his indictment.

You were chosen because of your crimes as nonbelievers!

With trepidation she turned toward the far corner and the tripod with the camera. It was then, for the first time, that she noticed the large knife leaning against the wall...*waiting.*

Let me show you what happens to nonbelievers!

She shut her eyes and prayed, then heard the

subdued jingle of a chain as Billy stirred, groggily positioning himself with his head in her lap. Lori caressed his hair, hoping he wouldn't feel her shaking fingers or her body trembling under him as her mind raced with a million fears, rocketing her back to her time in California, back to that night in Santa Ana...

...*coming off a long night shift of piddling pain-in-the-ass calls, a suspicious vehicle, loud music, barking dog, homeless guy sleeping in a home-owner's flower garden... Tim's supremely happy... he and Charlene are trying for their first baby. They pull into a twenty-four-hour store for one last coffee to end the tour...says he's dreaming of daddyhood...shifting the car into Park...joking about names—Brad for a boy, Angelina if it's a girl...he steps out of the car away from the door, then he sees him...the guy's backing out of the store, sparks blazing from the handgun he's firing at people inside... Tim goes for his weapon...in a heart-beat... Lori's coming around the car behind Tim and sees it all...in a heartbeat...the world slows... every second thudding in her ears...in a heart-beat...the shooter wheels, fires above the vest... a gout of blood blasts from Tim's jaw, a clump of flesh rips from his neck...another round tears into his shoulder, knocking him back into her...sending them both to the ground...in a heartbeat...a deaf-ening roar swells inside her...she catches Tim, her partner, a future dad...thinking...training...acting... she's reaching for her weapon...in a heartbeat... the shooter's firing again and she feels every round*

*pounding into Tim...his body's shielding her...in
a heartbeat...gripping her weapon...raising it...
Tim's spasming torso absorbing rounds...and she's
firing...the shooter's angry eyes fill with surprise...
she empties her magazine into his chest, putting
him down...in a heartbeat... Tim's blood warming
her... Brad for a boy, Angelina if it's a girl...shout-
ing...screaming...sirens...blood drenching her as
Tim empties of life...she's holding him...like she's
holding Billy now...*

Lori opened her eyes, looking back at the trees.

In the time after they'd buried Tim, she'd helped
the investigators and the district attorney, answering question after question. "You were where? Then
what happened? What actions did Officer Rowland
take? What actions did you take?" She'd gone to
counseling, done all she could to hang on while
inside she was descending into an abyss of pain,
guilt, fear and rage.

Lori had been shown photos of the shooter, Malcolm Jordan Samadyh, who was only twenty-five
years old and had already done time for armed robbery. Though her actions were justified, she had
taken a life and it haunted her.

Then, on the steps of a civic building during
the investigation, she'd run into Samadyh's mother
and brother. The devastation in their eyes had cut
through her and she'd spoken from her heart.

"Every second of every day, I wish for everyone
that it never happened," she'd said, hoping that they
might forgive her.

But Samadyh's mother's face had twisted into a

mask of fury and she'd spat on Lori while the little brother's eyes burned with hate, and then…then…everything clicked.

Lori looked to Thorne working on the laptop and suddenly knew. She'd barely recognized him from that chance meeting all those years ago, but now she knew without a doubt who he really was.

"You're…Malcolm Samadyh's brother, aren't you? You're Jerricko."

He stared at her for a long moment but said nothing and turned back to his computer.

"Is that why you're doing this?" she asked. "Because of what happened in California?"

He ignored her questions.

"Jerricko, your brother killed my partner, wounded others and tried to kill me."

He threw her a chilling glare.

"My brother was a *martyr.*"

"Jerricko." Lori kept her voice soft and quiet. "What happened was a horrible thing. I never wanted to hurt your brother but he killed my partner. I did what I did because I had no choice. You do. You don't have to hurt more people. You can end this now—just let us go."

He continued to work without speaking and Lori grew desperate.

"Please, Jerricko. Let us go. Please. I regret that night, you have to see that. I live with it every single day and I swear I wish it never happened."

He stared at her, his face reddening with anger, letting a long silence pass.

"But it did happen," he said.

"I'm so sorry." Lori let a long tense moment pass. "I understand how you feel."

"Understand? You don't understand. Ignorant, arrogant people like you and other Americans like you, will never understand."

"I want to understand. Help me to understand, so no more people get hurt, please."

He stared at her, his eyes flashing with anger and pain.

"My mother never wanted to come to this country, but she loved her husband and followed him here. You cannot comprehend what that meant, leaving her home. She did her best to adjust. She's a spiritual woman, she fasted, kept the holy days, our house was filled with prayer but what she saw every day all around her was the filth of this country."

"What're you talking about?"

"I'm talking about the racism, the worship of sex, drugs, pornographic dancing and music. We were exposed to that filth every day and it infected my brother. He began drinking, smoking, pursuing women. It broke my mother's heart because he was being disrespectful to God. She was losing him to your disgusting culture, which had poisoned him."

"Yes, there's a lot wrong with this country, but that's because it's a free, tolerant society. Jerricko, deep down we're good people who want to live right and do the right thing."

"Right thing? Is it right that you hate our babies and plan to kill them?"

"What do you mean? We don't hate babies."

"In Iraq, Syria, Afghanistan, you bomb our people, kill our babies and orphan our children. Look at the lives you destroy with your aggression, with your arrogant, evil foreign policy, you meddle in our affairs. By your actions you tell our people in all walks of life all around the world that you hate them and will kill them."

"That's not true. We don't wish to kill children. It's much more complicated than that."

"No, it's very simple."

He stared at her.

"When we came to America my mother studied American politics and foreign policy. She taught us how 9/11 was created by the American government to make the US hate us, so it could lead an invasion against us. While she was here my mother kept in touch with family back home. They told her of the bombings, the killings that still continue day after day."

Jerricko pointed to Cutty.

"He lost family in the bombings. So did the other two brothers on our team. We all did."

Jerricko paused to reflect.

"When Malcolm went to prison he found God again. My mother was so pleased that her son had returned to his righteous path. In prison, he'd vowed to become a soldier in the war against this evil American genocidal policy. The night you killed him, he was trying to raise money for an operation to support the cause."

Jerricko stared off.

"I loved him. My mother was drowning in grief.

She called out for vengeance. For me, losing Malcolm was like an amputation. Part of me died that day, too, and I blame you, the face of the police—the tool of the US government in its war on my people."

"Jerricko, it's not like that. I'm so sorry about Malcolm, but it's not like that."

"Oh, yes, it is. You see, losing my brother hammered home the truth about the crimes committed by people like you in the name of your country. It meant I had to do something about the atrocities committed by your lying government. They force me to pay taxes to pay people like you to kill our brothers and sisters, here and in our homeland. *You* support this government. *You* are a tool of this government. *You* have blood on your hands. You are guilty and you will be punished. They call us radicalized, but the truth is we are blessed defenders of an oppressed people. We embrace our responsibility and will sacrifice our souls to it."

"But my family…they're innocent."

"After my brother's sacrifice, I spent a lot of time thinking about you and what you did. I studied your family and I learned that your husband was a banker—a greedy nonbeliever. It was then that I decided that the way to make you pay for your crimes would be one that would help me on my path. My brothers and I needed funds to accomplish our goals, so we tracked you down."

"But *I* was the one involved. Punish me, but let my son and husband go. They're innocent."

"Innocent?" Jerricko sneered. "When I informed

the council of your crimes and our plans, they convened a tribunal and ruled that you *and* your family are guilty. You're all guilty. We're going to make examples of you."

"But my son…" Lori said. "He's just a boy!"

"This is war. This is your fate. There's nothing you can do."

Jerricko closed his laptop, left the cabin to stand on the front deck.

Lori was numb on the mattress, her mind reeling.

…in a heartbeat…

Her lower lip trembled as she looked down on Billy.

… She saw Tim bleeding on her…

… She imagined Billy's severed head…

Lori clamped her hands over her mouth, but inside she was screaming and screaming.

48

Miles from where Kate Page stood with investigators and reporters, Dan Fulton battled the dread gnawing at the edges of his mind about what was awaiting him.

Still under the tarp of the moving SUV, he'd tried to determine how far they'd traveled, but it was impossible because since they had taken him from the car they'd stopped a number of times, and for long periods.

During those stops Dan had heard the men talking to each other, then on the phone, but he was unable to make out their conversations from under the tarp.

Now that they were back on the road they'd made no other stops and Dan sensed that they'd been driving for a great distance. The whole time he thought of Lori and Billy, imagined their faces, heard their voices and prayed to be with them again. He ran his thumb over the edge of the utility knife tucked under his sleeve. Not much of a weapon against guns, but it was all he had—and he would use it to fight back. To save his family.

Eventually, the sound of the road changed, indicating they'd turned on to some kind of gravel path.

Dan took in a long, slow breath.

Stones pinged against the undercarriage, and he was bumped and shifted as the SUV twisted and turned along what had become a long, rough stretch. They continued for what seemed like miles, curving, dipping and tottering but always climbing.

Dan's heart galloped.

The blinking red light of his suicide vest continued its relentless countdown, and Dan was overwhelmed with the realization that they were heading to a remote area, and soon he was going to die.

This is it. It's—

Bang!

The sound of the explosion filled his ears and the SUV lurched off the road.

49

Somewhere in New York State

Warm tears rolled down Lori's cheeks.

Several long moments passed before they dried. She could no longer hope and pray for the best; she accepted what she now believed to be true.

They've killed Dan and they're going to kill us. They're just waiting for the others to bring the money.

The red light on the battery pack of her suicide vest continued flashing.

No one was coming. No one would save them.

It's just me.

Drawing on her counseling experience, Lori took deep breaths. She couldn't lose to hysteria. No matter the odds, she couldn't give in. She needed to turn her fear into action. She'd been a cop, a good street cop. She needed to use her training. To think. Take stock. Assess options.

I won't let Billy die here.

Lori looked at Cutty, who'd seemed indifferent the whole time she and Jerricko spoke, immersed in the chiming of the video games he was playing on his phone. Jerricko had returned to the table and was working on his computer.

The swish of bottled water meant Billy was awake, taking a drink.

She glanced at the persistent blinking light on his vest, then caressed him while cooing soft words of encouragement and love.

"Do you think Dad's coming with the police to get us?" he whispered in her ear.

"I do, sweetheart."

"Maybe he'll bring Sam?"

"Maybe." Lori smiled, holding him close, feeling his skin next to hers, inhaling his scent, fortifying her resolve as she began forging a plan.

Again, she took stock of the cabin—the beds, the bags, the kitchen area, the table with the backpack and laptop. Then she considered the duct tape wrapped around their wrists over the plastic cuffs, the metal handcuff around their ankles, secured to the long chains. The video camera in the corner mounted on the tripod.

The knife.

Lori searched for potential gaps and weaknesses but there was nothing.

Except the obvious.

"I have to go to the bathroom," she said.

"You just went," Cutty said.

"The sandwich didn't…agree with me. I need to go."

Cutty muttered, tucked his phone in his pocket, grabbed his rifle, then got the handcuff keys and used them to release her. Then he tossed the keys back on the table next to Jerricko.

"If the kid has to go, you're taking him. It's your turn," Cutty said, then raked the muzzle of his gun at Lori to the back door. "Let's go."

With her wrists bound in front of her, she stepped carefully to keep her balance while walking along the twisting, narrow trail to the outhouse. The low sun cast long shadows, but she drew upon all of her concentration to analyze the surrounding geography, searching for neighboring cabins, cars, people, any signs of life she could use to her advantage.

There was the van, but Lori didn't know who had the keys and was not confident in her ability to hotwire it, even if she had the chance.

At the outhouse she again endured the humiliation of being forced to keep the door open. She watched Cutty test his phone for a signal. By the face he made, it appeared to her that service didn't cover this area, something she noted as Cutty resumed playing his games on his phone.

When they walked back, Lori studied every aspect of the trail at every step. There was nothing. Nothing she could see that would help.

Time was running out, and hope, like the day, was fading fast.

Panic was churning in the pit of her gut as they neared the cabin, when a sudden *bang* stopped them in their tracks.

The sound echoed over the hills.

50

Somewhere in New York State

The explosion stopped the SUV and it was sagging on the right side.

Dan exhaled.

I'm still alive.

Looking down at his vest, he was relieved to see the little red light still blinking away. Then he heard the front doors open, his captors getting out to talk.

The rear opened.

The tarp was dragged off of him and he was yanked from the back by Percy while Vic held him at gunpoint. Squinting in the waning light Dan noticed that both men had removed their coveralls and were wearing military camouflage pants and dark T-shirts. He examined the surroundings. They were high in the hills, isolated amid vast forests. He drank in the cool, sweet air and tensed, like a condemned man.

This is it. Keep your hands clasped. Focus. Be ready.

The red light on his vest continued ticking down…

As Vic shoved Dan around the side of the vehicle, Dan saw that the front passenger tire had been shredded by jagged rocks.

Not an explosion, then, we just blew a tire.

Percy began removing the jack, wrench and spare, dropping them on the ground to change it.

He'd set his gun next to the tools.

Vic reached into the SUV for the bag with the money, hefting it over his shoulder. "Get up to the cabin after you fix that and we'll get started," he said to Percy.

Get started?

"Move!" Vic pointed with his gun and Dan began walking uphill ahead of him.

As they navigated the trail, Dan's pulse quickened as he took stock of his situation. Vic had the bag and his gun, making his balance a small challenge on the winding path. Dan could free his hands at will and he had the utility knife.

He may never get this chance again.

He began slipping the knife from under his sleeve, getting a solid grip on it. As he extended the blade, they came to a van parked on the road and his heart flooded with hope.

Lori and Billy!

Vic urged him on until they reached a pathway that twisted atop a narrow ridge and Dan saw a cabin a few dozen yards ahead.

Color flashed in the trees to the left and Dan saw a small outhouse—and two people on a path that wound near his trail. His heart soared.

Lori!

* * *

Cutty appeared relieved when he'd spotted two people near them on the adjacent trail.

He lowered his rifle and loosened his grip. The loud discharge they'd heard couldn't have been a threat.

"Brother!" Cutty called.

He pointed with his gun for Lori to lead him to the others on the ridge. Moving through the branches, her heart nearly burst when she saw her husband.

She rushed toward Dan, but Vic and Cutty moved their guns like a gate before her. Contact was forbidden.

"Lori, are you all right?" Dan asked. "Is Billy—"

"We're okay. He's in the cabin—"

"Shut up!" Vic ordered.

"Peace be upon you, my brother," Cutty said. "By God's grace, we've succeeded!"

Vic slapped the money bag and grinned.

"Peace be upon you. Yes, my brother, by God's grace we've been victorious." Vic laughed.

As their captors continued boasting, Dan and Lori stared at each other with such desperation, tears filled their eyes. Lori saw the intense, adrenaline-fueled emotion in Dan that she felt herself. Then, with a subtle nod, Dan showed Lori the knife's tip and she knew that this was their life-and-death moment.

"...a quarter million for the operation," Vic said, slapping the bag again. "Now we carry on as planned with our message and warning to the—"

The peel, rip and snap of the tape and plastic cuffs sounded as Dan jerked his wrists free and blitzed Vic, knocking him to the ground sending his rifle clattering down the hillside as he slashed at him with the knife.

Drawing on her police training, Lori dropped, hurtling her body full force into Cutty's knees, sending him to the ground before he had a chance to react. His rifle bumped down the ridge side with Vic's. She sprang to her feet and kicked wildly at Cutty's face, gut and groin.

Dan continued struggling on the ground with Vic, but his knife had slipped from his hand and tumbled down the rocky hill with the other weapons.

Lori picked up a baseball-sized rock with her bound hands and smashed it on Cutty's head. As he lay dazed on the ground she made her way to Dan as he continued fighting Vic.

"No!" Dan yelled. "Go get Billy! Hurry—I'll be right behind you!"

Alarmed by shouting along the road, Percy dropped his tools, grabbed his gun, left the SUV and flew toward the voices.

At the cabin, Jerricko seized his weapon, tore out the front door and down the trail.

Neither one saw the woman.

Lori had rushed into the forest, taking the outhouse path toward the cabin's rear. In the seconds she ran, she contended with her desperation to return to Dan and to run ahead for Billy, knowing their captors could set off their bombs at any time.

She blazed through the back door of the cabin, relieved to find Billy alone and unharmed. The handcuff keys were on the table, next to Jerricko's laptop. She snatched them, Billy standing, his eyes saucers of fear at hearing the shouting.

"Mom?" Billy's voice broke as she frantically worked the key to unlock the cuff and free him. "What's going on? Is Dad out there?"

In the instant she'd freed her son the blasts of automatic gunfire pierced the air outside. Lori looked out the window in time to see Dan rushing up the path, Jerricko and Percy behind, cutting him down with bullets and sending him toppling over the side of the ridge.

Dan! No! Oh God! No! They've killed him!

Shock paralyzed her with disbelief. Dan was gone. His killers took stances at the edge of the cliff and continued pouring bursts of gunfire downward to where Dan had fallen.

Numbed, horrified, Lori was rooted where she stood, wanting to cry out—*bastards!*—to the men who'd just murdered her husband.

Suddenly Percy whirled, fired. Bullets tore through the cabin.

Lori crouched, pulling Billy down beside her shielding him with her body.

She saw Jerricko's backpack with food and water. She seized his laptop and, fumbling with her bound hands, shoved it in the bag and took it.

"Hurry!"

She rushed out the back with Billy and they crashed into the forest, running for their lives as bullets flicked through the trees.

51

Somewhere in New York State

When the shooting ceased, Cutty rushed down the slope, surfing on the gravelly dirt, hopping over rocks toward Fulton's body splayed at the bottom of the cliff.

Motionless.

Vic had ordered Cutty to verify Fulton's condition.

Cutty bent over him for closer inspection. His blood-soaked clothes were ripped and torn. His bullet-ridden arms and legs were twisted into impossible angles. His face was a bloodied, pulpy mass. Cutty gave him a hard kick, listening for a groan, watching for movement.

Nothing.

"He's dead!" Cutty called up to the others, quickly covering the body with large branches and undergrowth. "The animals are going to feast on you. Too bad you won't live to see what we're going to do to your bitch wife *in front* of your kid, you greedy banker nonbeliever asshole, one-percenter prick!"

Cutty touched the back of his hand to his throbbing face, assessing his own wounds as he climbed back up, cursing Lori Fulton.

"That bitch is dead!"

Above him, Percy and Vic had collected the two lost rifles and were inspecting them for any damage when the sound of new gunfire erupted around them.

Percy and Vic turned to the cabin to see Jerricko was behind it, firing into the woods.

"She got away with the kid! Let's go!" Vic shouldered his weapon, then tossed the bag he held to Percy. "Carry the money. Come on!"

Behind the cabin, all four unleashed sustained gunfire into the dark woods before Vic ordered them to regroup inside.

Breathing hard, cursing and gulping water, they assessed their situation. Jerricko was searching the cabin and the area near the beds.

"How the hell did this happen?" Percy said.

"Forget the how. What do we do now?" Cutty said.

"I say detonate the bombs," Percy said. "Blow the mothers up, end of story."

"Cell phones don't work up here," Cutty said. "We can't send the signal."

"That satellite phone works. Use it to call the numbers and boom," Percy reminded them.

Vic pulled the satellite phone from his pocket, looked at it then looked at his crew while weighing the call.

"Don't do it!" Jerricko said. "She's got my bag—

and our laptop with everything on it! Everything! You blow her up, you blow up everything we've been working for! We have to get it back!"

They all looked to Vic, waiting for him to decide their next move.

He put the phone away.

"We're done here. The gunfire is going to bring hikers or police this way. We're not blowing anything up. We need that laptop. The police found both cars—we heard it on the news on the way up. They're getting closer, but we have time. We'll go after her and the kid."

"Yes!" Cutty said.

"Divide the money into other bags, so it's easier to carry," Vic said. "Get what gear you need—fast!"

Percy went to the duffel bags by the beds where there was more ammunition and food.

"It's dark. She's a woman, handcuffed, dragging a kid and she's unarmed in a dense forest. There are four of us. We have automatic guns, plenty of ammo and equipment. We know these woods. We'll hunt her down, recover our laptop, salvage our operation and carry out our plans to the glorious end. Agreed?"

"Agreed!" the others said.

"Allah is the Greatest!" Vic shouted.

"Allah is the Greatest!" the others repeated.

52

Manhattan, New York

Kate lifted her head from her work to the glittering spires of Manhattan's skyline rising before her.

She and Stan were crossing the Hudson on the George Washington Bridge into New York City. It was late. She'd worked nonstop the entire return trip, filing story updates and making more calls in pursuit of information about Lori's ties to Jerricko Blaine or Malcolm Samadyh. Most people she'd reached met her questions with, "Who? Never heard of him," or "Not us, wrong Blaines." She dialed another number, this one in Southern California, with little hope of a lead. The line was answered by a woman.

"Is this the home of Ramone and Wanda Blaine?"

"Yes, this is Wanda. Who's calling?"

"Kate Page. I'm a reporter with Newslead in New York. I'm trying to reach relatives of Jerricko Titus Blaine. Are you a relative?"

The woman on the phone hesitated, then replied that, yes, she was related.

Kate sat ramrod straight.

"You're related to Jerricko Titus Blaine?"

"Yes." The woman sighed. "We figured someone would call us sooner or later—we've been watching the news all day and we weren't sure if we should get involved, or what. We're not sure how we could help."

Pressing the phone to her head, Kate made a one-handed scramble into her bag for her pen and notebook, flipping through it to a clean page.

"You could talk to me—help me get the true facts?"

"All right. But listen, we've got nothing to do with him, or what he's involved in."

"Of course not. Can you tell me how you're related to Mr. Blaine?"

"We're cousins of Andy Blaine, Jerricko's father. He was a great guy—real salt-of-the-earth man."

"Was?"

"Oh—yes, he died in a car accident a long while back."

"I'm sorry about your loss," Kate said. "What about Jerricko's mother? Do you know her very well?"

"I think she's crazy. All Andy's trouble seemed to start with her. Ever since they moved back to the States, all she did was rant about how much she hated living here, telling the boys this was a terrible country right from the start."

"Sorry—can you backtrack a little bit? The boys?"

"Jerricko and his older brother, Mac."

Kate couldn't believe her luck, discovering that Jerricko had a brother. This call was good. "Jerricko's brother—his name is Mac?"

"Yeah, short for Malcolm. That one was always trouble, especially after Andy passed away. Got in with the wrong crowd—no thanks to his mother— and did some…pretty horrible things."

"Horrible like what?" Kate asked.

"Robbing convenience stores and that sort of garbage. He eventually went to prison, but when he got out he was right back to his old ways and… Well, a few years back he shot a police officer who caught him mid-robbery—ended up shot dead himself."

Kate was stunned. *Malcolm—the man Lori Fulton had shot after he murdered her partner…*

"And just to confirm—this shooting, was it in Orange County?"

"That's right. Santa Ana. About five, six years ago now I think."

"Wait," Kate asked, still trying to puzzle out one last detail. "Can you spell Malcolm's last name for me, please?"

Wanda spelled it for her, S-A-M-A-D-Y-H, adding, "It's Sam-a-dee-*hah*."

"Got it. Thanks. But do you know why his last name isn't Blaine, like his father's and brother's?"

The woman snorted. "Just more of his mother's influence. He took her name when he got out of prison. She'd convinced him that there was nothing good that came from America, so he wanted to reconnect with his mother's roots."

Bingo! Kate thought, everything finally falling into place. *Malcolm Samadyh is Jerricko Blaine's brother. Lori shot Jerricko's brother.*

"Do you have a number for Jerricko's mother, Nazihah?"

"No, sorry. She went back to Afghanistan, or Syria, someplace after Malcolm died—and we were never close. Like I said, she hated America and everyone in it, and that seemed to include us and the rest of Andy's family."

"Do you know why she hated it so much?"

"Well, she used to go on about how immoral we were here. And Mac's death only solidified those beliefs."

"Does Nazihah have terrorist, or jihadist sympathies?"

"It wouldn't surprise me," Wanda said.

"Have police talked to you?"

"No."

"Have any other reporters talked to you?"

"No, you're the first. But, hey, I should have said this from the start—I don't want you putting our names in any news stories. We've got nothing to do with this mess, and I don't want anyone thinking otherwise."

"But I identified myself as a reporter at the start of this call."

"Well, we were just talking!" Wanda said. "You never mentioned anything about a formal interview or anything. You don't have permission to use our names."

"Okay, how about this? If you can help me get

in touch with some of Jerricko Blaine's other relatives, I won't use your name. I'll just identify you as a relative." Wanda took a moment, covering her phone for muffled discussion before returning to the call.

"My uncle wants to know how much you pay for the contact info we'd give you?"

"We don't pay for that kind of thing, sorry. The best I can do is offer to keep your name out of my story."

Wanda covered the phone again to deliberate.

"All right," she confirmed when she was back on the line. "I'll help you if you guarantee to keep our names out."

"Absolutely. I will."

"All right, why don't you give me your number? I'll call some relatives and tell them to give you a call."

"Promise?"

"Yes. There's a few people I can think of, cousins around the country, especially one in New York you should talk to. He knows way more about the boys than me. I'll make some calls and tell people to talk to you."

Kate thanked the woman and then spent the rest of the drive waiting.

But no calls came.

Block after block rolled by as Strobic drove through Manhattan's West Side and Kate was filled with the sick feeling that something critical had slipped through her fingers. In an act of desperation, she called Wanda Blaine back, but no one answered.

I had her on the line, and she was talkative. I should've pressed her harder.

But exhaustion had clouded Kate's thinking, and now it was too late.

Images of the day replayed in Kate's mind when she was alone in the elevator on the way up to pick up Grace. As it rose, the hum lulled her. She leaned against the wall and almost drifted off.

Nancy greeted Kate with a warm smile, letting her in to wake Grace from a dead sleep on the sofa.

"Thanks a million, Nancy."

"No thanks needed."

Kate then brought her groggy daughter to their floor, into their apartment, into her nightshirt and into bed. After kissing Grace good-night, Kate saw that Vanessa was in her room asleep. Knowing she'd have just finished a night class, and that she'd be up early for a morning shift at the diner, Kate was careful not to disturb her as she moved down the hall toward the bathroom.

Kate climbed into the shower, the needles of hot water soothing her. As she let the pressure of the water slowly relax the tense muscles in her neck, she contemplated her next steps.

She needed to dig up more about Jerricko. Now that the link between him and Lori was clear, she needed to find out whether this whole thing was cold-blooded revenge or something more. Why rob the bank and take the family hostage? Why hadn't he just gone straight after Lori? And the big question: Who was helping him?

She still had a lot of work to do. But she'd just landed a big exclusive, which should make Reeka happy. Kate would start writing her story in the morning, and she'd press Agent Varner with this new information to try to leverage anything more. And, keeping her promise, she'd also share her information with Ben Keller in LA about thirty minutes before Newslead released her story.

After showering, she brushed her teeth, dried her hair, pulled on her robe, then slipped into Grace's room to check on her. Kneeling at her bedside, Kate adjusted her blanket, tenderly pushing aside strands of Grace's hair and looking at her.

"I'm sorry I've been working so much, sweetie," Kate whispered, grateful to have Grace safely by her side. Her heart ached for Lori, Dan and Billy Fulton. "I love you so much."

Kate kissed Grace's cheek and left the room.

Since the door to Vanessa's room was opened a crack, Kate tiptoed in and knelt at her sister's bedside.

Sometimes I still don't believe that you're here with me.

Kate marveled at Vanessa, a beautiful young woman who'd triumphed by crawling victoriously out of the hell she'd been cast into. She was working so hard at reclaiming the life that had been stolen from her.

You're my hero, kiddo.

Kate then climbed into her own bed. Sleep came

quickly and soon her mind was filled with stressful dreams of making calls, the sound of her phone ringing, then vibrating, so loud…

Kate woke, head spinning as she grabbed her phone.

"Hello?"

"Hi… Is this the reporter who was asking about Nazihah Samadyh's sons?"

"Yes, who's calling?"

"Bert."

He had a heavy accent—maybe Middle Eastern, Kate thought.

"Bert who?"

"Only my first name, okay? My cousin in California told me about you. I'll talk, but not now. It has to be early tomorrow."

"Can't we talk on the phone, Bert?"

"No, it has to be in person."

"Why not now?"

"Because I'm going to the FBI tomorrow."

Kate sat up and grabbed a pen.

"All right, where do you want to meet?"

"At Grand Central Terminal, by the Grabbin Run Deli. You know it?"

"Yes."

"Meet me at seven-thirty. I'll tell you everything before I tell the FBI, because you should know the truth. You're my safety net for the truth."

The call ended with Kate staring at her phone.

How about that? Wanda Blaine came through, Kate thought as she absorbed the information.

"You should know the truth."

Her head was swimming.

She settled back into bed, though it took several long moments for her pulse rate to slow down. Waiting for sleep, she looked through her window and up at the crescent moon. Staring into the night, she thought of Dan, Lori and Billy Fulton and wondered if they could see the same moon from where they were.

Are they even alive to see it?

53

Somewhere in New York State

Lori ran with Billy through the dark woods, terrified, breathless, her heart bursting.

Images of her life streaked before her: Dan's smile when she first met him at college; their wedding day; his tear-filled eyes above the surgical mask in the delivery room when they had Billy; his last words...

"Go get Billy... I'll be right behind you!"

Something had cleaved inside and Lori needed to let loose a great guttural, animal shriek at the horror she now faced. A wail was about to erupt and shoot to the heavens, beseeching God to turn back time and release her from this netherworld.

Why, why, why?

But she couldn't scream. They would hear her. She choked back her sobs and fought against the shock, the cold, the painful stomach spasms, helping Billy as they ran.

The whip-snip of bullets in the trees had ceased; the distant echoes of voices had long faded. How long had it been? She didn't know. How far had they fled? She didn't know. But fear compelled her to keep moving.

Fear that the murderers were gaining on them.

Fear that at any time they could detonate the vests. If they got far enough away maybe they'd be out of range. Lori held fast to that hope.

As it grew dark, they had to slow down. It was harder to see now and the cumbersome vests and Lori's bound hands made it difficult to travel. Lori refused to jettison the backpack of food, water and laptop, despite the extra weight. It was all they had now, along with their will to survive.

Keep moving, keep moving.

Legs numb. Sides and arms aching, lungs sore, throats dry and ragged from panicked breathing. But they kept moving through the dense stands of sweet-scented woods. Branches scraped their faces and arms, snagged and pulled at them. The terrain was rocky, uneven and dangerous.

They stumbled often and when Billy had cried out, Lori comforted him.

As they continued, she heard him sobbing through his clenched jaw and she was pierced with the thought that he'd witnessed his father's murder.

Did he see it? Does he know Dan's dead?

She was uncertain. They hadn't stopped. There'd been no time to talk.

Eventually they could go no farther. They settled in along a small hollow in a soft hillside. In silence, they gathered branches to pull over them for cover. The temperature had plunged and they shivered quietly. The running had warmed them, but Lori knew the freezing air would make it worse for them while they were still.

She searched blindly through the backpack, opening the zipped pockets, desperate for anything that would help them survive. Feeling around, she let out a gasp of relief when her fingers found a folded pocket knife. She held it to her face to examine it for the groove she needed, then opened the blade and very carefully cut Billy's wrists free of the plastic cuffs, passing the knife, so he could do the same for her.

The freedom to move their hands and arms was a victory, and it gave Lori a measure of hope. She considered attempting to remove the bombs, which she thought might be possible by moving their arms, sliding the vests up and over their heads. But the way they were rigged, zippered and Velcroed, with wires running across the front, drove home her fear that any attempt to free themselves might cause the bombs to explode. They'd had them this long and they were still alive. She'd only try removing them as a last resort. Besides, now they offered warmth.

She continued searching the bag, finding a sweatshirt and ball cap. Taking her time, she put them on Billy. Swishing sounds in the backpack led her to discover a plastic bottle of water that felt nearly full.

"Easy," she whispered to him as he drank. "We have to save as much as we can."

She felt the laptop and debated whether to turn it

on and use it. Maybe, just maybe, if there was service, the computer could be a lifeline to help. But she decided against trying to find out right now, worried that the light of the screen would give away their location or activate some other tracking feature she might not be aware of. No, she didn't want to take that risk. Not now.

She pulled Billy close, both of them trembling, gasping erratically as they fought to stay warm. The night carried the intermittent sounds of nocturnal animals moving through the forest.

"I'm scared, Mom," Billy whispered.

She held him tighter.

"We'll be okay. Try to rest. It's the best thing."

"But…what happened to Dad?"

His question cut through her. She pushed back a sob and anguished over whether to lie to her son to protect him, or if it was best to just tell him the truth.

"I heard shouting," Billy insisted. "I heard Dad's voice. I know it was him. Then there was all this shooting. Mom, what happened?"

Lori swallowed hard and realized that, after all Billy had been through, he needed to know the truth.

"Yes, sweetheart, your dad was outside. The two other men brought him here, then Daddy did a very, very brave thing. He fought back, so fast and so hard, that we—" her voice broke "—that we were able to get free…"

"So where is he?"

"Honey, I'm so sorry, but he didn't—they—they shot him."

Billy pulled away from her, whispering harshly, "No! You're lying!"

"Shhh-shh."

Lori pressed her little boy's face tight to her body, practically feeling his heart break, feeling him shake as he sobbed against her.

"He saved us, sweetheart. Daddy did what he had to, so that we could get away. He saved us and now we have to do our best to get home, so we can tell police what they did. Promise me we'll fight hard, together, for Daddy, okay?"

Lori felt his head moving up and down against her as she stared up to the sky at the crescent moon and prayed.

54

Blue Coyote Mountains, New York

In Greene County, deep in central New York State, to the southeast and west of the Hudson River, the lowlands rose into the Blue Coyote Mountains.

The short line of beautiful highlands stood between the Blackhead Mountains to the north and, to the south, the Catskills, which stretched over six thousand square miles of forests, rivers, waterfalls and farmland.

The Coyote range was largely unknown to most people, except those with ties to the remote region or locals who lived there.

Sidney Ferring drove his battered Ford pickup along a ridge that climbed into an isolated corner of the Coyotes. The truck lumbered up the rugged, twisting pathway until he came to an SUV.

Sidney shifted the transmission into Park and killed the engine. As it ticked down, Caesar, his Belgian shepherd, yipped and jumped from the rear to explore.

"What do you think?" Sidney asked, turning to

his brother Tyree, who was nursing a hangover in the passenger seat.

"Get out and check it, dim wad," Tyree said. "You're the one who heard all that ruckus coming from here last night. You wanted to come up here."

"You'd have heard it, too, if you wasn't drunk." Sidney got out of the truck to look around.

The SUV had dipped to the right, resting on the rim of a flattened front tire. The spare and tools were placed next to it, as if someone had started to replace it but changed their mind instead.

No one was in sight. No note on the windshield.

Sidney whistled to Caesar and they got back in the truck.

"Weird," he said, continuing up the ridge until they came to a van parked a few yards from old man Vanderhooven's cabin.

Vanderhooven was a retired farmer who lived in a seniors' residence in Albany. Sidney and Tyree's mother, Irene, ran a property management company and rented the place for him to fishermen and hunters, while her sons occasionally hired themselves out as guides or did odd jobs on the properties. The boys lived in a double-wide in Owl Pond Valley, a couple of miles below.

Last night when Sidney had gone outside to relieve himself, he'd sworn he'd heard gunfire—a lot of rapid gunfire—echoing down from the old man's cabin in the mountains. It motivated him to investigate this morning.

"Hello?" Sidney called as they got out of the truck and approached the cabin. "Hello?"

"Not so loud, dim wad."

The brothers had no idea who their mother had rented the place to. It was usually all done online. People could transfer her the money and she'd send them a code for the key lock. The front door was wide-open, so they stepped inside. They scanned the place quickly—the beds, the kitchen area, the table. Nothing. Nobody. Then—

"*Jee Zuss!* Look at that!"

Sidney went to the mattresses in the corner, finding chains attached to the wall with handcuffs linked to the ends.

"This don't look good, Ty."

"It sure as hell don't."

"What do you think? They making porn or something?"

"How the hell would I know?"

Suddenly Caesar let go with nonstop barking outside.

"Better see what he's yapping about," Sidney said.

They went out and down the pathway where the dog was perched at the edge of the ridge, barking at something down below. As if cued by their arrival, Caesar disappeared down the hillside, woofing all the way. Sidney squatted to look at whatever was exciting his dog.

Tyree felt a crunch and heard tinkling under his boots.

"Hell, look at all these shell casings! You for damn sure heard gunfire last night, Sid!"

"I told ya!" Sidney surveyed the area. "Damn, there's a lot of 'em. What the hell were they shootin' at?"

Caesar scampered to the ridge top, returning to Sidney with something in his jaws. Petting his dog, Sidney took the item in his hand. It was about the size of a sheet of tissue, a torn piece of fabric, damp with red—

"*Jee Zuss*, that looks like blood!"

Sidney's attention followed Caesar, who'd galloped back down the hillside to the brush heaped at the bottom.

Sidney put one hand over his eyes to block the sun, squinting until he saw a bloodied hand among the branches.

55

Manhattan, New York

At 7:15 a.m. Kate Page joined the bustle of Grand Central's main concourse, loving its sweeping staircases, glimmering chandeliers and cathedral splendor.

Striding with thousands of commuters, she made her way to the lower level, aware that she was being watched on Grand Central's closed-circuit security camera system. Kate knew about the electronic sensors, the radiation detectors, and that you couldn't go twenty feet without seeing a cop. Since 9/11, Grand Central was considered one of the world's top targets for terrorists—just another part of life in New York.

But this morning it all underscored her unease over her meeting.

Bert was a complete stranger, but meeting with strangers was part of her job.

As a reporter, Kate had met sources like this all the time. She was not fearless and she was not a fool. She always took precautions. She was extremely careful never to meet anyone alone, unless it was during the day and in a very public place.

Bert could be luring her for his own reasons. He could be a nut who wanted to be part of the story, but, if her instinct was to be trusted, he could also be a genuine source of critical information.

At the food concourse she was greeted by appetizing aromas of freshly baked bread, bacon, coffee and fresh fruit. She threaded her way among commuters, moving under the marble arches along the many food kiosks and joining the line at Grabbin Run Deli.

She studied the sea of faces, trying to guess if she could match one to Bert's voice. He'd called her again this morning to say he was bringing someone with him and ensured Kate that he'd recognize her from pictures he'd seen online related to news stories.

Kate bought a tea and a bagel with cream cheese. She got lucky when someone vacated a table with three chairs. She took a seat and unfolded her copy of the *New York Times*. She'd managed two bites, two sips and got to page three before two men stood at her table.

She lowered her paper.

"May I help you?"

"You're Kate Page, the reporter?"

She nodded.

"I'm Bert, and this is my son, John."

Bert was in his mid-fifties. His dark-complexioned face was covered with salt-and-pepper stubble. His dark, oily hair was parted neatly to one side.

He wore a sport jacket with a newspaper rolled in one pocket—Arabic, Kate noticed from the headlines.

His son was in his early twenties, with white earbuds collared around his neck. He wore a Lady Gaga T-shirt and jeans and was chewing gum.

"Please, sit down," she said.

"We have very little time before we catch the train to Federal Plaza."

"I understand." Kate set her phone to record and took out her notebook.

"No pictures, please."

"Got it. What do you do for a living, Bert?"

"I'm a contractor. I have a small carpentry business in Yonkers."

"And John?"

"I'm a student at Hunter College."

"What're you studying?"

"Chemistry."

"Okay, let's get to it. Why did you call me? What is your relation to Jerricko Blaine and his family?"

"His mother, Nazihah Samadyh, is my cousin," Bert said. "I want you to know that we've not had contact with her for years. To be honest, we never got along. We're going to the FBI to tell them the truth about her son Jerricko."

"And what's the truth?"

"First, you must know that I am an American citizen. I came to this country because I respect it and love it for the freedom and dignity it offers to everyone who is willing to work hard."

"Understood."

"John, my son, is also an American citizen, born here in New York."

"Okay."

"Nazihah and her sons have brought shame upon our family. When she came here, she always complained, she never even tried to fit in. Her husband, Andrew, was a good man, but she was not happy here. She was always critical of US policy. You know that her son Malcolm went to prison for robbery, then murdered a police officer and was shot."

"Yes."

"In her twisted thinking, Nazihah said it was the fault of the US government and its policies that Malcolm was shot. She believed in some fantasy conspiracy and moved back to Afghanistan. Jerricko, Malcolm's brother, didn't want to leave the US at first. He was never the same after his brother's death. He started hanging out with the wrong people. We know because he recently tried to pull John into his circles."

Kate turned to the younger man.

"It's true. He messaged me online, told me how much he respected and admired me for my work at Hunter."

"Did you hang out with him much?"

"He came to our place and we went out a few times. But he was just like his mom—all he ever wanted to talk about was the corruption of America and how everyone here was greedy and sinful. But he was never open to talking about it or letting anyone argue with him. I knew things were getting out of control after he'd told me that he'd used a

stolen and altered passport to go to Afghanistan to
visit his mom. When he came back, he kept sending me online links to read, extremist stuff that his
mom had sent him. He was always denouncing the
US and Israel as part of a global system of oppression. I mean, some of the stuff he talked about was
true—there are tons of pretty horrible things that
happen all the time. But he'd show me all these ji-
hadi sites, stuff that was way too intense, and tried
to convince me to join him and his friends."

"Were you interested?"

John shook his head.

"People are entitled to their opinions," John said.
"You can argue that US foreign policy is flawed
and Jerricko's friends make good points, but it
doesn't mean I should rush out and cut somebody's
head off. That's doesn't improve things. I think
these guys are off-the-chart crazy with their need
for revenge."

Kate nodded.

"So," Bert said, "when we saw the news about
Jerricko and the bank manager, the robbery and the
bomb vests in Queens, we were so ashamed and
disgusted. That's why we're going to the FBI this
morning—in case we can answer any questions
that could help them."

"They don't know you're coming?"

"No. We'll show up and tell them what we just
told you," Bert said. "I'm certain they'll be very
interested in talking with us. Last night, when my
cousin in California called about you, I'm thinking, I must have the truth be known that our family

denounces this and we have no part in it. That is why we're speaking to you first, so the press hears this, too. Please, you must understand."

"I do."

"Okay, so here's the thing," John said. "Jerricko was trying to recruit me to their cause because I'm a chemist. They said if I helped them it would be part of something 'really big, glorious and monumental,' and that was going to happen very soon."

"Did they mean the robbery using the bomb vests?"

"No," John said. He looked around nervously, but Kate gave him a reassuring smile, nodding at him that it was okay to continue. "I think the robbery's only the beginning."

"Beginning of what?"

"I'm not sure. Something bigger," Bert said, glancing at his watch. "We have to go now."

"Wait," Kate said. "I need to see some ID, so I know who I'm talking to?"

Unease spread across the older man's face.

"My editors will think I made this all up," Kate said. "I need to confirm your identity, but we won't publish your names. I'll protect you as sources, but I need to see ID."

After a moment's hesitation, both men produced wallets with photo ID. The father's real name was Walid Sattar, and his son was Omar. After she photographed their IDs and made notes, both men got up and disappeared into Grand Central's chaos.

Kate sat there for a moment absorbing what she'd just heard. It was astounding. Then she left and hurried down East Forty-Second Street half a block to the lobby of the Grand Hyatt, glad she'd alerted the photo desk to her meeting. Nothing was going to slip through her fingers this time.

Kate sat on one of the cushioned benches near the registration desk. Two minutes later, Strobic joined her. During her meeting at the Grabbin Run with Bert and his son, Strobic had positioned himself unseen at the next food vendor, taking pictures of Walid and Omar.

Strobic showed them to her, a series of crisp shots, clearly identifying the faces of the men, frame after frame. Kate would protect their identities, but if anything happened, she now had evidence of the meeting.

"Good work, Stan," she said as her phone rang.

"Kate Page, Newslead."

"Kate, it's Thane in the newsroom. You're with Strobic, right?"

"Yeah, what's up?"

"We need you to get up to the Blue Coyote Mountains, about two or three hours north. I'll get you directions. We've got a major break."

"What happened?"

"They found Dan Fulton's body."

56

Coyote Mountains, New York

Lori kept waking, sleeping and waking again.

We're still alive.

She lay there in the twilight, shivering under the vest as Billy slept with his head on her chest. Birdsong echoed with the rustle, cluck and screech of small creatures moving through the forest. Lori listened for sounds of any approaching threat until the sun rose, bathing the woods in light and the horror churning inside her erupted.

Dan's dead! Oh God! Dan!

She covered her mouth with both hands to silence her sobs, but her anguished spasms woke Billy. Cold replaced his warmth against her as he went behind a tree a few yards away and relieved himself.

Lori regained a degree of composure and studied him closely, touching his cheek when he returned to her side. His eyes were reddened because he'd cried much of the night. Stress lines were carved deep into his face.

"How are you doing, sweetie?"

Billy shrugged.

"Do you want to talk?"

He shook his head, but then he nodded.

"What is it, honey?"

"Did they really kill Dad?"

Lori stared into his eyes and nodded, pulling him to her and holding him as they both wept. She was numb. None of this was real. How could it be real?

Dan, tell me. What am I supposed to do now?

When their tears subsided, she brushed his cheeks.

"We just have to keep going, okay?"

"But how can we, without Dad?"

"I know, honey. I know it's hard, but we have to do this. Dad would want us to keep going."

He nodded.

"Do you think they killed Sam, too?"

"No, I don't. I believe in my heart that Sam's okay and he's waiting to see you again."

Billy considered her words carefully as he absorbed them.

"I'm thirsty," he said. "And hungry."

"Me, too. Let's see what's in here."

She hefted the backpack, positioned it on her lap and pulled out the bottled water, which she passed to Billy. As he drank she opened a package of twelve chocolate-iced donuts. They ate two each, careful to save the rest.

"Mom, what are we going to do?"

"We're going to find a way out of here."

Lori pulled out the laptop and turned it on. The

computer came to life, and she immediately tried to get on to the internet. But it was futile. There was no signal and no capability to find one. They had no way of reaching help.

"Can I have another donut?" Billy asked.

"I'll give you half of one. We need to save the rest."

As Billy ate, Lori scrutinized the laptop with heightened intensity, searching for anything that might help. Other than a couple of standard icons, the desktop was clean. She went on to the drives, found several folders and began opening them. Reading as fast as she could. One held files that contained detailed maps of New York City. Another file contained a list of names, addresses and emails for several people. Most were in the United States, some were in Canada, Germany, Australia, Britain, Kuwait, Iraq and Syria.

Another file contained four videos.

She played the first and was greeted by the face of Percy. The running time was a few seconds. She kept the volume low, hit Play, and Percy spoke directly into the camera.

"Greetings from paradise. At this moment, you're asking why. We'll enlighten you. Because your elected government continuously perpetuates atrocities around the world, your support of them makes you, the people of America, responsible, just as I am and my brothers are responsible for protecting and avenging our people. Until we feel safe from your oppression, you will be our targets. What you have witnessed in New York is only the beginning. More acts will come and they will be stronger until you cease committing atrocities. Allah is great."

The three other videos showed the other captors making similar short statements.

"Those don't sound good. What are they?" Billy asked.

Lori knew but didn't answer.

She opened more files, finding another map. This one was of Manhattan, clearly marked with four locations, the Staten Island Ferry, Times Square, Penn Station and Grand Central Terminal. A name was affixed to each location, causing the tiny hairs on the back of Lori's neck to stand up.

"Oh my God, no!"

"What is it, Mom?"

She opened files containing notes, one detailing how the group had planned to give the money from the bank operation in Queens and names of "young American believers" to a network, so that it could fund more "glorious operations."

Lori shut off the laptop and took several deep breaths.

"We've got to get out of here and warn people."

"Warn what people about what, Mom?"

"Something very bad is going to happen and we've got to stop it. Come on, we've got to find our way out."

As they stood to leave, they froze.

Voices carried from the distance.

57

Coyote Mountains, New York

Daylight slowly began filling the forest.

As it fingered through the trees, Cutty could feel it needling him for his failure. His prisoner had defeated him and escaped.

The cuts, the bruising and the fractures he'd suffered from her surprise attack only fed his rage. He was the biggest, the strongest of the group, and he'd had his ass handed to him by a stupid nonbelieving woman.

His flashlight raked through the waning darkness as he and Percy hunted Lori down. Jerricko and Vic were hunting together another forty or fifty yards to the north. Both teams communicated to each other by way of signal bursts from their flashlights.

Cutty's thoughts shifted to his family and the images his relatives had sent him from northern Iraq. The dead little babies, their mouths agape, buried in the rubble of shelters destroyed by American drones. His anger warmed his blood as he nursed his humiliation at losing his prisoner. He would personally exact payback from that bitch—right in front of her kid. He'd get Percy to record it before he and the others took their turn.

Problem was, Cutty was not sure if he would enjoy that more than just cutting off their heads and showing the world the price to be paid for oppressive regimes.

Soon every person on the planet will know me and my brothers and the glory we've attained.

As the sky brightened, Percy signaled—he had something.

With the rising sun Percy saw a flash of color in the distance.

He signaled to the others, then got on the ground and took a position, raising his small binoculars. Deep among the branches and needles, he saw a postage-stamp size patch of blue. He couldn't discern movement or details, only that whatever the object was, it didn't belong there.

"It's them," Percy whispered to Cutty, who'd joined him.

Percy, who was the best shot of the group, raised his gun and sighted the target, easily more than a hundred yards off. But he knew his gun's limitations.

A thought arrived.

Percy lowered his gun and reached into his pocket for his cell phone, wishing right now that he had Vic's satellite phone. Cell service was spotty, but there were brief periods when his cell worked, and if God willed it, this would be one of them.

"What're you doing?" Cutty asked.

"I'm trying the code. Let's blow them up!"

"But Vic and Jerricko said she's got the laptop."

"Yeah, well, I say we take our chances and kill them now. What good is the laptop going to do us if they get away? Besides, we've got the money. Vic's got the sat phone. We know what to do, so let's get on with it." Percy held up his phone. "Look, I've got a signal! I'm making the call."

58

Coyote Mountains, New York

The air ambulance helicopter whipped dirt and stones into the air, forcing emergency crews on the ground to turn away as it landed in a small clearing on the jagged hilltop.

Less than an hour earlier, after the Ferring brothers had gotten down from the ridge, Sidney Ferring had made a 911 call to a Greene County emergency services dispatcher who then set events in motion, alerting several agencies to a mountain trauma rescue.

On the scene now as the chopper put down were Greene County deputies, state police out of Cairo, forest rangers, and a K-9 unit that was checking the cabin and the trail to the outbuilding.

Crouching as they left the chopper with medical bags, the flight paramedic and flight nurse stepped down the hillside to join Greene County paramedics who'd arrived earlier with a scoop stretcher and gear.

They'd cleared away the branches and had set

out working on the male patient when the chopper team arrived at the base of the slope.

"We've got vitals! He's got multiple GSWs, multiple fractures, maybe spinal injuries," one of the paramedics shouted. "Lost a lot of blood. Doesn't look good."

As they worked to get the patient on the stretcher and start an IV, one of the county paramedics shouted, "Stop!"

Everyone halted.

"He's wearing a bomb vest! Everybody step back!"

Amid the blood-caked dirt and needles covering the patient, a canvas vest with various compartments, wires and a blinking red light of a battery pack was now visible.

The teams backed off several yards, using a rock formation as a shield as they shouted over the thud of the waiting helicopter.

"He's that bank manager from Queens!" one of the county paramedics said.

"If we don't move him now, he'll die," the flight paramedic called out.

"Yeah, but if that vest blows, we could all die! We need the bomb squad," the flight nurse said.

"There's no time. He'll bleed out before they get here!"

"Wait! One of the deputies up top did bomb disposal work when he was with the army or marines." The county paramedic shouted for help into his radio.

Less than a minute later, Greene County deputy sheriff Kyle O'Mara, who'd served with the US Army in Baghdad, hurried down the hill and huddled behind the rock with the paramedics, listening and looking toward the patient as they told him what they'd found.

"I'll take a look," O'Mara shouted then moved toward the patient.

He knelt over the bleeding man, studying the vest. The packs looked to him like C-4, which was material that was hard to obtain. He sniffed them for the characteristic smell of C-4 but was still not certain. He knew C-4 would not explode when moved or dropped and given the man's injuries, he likely tumbled off the edge of the climb without detonating the bomb. Still, he was wary. The arming mechanism looked genuine and rigged to a remote detonation pack, but it wasn't that sophisticated by his estimation.

With the helicopter thundering, the vest's battery light ticking down and blood oozing from the patient, O'Mara knew he had to make a decision now.

Betting his life, he reached for the wire he believed would disarm the vest.

"It's just you and me, buddy," O'Mara said as he pinched a yellow wire, getting ready to pull it. "Our Father, who art in Heaven…"

59

Coyote Mountains, New York

Percy pressed the send button on his phone, but nothing happened.

No flash. No bang. No nothing.

He looked at the screen for an answer. He still had a signal, so he tried the number again.

Nothing happened. The blue patch was still there, tiny among the woods in the distance.

"What the hell?" Percy thumbed the send key repeatedly.

"What'd you think you're doing?" Vic said, keeping his voice low as he arrived with Jerricko.

"I found them." Percy indicated the colored square far off. "And I'm going to kill them."

"Stop! You were ordered not to detonate the vests!"

"But you know it's the best way to stop them."

"She's got all of our data—you could destroy everything!"

"What the hell're you thinking? We killed the

husband. We don't need the data, we know what to do."

"We *need* that laptop. You don't know what's on there."

"We know the operation. I say we stop running around and finish the rest of them—now!" Percy held up his phone. "I got a signal here but the code's not working. Why isn't it working?"

Vic didn't answer.

"I asked you a question!" Percy said.

Percy, Cutty and Jerricko stared at Vic as he considered the question, letting a long tense moment pass before he said, "The bombs aren't real."

"What do you mean they're not real?" Percy asked.

"The C-4's modeling clay, and the batteries just make the light flash. The wires are for show."

Percy and Cutty glared at Vic.

"We needed the family to think they were real—especially Dan—to guarantee they'd cooperate. I needed you, the squad, to believe they were real, so that we could convince them."

"Why the hell wouldn't we use real bombs?"

"We didn't have the time or resources to make them for this part of the mission. Look, this was the only way to protect the entire operation." Vic looked at each of the men in turn. "Do you get that?"

One by one they nodded.

"Now, we need to get that laptop, dispose of those two, then make our contact so we can proceed to the next stage before it's too late."

"Look," Jerricko pointed at the moving patch of blue.

"We can't waste another second," Vic said. "Jerricko, you swing north. I'll go south. You—" Vic tapped Percy's shoulder "—swing east." He nodded to Cutty. "Take the west. We'll box them in, then tighten the noose."

60

Coyote Mountains, New York

The East River dropped under Nick Varner, and skyscrapers reached up as the state police helicopter lifted off from Pier Six in Lower Manhattan.

Marv Tilden and two other investigators were also belted to their seats as the chopper thundered north to the Coyote range where two locals had found Dan Fulton.

Fulton's condition was critical and he was not expected to live. He'd been airlifted to a trauma center in Albany where he was now undergoing surgery. If he survived, they'd need to talk to him. But first they had to get to the scene, which, by helicopter, was twenty minutes away.

The metropolis unfurled below, giving way to New Jersey, then the forests, hills and mountains of New York. Varner missed much of it because he was working on his phone, reviewing the recent progress they'd made on the case.

When the FBI had been alerted to Fulton's discovery, Varner and Tilden had been in the process of interviewing Jerricko Blaine's uncle Walid Sattar and his son, Omar Sattar. Alarmed by the news reports, the Sattars had come forward with information. They'd revealed that Jerricko had stayed with them in the weeks prior to the bank robbery/abduction in Queens.

"We had not seen him or his mother for years since his brother's death, so we let him stay. It was out of respect," Walid had said. "He's family. But Jerricko upset everyone, always talking jihad, ranting about the evils of America and his duty to fight against it. He tried to recruit my son to his way of thinking."

Omar had given Varner and Tilden as much information about the "big operation" as he could, and about Jerricko's talk of action.

"He said they could use me as a chemist in an event that would make us famous forever. He didn't tell me what it was. He was very cryptic," Omar had said. "But I do know that he went to the public library to use the computers there, probably to talk to his friends."

This all fit with the information they'd received from FBI agents in LA, Varner thought as he'd continued making notes.

"You see," Walid had said, "we're proud American citizens. We have nothing to do with Jerricko's craziness."

Varner knew that the Sattars had handed them a key piece of information, but it was not the only break. More information had come in around the same time.

As the chopper pushed north, Varner reviewed video footage collected from residential security cameras in the Fultons' Roseoak Park neighborhood. It showed four male figures entering the Fulton home. There was footage of Lori and Billy being forced into a van, and later of Dan driving off with an SUV following him. It confirmed what they'd suspected from the start: Jerricko Blaine did not act alone.

They'd also learned that the bomb vest the suspects had put on Dan Fulton was nothing but a prop. Combined with the fingerprint evidence and other mistakes they had made, the suspects were untrained, inexperienced amateurs, possibly homegrown, self-radicalized extremists, and questions raced through Varner's mind.

What was the "big operation" they were planning? Was it this—the robbery and abduction—or something bigger? Did they take the cash to get rich? Or was there another use for it? Were they acting on their own or being guided?

The FBI had moved to expedite warrants to search the Sattar home in Yonkers and the public library branch Jerricko Blaine had used. And again, Varner submitted Jerricko Blaine's name into the Guardian database, the networks for Homeland, Justice, the State Department and several others.

He double-checked to ensure he'd also made submissions for Blaine's mother, Nazihah Bilaal Samadyh, and brother, Malcolm Jordan Samadyh.

Pieces were coming together.

Now we've got to connect the dots.

* * *

The helicopter skimmed treetops as it descended, agitating branches and whipping up dirt as it put down.

Bending under the whomping rotor wash, Varner's team hurried to meet investigators from the state and county. The State Police Crime Scene Emergency Response techs were working with the FBI's Evidence Response Team. "Agent Varner. I'm Fred Dylan, New York State Police." Dylan handed the newcomers shoe covers and latex gloves. "This way. Follow the red ribbon closely to protect the scene, please."

Along the route to the cabin, Dylan updated them on Dan Fulton's condition. Then they arrived at the SUV, which was consistent with the vehicle in the footage. Crime scene technicians were photographing it, swabbing and analyzing the interior, bagging shell casings and marking their locations.

Varner was confident evidence would surface that would bring them even closer to the suspects. He was optimistic that the fake bomb vest would yield leads. Crime scene experts were also at work down the hillside where Dan Fulton had been found and at the second vehicle, the van, which was parked near the cabin.

"It's a rental," Dylan said. "A man named Robert Smith paid cash to have it for a month. We suspect that's an alias."

The cabin's interior was being processed, but what Varner and Tilden saw inside pushed their concerns to a higher level. In the corner were mattresses, chains and a tripod.

"We believe the family was held here," Dylan said.

"Looks like someone left in a hurry," Tilden said.

Varner noticed the large knife resting against the wall near the tripod and lowered himself to study it without touching it.

"Is that ceremonial, like the one they used in Northern Iraq to behead that aid worker?" Tilden asked.

As Varner nodded slowly, they heard the yip of a dog with one of the K-9 units and two-way radios crackled.

"…we might have a trail…"

What was now clear was that the suspects, and possibly Lori and Billy Fulton, were out there somewhere in the Coyote Mountains.

Now it's a manhunt-hostage-rescue, tied to plans for an attack.

Varner studied the vast mountain forests.

And we're running out of time.

61

Coyote Mountains, New York

"That's as far as you go. All press over there."

The state trooper standing on the road at the intersection directed Stan and Kate to the parking field. It was beside an abandoned church, which investigators had designated as the media center.

The lot was filling with news vans and TV satellite trucks, more than at yesterday's scene when they'd found the car. Today's discovery of Dan Fulton had pushed the story to a national lead and Kate knew that meant she had little time to tie up the loose ends on her exclusive and get it out. Lori's connection to Jerricko Blaine and his brother, Malcolm Samadyh, was a huge scoop. But the most chilling aspect that she'd uncovered was the possibility that Jerricko, driven by his brother's death and his mother's call for jihad, was tied to an extremist group plotting an attack.

Kate had written most of the story on the drive along the Thruway but she hadn't sent it to the desk yet, nor had she alerted them. She had to be doubly sure of her facts. She needed more confirmation and she needed it fast.

"I don't like this setup." Strobic nodded to the mountains as they left his truck and walked to the media center. During the latter part of the drive, while Kate wrote, he'd used an earpiece to listen to one of his emergency radio scanners, which allowed him to monitor parts of the investigation and search as they were unfolding. "We're three miles from the scene up there."

"That's not going to work for me," Kate said. "I've got to get close to the action. We've got to figure something out, Stan."

Kate's phone rang. It was Reeka.

"The *Daily News* says Dan Fulton's dead."

"What?"

"The *Post* has him on life support. Which is it? Can you confirm?"

"We're working on it, we just arrived."

"We've got to keep leading on this, Kate. We need another exclusive angle or our subscribers will turn to AP and Bloomberg."

"I'm aware of that, Reeka, and I'm working on it."

"What're you working on? I want to put it on the sked to interest subscribers."

If I tell her what I have, she'll go crazy and oversell it. I can't let the story go yet without solid confirmation, I just can't.

Phone pressed to her ear, Kate searched in vain for Nick Varner and Marv Tilden.

"Did you hear me, Kate? What're you working on?"

"Just some background."

"What sort of background? Do you have a lead on something?"

Kate had to stall.

"Sorry, Reeka, you're breaking up. Service is weak up here."

"I can hear you fine."

"What? What? Sorry, Reeka. Hello?"

"I'm here."

"Hello? I can't hear you. Sorry. I've got to go."

As soon as Kate hung up she put in a call to Varner but it went to his voice mail. She left an urgent message before entering the center.

Inside the reception area of the old church, amid the sound of radio cross talk, a few rangers, deputies and state troopers were hunched over wooden tables studying maps. Others were at a table with a coffee urn and boxes of donuts. Newspeople were coming and going. Technicians were on the phone to their stations, while some helped themselves to the refreshments.

Varner and Tilden were not there.

To one side, several reporters had encircled a man wearing a nylon FBI jacket. He was explaining information while passing out sheets of paper. Kate held up her hand for one. It was a press release confirming that Dan Fulton was alive but in critical condition in an Albany hospital. It added that a search was under way for Lori and Billy Fulton and the suspects wanted in connection to the robbery, kidnapping and assault arising out of Queens.

"It's just like I told CBS," the FBI agent said,

"the airspace over the crime scene and search areas is restricted."

"But we need to get our people up and over it," a woman wearing a FOX ball cap said.

"No TV or still news cameras can fly over the area because it's dangerous to aerial search operations."

This angered the networks who were arguing with the agent about establishing elevation levels for the press, or at least pool access. In addition to protecting the crime scene, law enforcement and search officials were contending with other challenges.

The Coyotes bled into the Blackhead Mountains, which were part of the Catskills. In all, they had a potential area of nearly one million acres to search. They were bringing in more planes, helicopters, dogs and people on horseback. In much of the rugged region, cell phone service was spotty, satellite phones were unreliable and even radios had their limitations.

"We've essentially got a needle-in-a-haystack search for armed, dangerous suspects, a missing mother and her son," the agent said. "We're alerting the residents who live here. The press can travel the perimeter roads, but be advised we're setting up checkpoints as fast as we can and wherever we can."

Strobic was shaking his head.

"This sucks," Kate said. "We can't just sit here. We need to get closer. Want me to talk to somebody?"

"Leave it to me. I'll meet you back here, Kate."

Like Strobic, Kate was experienced in shaping order out of chaotic situations. She found a chair in a quiet corner and worked on her story while her deadline and her dilemma with the story hammered in the back of her mind.

She read over her piece; it had everything. It was dynamite and ready to go but she couldn't send it, not yet. Yes, she was certain of her facts but at the same time her information was so significant it scared her as a parade of journalistic screwups blazed by her.

In the Boston Marathon bombing, a New York newspaper identified the wrong suspects. In the bombing of the Atlanta Olympics, news organizations identified an innocent man as the bomber. In the Oklahoma City bombing, a Chicago news organization identified a Middle Eastern man as the suspect and was completely wrong; and there were many other massive mistakes. In each one, they ruined lives, damaged criminal investigations, led to firings and lawsuits.

Kate needed to be absolutely one hundred percent certain of her work.

So much was at stake.

She stared out the nearest window to the mountains. A helicopter thudded in the distance and her thoughts went with it to the Fultons.

Is this where they die?

Her phone rang.

It was Varner.

Relieved, Kate answered while rushing out of the center, so no one would overhear her.

"What is it, Kate? You've got about one minute."

She told Varner everything she had. Everything.

"I need to confirm this—all the connections, the revenge motive, the links to jihadist groups and the threat?"

A long static-filled silence passed between them.

"Who's your source?"

"Come on, I'm not giving that up, just like I wouldn't give up your name."

Another long silence.

"Nick, I'm going to hit Send on my story, and in about fifteen minutes it'll go live across the country and online. I've held back long enough, longer than any right-thinking reporter ever would. Is any part of my story wrong?"

Varner let another long silence pass.

"Nick? Come on!"

"Everything you have is correct. Now I'm going to be up-front with you, no BS because we don't have the time. You're one of the best reporters I've known. I don't know how you did it, but you've nailed everything and you've been exceptional at holding back and doing the right thing. That's why I'm putting all my cards on the table to ask you to continue doing the right thing."

"What're talking about?"

"Kate, if you make public what you have about a possible attack you'll tip off the suspects about our progress and we could lose them and the Fultons. We're close, Kate, and if you let them know how close, then you'll be putting everything at risk."

"That's what you tell me every time."

"Because it's true."

"Do you know the target for the larger attack?"

"I'm not revealing that. Kate, listen to me—"

"No, you listen to me. Homeland puts out vague threat warnings all the time 'based on chatter' and they scare us all half to death. Why is it so different when we report about it? I'm not naming any locations. I'm just sharing the information we have."

"The difference is these suspects don't realize how close we are to catching them, and you're about to tell them."

"Give me a break, Varner. Look around! The sky is full of helicopters, the forest is full of cops and dogs searching—it's not exactly a quiet operation. They've shot Dan Fulton, and they know that we found the note and the cars. Be realistic here. I think they get that you're close."

"Kate, they know we're pursuing them for the Dan Fulton attack, the abductions and robbery. They don't know that we know what they're planning next and that others are helping, unless you tell them. Do you want to be responsible for aiding them?"

"No."

"All I'm asking is to consider holding back on that part of the story. I'll give you confirmation on everything else. I owe you that. You'll have way more than anyone in the press. It's yours, you dug it up, you earned it. Okay?"

Kate was silent.

"Kate, all I'm asking is that you think this through and don't tip them off."

"I'll think about it."

Kate hung up and reread her story with her finger hovering over the send button, biting her lip and considering Varner's plea. She already had a scoop with all of Lori's ties to Jerricko and his family. The fear of a planned attack was a huge aspect. But the location of the attack and exactly how or when it would occur were still unknown.

Kate went back into her story and removed aspects about Jerricko's plans "for a big operation," replacing it with "law enforcement sources would not rule out a terrorist link to the case"—something they'd already stated publicly.

Everything else in the story was solid.

Kate sent her story to Reeka, then, as promised, alerted Ben Keller at the *LA Times* just as Strobic approached.

"Come on, we've got to go," he said, trotting to where his pickup truck was parked.

"Where we headed, Stan?"

"I spent most of my teen summers up here. I know the back roads and I'm pretty sure I can get us closer to the action."

"Good. We can't let these guys corral us. But what if there's a development here? I don't want to miss it."

"I can take care of that."

He opened the rear of his Silverado, the cap and tailgate.

"Good Lord, Stan. It looks like a homeless person's shopping cart exploded in here!"

Strobic ignored her as he rummaged through

blankets, pillows, boxes of chips, crackers, canned beans, jackets, boots, tools, digging toward one of his silver metal lockers. He pulled out scanners and antennas and started adjusting them.

"We'll be plugged in. If something happens, I'll hear it. One of my old buddies is part of a volunteer search group—that's who I went to talk to just now. He told me the best sectors to start with. Buckle up, Kate. We've got a lot of ground to cover."

62

McLean, Virginia

The staccato clicking of Shane Hudson's keyboard was unrelenting as new data on the suspects in the Queens case streamed into the National Counterterrorism Center.

He glanced at the framed photo of his wife holding their two-year-old daughter in her arms at the beach. Emerging on the monitors before him was one of the most serious threats to the nation.

Warrants executed by the FBI and local police at the Yonkers Public Library, the Yonkers home of Walid and Omar Sattar and several other key points were yielding crucial information with each passing minute.

The FBI's cyber experts zeroed in on Jerricko Blaine's use of a public library terminal to determine whom he'd communicated with recently. Working with internet service providers, they'd unraveled an intricately deceptive trail leading them to accounts used by his associates. Agents were dispatched to physical addresses and executed more warrants, resulting in more information.

In California, a sharp-eyed analyst with the Department of Corrections and Rehabilitation retrieved a key report from a gang intelligence officer concerning an extremist prison group that called for Muslims to kill those whom they'd deemed enemies of Islam.

The group was led by Bartholomew Drum, who was serving a life sentence for stabbing a US Marine in a mall parking lot. The intelligence officer had been using inmate informants while confidentially monitoring all of Drum's secret communications, even those he'd cryptically made through his own visitors and visitors of other prisoners who followed his teachings.

Malcolm Samadyh had been a devoted follower of Drum's, and upon Samadyh's release Drum had ordered him to recruit people without criminal records to carry out attacks on the enemies of Islam. But when Samadyh was killed, Drum had reached out to his grieving mother, urging her to honor her son's death by carrying on the cause.

Nazihah Samadyh had agreed and proposed to use "powerful friends" in Afghanistan, where she'd returned, to help establish the group. She'd started by recruiting her surviving son, Jerricko, to lead the group.

Then she'd gone online, scouring postings for malcontent young Americans. The first person she'd recruited was Jake Spencer, a college dropout from Minneapolis who'd written passionately about his disgust with US actions in the Middle East. Spencer also had experience with the US

Army before he left because of his growing negative views on US foreign policy. Samadyh named Spencer the group's operations commander.

Then she'd recruited Adam Patterson, a despondent arts student from Chicago, and Doug Kimmett, a part-time mechanic out of Binghamton, New York, who wanted to be "part of something big."

All were clean-cut young Americans who, through bloodlines or marriage had relatives overseas in Iraq, Syria, Afghanistan and Libya. Spencer, Patterson and Kimmett had become disillusioned with their country and had converted to Islam, ignoring the peaceful teachings and gravitating to extremism. Nazihah Samadyh had further radicalized them, convincing them to take action. She'd arranged for the group to communicate online with commanders in Iraq, Syria and Afghanistan who'd indoctrinated them and helped them adopt Arabic names. They became members of the YLOI, the Young Lions of Islam, an ultraviolent group. After swearing allegiance to the black flag of the extremist movement, they'd sought opportunities for a mission inside the country.

As Hudson paused to question why this intelligence was not acted on earlier, he found his answer in a supplementary note from the analyst in California.

"The report was in its draft stages and never finalized. It was found on the officer's computer after he'd died of a heart attack."

Hudson took a breath, shook his head and resumed working just as a new, updated alert concerning NSA intercepts on a potential attack came in from the US base in Menwith, England.

After breaking down the new information on the Queens case, the NSA analysts at Menwith linked Jake Spencer to a satellite phone purchased online and shipped to a post office box in Minneapolis.

Analysis of newer intercepted chatter between senior leaders of the YLOI in Iraq, Syria, Afghanistan and Kuwait showed that they were discussing an impending attack within the US. Intercepts of recent conversations showed the phone used by Jake Spencer was involved in these discussions.

The chatter had made cryptic references to a wedding with many gifts and guests, resulting in "a glorious celebration," but now there was heightened and excited discussion concerning the "most beautiful gift," and how it would come from "the clock maker."

The analysts translated that to mean bomb maker.

"He's finished," one of the intercepts stated.

A new alert from Menwith flashed on one of Hudson's monitors.

The bomb maker was an American living somewhere in the eastern United States.

Who? Where?

Identity and location were still to be determined, the NSA responded.

Hudson continued working as fast as he could.

63

It's them!

Lori and Billy held their breath to listen.

The distant sound of voices was unmistakable. Lori looked in all directions, not seeing them but *feeling* them.

She searched the dark foliage in vain for an escape route. *Which way, which way?*

The smooth earthen line to the left would be the obvious choice, but the men would spot it. The dense thicket to the right would be tougher and the agitation of the branches against the suicide vests could end everything.

Either choice was a risk.

"This way!" she whispered, shouldering the backpack, seizing Billy's hand and rushing into the thicket.

Branches pulled and scraped against them as they knifed through the undergrowth. With each step, Lori feared the slapping and tugging might detonate the bulky vests.

They moved quickly and quietly. The ground undulated with jagged little cliffs hidden by the dense growth. At times she lost her balance; at times Billy stumbled. But they never stopped. They accelerated where the terrain allowed. Lori's tears for Dan became tears of rage as she vowed to fight to the death for her family. But her heart sank when she glimpsed a movement of color through the trees to the distant left.

That's one of them!

Far off to the right she saw a flash of a T-shirt.

Another one!

Casting back over her shoulder, she glimpsed a third one gaining on them. Turning to look ahead she saw the fourth one moving into position. There was no escape. Squeezing Billy's hand, she veered into the darkest part of the woods where the forest was most dense. It swallowed them as they knifed through the tangles of trees. For a few moments they'd be out of sight, but Lori knew there'd be no escape.

They're going to kills us! They killed Dan and they'll kill us—but I'm not going to make it easy for them. We're not going down without a fight!

Then something occurred to her: they could have detonated the vests by now, ending this chase once and for all. But they hadn't—why? As she adjusted the weight of the bag on her shoulders, it suddenly made sense. The killers needed their laptop because it held the plans for the operation—information that would be lost if they detonated the vests. She scanned the dense groves then stopped.

"Mom!" Billy whispered full bore. "What're you doing?"

She reached into the backpack for the laptop and ensured it was on. It showed about seventy percent battery life. She concealed it inside a small rock pile at the base of a tree with three distinctive fork-like branches at the base. Then she pulled off a chunk of bark leaving a white patch on the tree's west side at her eye level. If somehow they survived, they could come back with help and experts who could maybe track the laptop.

"Let's go!" she whispered.

They pushed on until they stopped at a shallow hollow in a thicket on a gentle slope.

"We have to hide!"

Frantic, Lori gathered huge bunches of shrubs and branches, burying Billy and herself under a thick, convincing blanket of camouflage in the heavily wooded section.

With their hearts pounding, they struggled to quiet their breathing. Amid the smells of earth and moldy leaves, pine needles pricked at their faces and hands. They heard branches cracking and leaves swishing as their pursuers approached.

Billy was trembling and Lori held him.

At least two of the killers were within a few yards. She heard them panting and sniffing. Then the other two arrived.

"They should be here. Did they come through your lane?"

"No. I thought they went your way."

"They're here. They have to be."

"Okay, everyone shut up. They're in this area."

Everything fell silent.

Lori knew they were scouring their surroundings. *Likely looking right at us!* In the quiet, the entire woods waited. The wind waited. Lori could feel sweat webbing down her face. Billy began trembling again; his shaking rustled some of the branches covering them.

Lori held him tight.

Pulsing with fear she caught sight of a boot then a gun barrel.

A creeping sensation suddenly tingled along Lori's skin as a spider worked its way up her pant leg. She choked back her need to scream and swat at it; her entire body was paralyzed with fear.

The quiet was soon broken by the gunman standing nearest.

"I think I heard something over here."

Lori bit her bottom lip and held on to Billy.

"Right over here."

Lori and Billy could hear them raking the thickets beside them.

God, please! Please!

Lori clenched her eyes shut and held her panicked breath.

64

Coyote Mountains, New York

The gunmen froze, standing motionless as faint whomping rolled over the treetops.

"Hear that?" Cutty said. "It's a chopper."

"It's coming this way," Vic said. "To hell with this, let's go! We'll come back for them. Go, go!"

They moved on fast, climbing to a high point that gave them a view of the grove where their prey was cornered while providing a dense canopy of cover overhead. They watched the sky through a patchwork of light as the helicopter's thudding grew louder before fading away.

"They're on our trail! They'll be back!" Percy shouted. "We have to abort!"

Vic didn't respond; he was concentrating on Jerricko, who'd been monitoring news reports on his powerful portable radio.

"Well?" Vic said.

"They found Fulton." Jerricko yanked out his earpiece.

"They found him? Already?"

"In critical condition but alive. They've airlifted him to Albany."

"Maybe that's Fulton's chopper we heard?" Cutty said.

"He's alive!" Percy said. "What if he talks? We've gotta abort."

"Relax, he doesn't know anything. It's in the laptop," Vic said. Turning back to Jerricko, he asked, "Did the news say anything about our operation?"

"Nothing."

"Then we proceed as planned in the name of Allah."

"Are you crazy?" Percy said. "If they found Fulton, they've got the cabin and our vehicles—and the woman's got our laptop! They know everything! Let's just take the money, lay low, regroup and replan."

Vic tightened his grip on his gun and stepped into Percy's space, drawing his face so close Percy felt his hot, angry breath on his skin.

"Are you committed to your martyrdom?" Vic asked.

Percy searched the fire burning in Vic's eyes.

"Completely."

"Then shut your mouth and obey orders!"

Vic pulled his satellite phone from his backpack and confirmed that he had a signal from their elevated position. Then he made a call while the others stood near, listening to his side of it.

"Yes, we spoke earlier about the wedding...are the clocks ready?...Good...Unfortunately, we've had a breakdown...we'll need a ride to the celebration hall…so you'll pick us up at the meeting point…We'll be there in a few hours…Yes, we do have a substantial contribution to make as a financial gift…Yes, very substantial…In a few hours, then…Yes…Many blessings on this special day… Yes and to you, as well…"

Vic ended the call and scanned the grove where he knew Lori Fulton and her son were.

"The press attention will help us spread our message to America. This is not the time to falter." He repositioned his gun on his shoulder. "We're going to recover our laptop and make examples of those two. Then, by the grace of Allah, we'll carry out the successful completion of our glorious mission for the world to see."

65

Coyote Mountains, New York

Kate looked into the thick forests as Strobic's Sil-verado ate up the paved narrow roads that snaked through this part of the mountain range.

"We just passed Split Creek. Used to go fishing there with my dad," he said as dispatches from po-lice, rangers and search teams crackled from his scanners. Some transmissions were so static-filled they couldn't be understood, while others blasted with clarity. The steady flow of cross talk empha-sized the urgency and scope of the search.

"Are we close?" Kate asked.

"We're in the right sector," Strobic said.

They passed through a hilltop turn, providing Kate with a sweeping view that hammered home the vastness of the wilderness.

How will they find anyone in this?

Strobic's strategy was to stay on the marginal roads at the fringe of the search perimeters before those perimeters changed.

"This is how we're going to get inside," he said.

The backcountry was webbed with hunting trails and old logging roads. Strobic said none of them were mapped but he could pinpoint them. They would lead him into the heart of the search by using the tip his old friend had given him at the media center.

They'd gone about five miles without Kate seeing anything promising.

"Is it much farther, you think, Stan?"

"Hard to tell. Want to go back?"

"No. I want to keep going."

The road twisted and Strobic slowed when they spotted a couple of local volunteer firefighters on ATVs. After passing them, they continued on for about half a mile when Strobic slowed for three searchers on horseback moving along on the side of the road.

"Looks like they're still marshaling some people at this edge of things."

Less than half a mile later they came to flashing emergency lights and a Greene County sheriff's deputy's car blocking the road. The deputy swiveled his hand for Strobic to turn around.

"Great," Kate said. "This isn't good."

"Hang on." Strobic got out and approached the officer's car. "Press," he called out.

The deputy got out of his vehicle, adjusted his hat and approached.

"You've got to turn around," he said. "No one goes beyond this point."

Strobic held up his ID.

"We're with Newslead out of Manhattan."

"I'm sorry, but—" The deputy paused to study the ID, then raised his head. "Stan?"

Strobic smiled. "Harry?"

"Well, I'll be damned!" The deputy and Strobic laughed and clapped each other on the back. "How's Ellen and the kids?"

"Good, all good. And you? Peggy and the boys?"

"Growing too fast."

Strobic motioned to Kate, inviting her to meet his friend. "This is Harry Baker, my best friend when I spent summers here as a kid. Harry, this is Kate Page, one of our best reporters."

"Hi there, Kate."

"Nice to meet you."

"So, Harry," Strobic said. "This is where they're focusing the search?"

"Partly. They've got sectors all over." He pointed to the hills. "I'm just sitting on my point for this one."

"So what do you think? Can we go in?"

"No can do, Stan. Way too dangerous. I got my orders."

"Back at the center they said we could travel on the fringe roads."

"Sure, but not this way. Sorry—I can't swing this one for you. Too much at stake here."

Strobic nodded while biting his bottom lip in disappointment. He patted his friend's shoulder and shook his hand.

"Okay, rules are rules," Strobic said. "Look, I might get tickets to a game. You should come in and we can catch up."

"We'll do that," the deputy replied, smiling.

Back in the truck, Strobic wheeled around as the radios crackled. He ran a hand over his face, irritated at hitting yet another dead end. "I don't know, Kate. Maybe we should go back."

"No. We've come this far, we can't give up now. Let's find another road."

"You're a scrappy one." Strobic smiled. "All right, we'll keep going."

66

Albany, New York

The intensive care unit at Highland Sloan Memorial was on the seventh floor in the northwest wing of the sprawling brick and steel complex.

The unit's corridor gleamed with polished tile.

A uniformed Albany officer holding a rolled-up *Sports Illustrated* was among the people gathered at Dan Fulton's door when Varner and Tilden arrived. A ponytailed woman wearing a white coat and glasses pulled them away from the group to an alcove.

"Dr. Beth Valachek," she said. "You must be Tilden and Varner. The desk messaged me that you were on your way up. How was your drive?"

"Fast. My ears are ringing from the siren," Tilden said. "How's Fulton doing?"

"Not well. He suffered six gunshot wounds—once through his right arm, his left shoulder, left hand, abdomen, the left thigh and his lower back, thankfully just grazing his internal organs. He also suffered several compound fractures to his legs, arms and ribs, and he's lost a lot of blood. Had he not been found for another hour or two, he would've died."

"The forensic people are going to need those slugs," Tilden said.

"That's been taken care of."

"Can we talk to Fulton?" Varner asked.

Valachek removed her glasses.

"I advise against it. He's been heavily sedated since he arrived. He's just coming around now, in and out of consciousness. It's touch and go, he might not survive his wounds."

"We understand the situation. But Doctor," Tilden said, "we need a statement from him, anything at all to help us because—"

"I'm aware of the gravity of the situation with his family." The doctor tapped her pen on her clipboard as she considered. "Okay, I'll allow you a few moments with him—*after* you put on some protective gowns and coverings."

"Thank you," Varner said.

Valachek escorted them past the others and into the room.

The soft beeping and rhythmic hum of the equipment next to Dan's bed offered an air of calm in the dimly lit room. His blood pressure, heart and other vitals were monitored on the small screen above him. The doctor nodded to the nurse at Dan's bedside, who moved an IV pole so Varner could get closer.

An oxygen tube was fixed to Dan's swollen face, which was laced with cuts and bruises. His eyes were closed. Varner turned to Valachek, who nodded. Tilden stood at the other side holding a small recorder.

"Mr. Fulton. I'm Nick Varner with the FBI. Please, let us know if you can hear me?"

Nothing but stillness in the room, but then a slight change in hum of the monitoring equipment.

"There," the nurse said. "He moved his right fingers."

"Thank you, Dan." Varner held up his phone. "I need your help with a few questions. Please, if you can, hold up one finger for yes, two for no. Do you remember what happened to you today?"

Slowly Dan's right index finger lifted.

"Do you know the men who shot you?"

Dan lifted two fingers.

Varner cued up a photo on his camera.

"I'm going to show you picture number one. Can you tell me if this person was involved?"

Dan opened his eyes to Varner's phone at a photo of Jerricko Blaine. Dan looked into the face long and hard as if searching for something more, something greater beyond it. After a long moment, nothing happened. He raised no fingers.

"Okay, I'll show you picture number two."

Varner showed him a photo of Jake Spencer. Again he and Tilden looked at Dan's hand for a response, but nothing happened. Then the beeping of his monitor increased slightly.

"I don't think we should proceed any further," Valachek said.

"Just another moment, please."

Varner cued up a third photo. This time, Dan shut

his eyes and tears rolled down the side of his face as he moved his fingers. His index finger went up.

"Yes?" Varner was hopeful. "You recognize number three as the person who shot you?"

Then Dan extended his thumb at a forty-five-degree angle with his finger, confusing Varner, who looked to Tilden.

"A gun?" Tilden asked.

Dan lifted two fingers.

"I'm not sure what you're trying to tell us, Dan," Varner said.

Valachek's eyes flicked to the monitor. The beeping was increasing.

"Maybe an…*L*," Tilden offered.

Dan lowered his thumb, leaving his index finger extended—that meant yes.

"*L* for *Lori*?" Varner asked.

Yes.

"You want to know about your wife and son?"

Dan moved his index finger for yes and the beeping increased.

"We're searching for them. We believe we know where they are—"

The beeping got louder, faster.

"I'm ending this," Valachek said as the beeping evolved into a loud squeal. "Out—now!" Valachek slammed a palm on the alarm button over the bed. "Susan, get the cart! He's going into arrest!" She swiveled to face the investigators. "I said leave!"

Varner and Tilden left the room as emergency staff rushed in.

67

Springfield, Massachusetts

Through the image of his rifle scope, the sharp-shooter locked on to the living room window of the one-story house on Eddywood.

The tree-lined street was deathly still, except for the chirping of birds and the quiet work of Springfield's SWAT team. It was responding to a lead in the bank robbery abduction in Queens, New York, and Dan Fulton's shooting in the Catskills.

New information concerning a looming attack somewhere in the United States pointed to a suspect in Springfield.

At the perimeter of the scene, FBI agent Marilyn Chase, from the Bureau's Springfield office, was giving play-by-play updates over her phone to Nick Varner, the case agent.

At the National Counterterrorism Center in McLean, Virginia, operations officer Shane Hudson had connected more dots between the NSA intercepts from England and new incoming data from an array of top-secret networks in the US.

He broke down the new analysis on the chatter by YLOI leaders in Iraq, Syria, Afghanistan and Kuwait and, aided by security agents, they'd tracked calls to a key US suspect: Todd Dalir Ghorbani of Springfield, Massachusetts.

Ghorbani's name had surfaced in several highly classified databases of potential terrorist suspects. He was thirty, an American citizen who was born in Tehran, Iran. He'd been a toddler when his parents had been killed in 1988, while traveling in a commercial jetliner traveling from Tehran to Dubai. A US warship had mistaken the aircraft for an enemy fighter, shooting it down with a guided missile over the Strait of Hormuz in the Gulf.

"His relatives brought him to America to raise him after his parents were killed but they never told him the truth about the tragedy," Chase told Varner. "Our cyber people say he found out three years ago while going through family papers after his adoptive father's death."

"That must've been a trigger for him," Varner said.

"It was. The revelation traumatized him. He used an alias and began blogging about his story, finding sympathy with extremists, including Nazihah Samadyh. Our people say that she'd recruited him online."

Ghorbani had a PhD in chemical engineering from MIT. He worked as a forensic scientist for a global company that specialized in investigating fire and explosion incidents around the world.

In examining the most recent chatter, the CIA

and NSA tracked snatches of encrypted satellite phone transmissions between Ghorbani, Jake Spencer, Nazihah Samadyh and senior leaders of the YLOI in the Gulf and Middle East about "wedding plans" and the special gift from the "clock maker."

The FBI's ongoing execution of warrants tied Ghorbani and Spencer to Jerricko Blaine, Doug Gerard Kimmett and Adam Chisolm Patterson. However, no criminal history or fingerprints surfaced for either Kimmett or Patterson.

Drawing on further analysis of the chatter, US intelligence had now identified Ghorbani as the "clock maker" and that the wedding gift was a bomb that he'd constructed. More recent chatter involving Spencer's satellite phone had been intentionally scrambled and was still indecipherable. NSA technicians would need more time to extract the content of the transmissions.

Given what local justice officials called "exigent circumstances," law enforcement in Springfield took immediate action on Ghorbani's home and work addresses.

An intense debate among the FBI and national security officials ensued on whether to release photos and information on all the suspects. Going public could force the suspects to halt their plans, go underground and destroy evidence, making it difficult for prosecution. Investigators pleaded for more time to capture their subjects before information was released.

Calls to numbers associated with Ghorbani went unanswered. At the plant where Ghorbani worked, his supervisor told investigators that he'd called in sick that morning. The option of using a ruse to lure Ghorbani outside his home and arrest him was considered but ruled out. The option of using a robot to breach the door, out of concern that explosives may be present, was ruled out as it removed the element of surprise.

Under the circumstances, a dynamic, deliberate entry was chosen.

"No movement," the sharpshooter said softly over his headset to his commander.

Similar whisperings came from SWAT members in various positions around the small house. With everyone in position, the commander gave the green light.

Team members breached the front and back entrances. They entered rooms in pairs, gun muzzles raised, searching for threats in corners, within furniture and closets. They called "clear" when they'd checked each room. Within minutes, they'd reported to their commander that no one was present on the property.

With the house secured, the bomb squad began processing the house, concentrating on Ghorbani's basement worktable. There they found traces of several components used in making explosives, including C-4, black powder and triacetone triperoxide. It was a violation of his employer's policy to have any work-related materials leave company premises. More troubling: they found detailed street maps of Boston, Philadelphia, Chicago,

Washington, DC, and New York City. Landmarks were flagged with *X*s.

At that point, new intelligence concerning Ghorbani had been captured by FBI cyber experts from the "dark web," which was believed to host sites unreachable by search engines and normal channels.

In a recent posting to jihadists, Ghorbani had written: "The American government murdered my father and mother. It is my destiny to do all I can to honor their memory by supporting strategic martyrdom operations."

After Springfield detectives questioned Ghorbani's neighbors, they'd learned that one woman had thought she'd seen him driving away from his home earlier in the day. She wasn't certain.

"It was only a couple of hours before the police showed up," she'd said.

Attempts to pinpoint Ghorbani's location by tracking his cell phone or the GPS in his vehicle had failed, FBI agent Marilyn Chase reported to Varner.

"We've issued an alert for him and his vehicle. He's on the move, Nick. People here are convinced he's built a device and taken it with him, but we don't know where he's going."

68

The Pioneer Valley, Massachusetts

The New Age sounds of wind chimes, harps and flutes floated from the speakers of Todd Dalir Ghorbani's red Chevy Malibu.

This was a glorious day.

He was west of downtown Springfield when he left the Mass Pike for US 20, a two-lane strip that meandered through lush wooded farmland.

At first Ghorbani was nervous about the circumstances that had forced him and his brothers to fall back to their contingency plan for the operation. But he was calmed by his music and his confidence. For months his unit had planned, studied and prepared. God's merciful kindness would guarantee their success and Ghorbani was honored to do his part.

This mission would inflict a terrible wound on the enemy.

It would be a profound victory that would reap lasting glory.

The group of brave young lions that he was helping would provide two hundred fifty thousand dollars to fund more operations. They'd also give him names of US-born fighters, and others in Canada, Australia and Britain and around the world poised to carry out future missions.

After today's operation concluded, Ghorbani would post the videos of the young martyrs, ship the money and information to his commanders overseas and continue his work with new recruits.

He eyed the passing roadside, slowing and leaving the highway when he came to a steel gate with the Private Property–Keep Out sign bound by wires to the bars. He unlocked the chain and drove into the bramble along a path overgrown with tall grass.

He'd rented this isolated property well over a year ago.

After traveling about fifty yards he arrived at a barn with faded, weather-beaten slats. He wheeled to the side door, got out and unlocked the padlock. The metal pulley and rollers squeaked as he slid the door open. He drove his Chevy inside, dust and bits of straw rising in the columns of light piercing the gapped walls as he eased his car next to a vehicle shrouded with a canvas cover.

Ghorbani got out and pulled off the cover before opening the vehicle's trunk. Then he went to his Malibu and opened the trunk where four backpacks sat waiting. Grunting, he hefted the first one, setting it carefully in the waiting vehicle's trunk. He did the same with the others. When he finished, he dragged the back of his hand across his brow and admired his work.

He'd taken such loving care assembling the components—the initiator, the switch, the main charge and power source—within a large container. He'd used TATP, which had proven effective in the London attacks. He'd packed each container with twenty-five pounds of "enhancements" such as nails, glass and jagged steel fragments. Anyone within one hundred feet would be killed. Anyone within a thousand feet would be injured. In a crowded area, the casualties would be high. The psychological impact, the sheer terror, the disruption would be catastrophic.

Ghorbani prayed for a moment before taking care of other preparations he needed to complete. When he was ready, he got into the vehicle he'd just loaded and drove off, locking up at each step.

He resumed driving on US 20, then back on to The Pike, heading west to New York State.

69

Coyote Mountains, New York

Lori could breathe again.

"They're gone," she whispered to Billy, still trembling in her arms.

"You're sure?"

"Let's go, before they come back!"

Taking great pains, she very slowly moved the bushes enough to slip away. Adrenaline pumping, they continued rushing through the woods. Their legs ached. Their faces and hands were bloodied, stinging with cuts and scrapes from branches and needles.

They pushed on.

Lori thought of the helicopter that had passed in the distance. It was gone now but it might return. *Maybe they're looking for us.* The possibility gave her hope.

Lori begged God to let them find a hiker, a house, a road—anything.

Help us! Please!

They heard a rushing that grew louder as they

came to a clearing and a small cliff over a fast-flowing river. She crouched down with Billy and scanned the banks in both directions.

"We'll follow this river," she said. "There's got to be help along here somewhere."

"I'm thirsty."

Lori slid off the backpack, pulled out the water bottle, unscrewed the cap and passed it to him. Billy took a swallow—then froze. His eyes widened at something behind Lori. She turned to Jerricko Blaine, who'd stepped from the woods leveling his gun at them.

The water bottle hit the ground as Cutty appeared and seized Billy.

"Don't you hurt him!" Lori lunged at Cutty but Percy jerked her back and punched her in the gut, forcing her down to her hands and knees, gasping for air.

Vic snatched the backpack and pulled it open.

"We're losing time," Jerricko said. "We'll prosecute them right here. Cut those vests off. We don't need them anymore. Record the video. We'll do the boy first."

Cutty produced a large serrated knife and sliced off the vests.

The bombs were never real, Lori realized. But what did it matter now? She and Billy were backed up at gunpoint to a flat patch of earth. Percy pulled Billy's arms behind his back and tied his hands with a strip of rope. Then he tied Lori's hands. Vic had been rummaging through the backpack and dumping the contents on the ground.

"It's not here! The laptop's not here!"

Jerricko's eyes narrowed at Lori.

"Where's our computer?"

Lori refused to speak.

In one clean motion, Cutty clenched Billy's hair, yanked back his head to expose his throat and pressed his knife to his skin.

"No! Don't hurt him!"

Billy shook with fear as tears streamed down his face.

"We killed your husband. The kid's next!"

"Mom!"

"Don't hurt him!"

"Where's the laptop?"

Lori looked at Billy.

I need to buy time.

"I—I hid it."

"Where?"

She pointed her chin to the forest in the proper direction.

"I marked the spot."

Jerricko stared at her. "You're going to get it for us. You two stay here with the boy. Untie her hands, so she can move faster. Let's go!"

70

Coyote Mountains, New York

What can I do now?

Lori's heart pounded like a jackhammer; panic burned through her mind.

Yes, she'd bought time, but she was losing it every second as they marched her back through the forest at gunpoint. Her brain roared at her to do something, anything, to save them.

I have no options. I have nothing.

Locating the tree was not easy. The woods looked different to her traveling in this direction.

Oh God, what if I can't find it?

Each time she stopped to cope with indecision on which way to go, Jerricko jabbed her with his gun.

"Stop wasting time!"

The faraway sound of a helicopter faded in and out, like a distant dream. Whenever Lori paused to look skyward he prodded her with his gun.

"Stop stalling!"

She'd stumbled over outcroppings and stepped

through twisted masses of fallen trees as she led them back through the area where she and Billy had hidden. Vic and Jerricko grew impatient each time they heard the intermittent whump of a helicopter.

But Lori grew hopeful.

Please, find us! Please!

They came to a dense, terraced section. Lori spotted a patch of white on the forked-branched maple tree where she'd stripped a piece of bark.

"This is it."

She bent down to the rock heap at the base of the tree, reached into it and pulled out the laptop. Vic took it from her, sat down and quickly browsed through its folders. Satisfied everything was intact, he slid it into his backpack, stood and pointed his gun at Lori.

They started back.

Billy's shoulders rose and fell as he cried, sitting on a rock, his hands bound behind his back.

Cutty and Percy stood near him, their guns strapped over their shoulders.

Lori's heart quavered as she was escorted back along the cliff above the river. Over the water's rush, fear throbbed in her ears.

She knew what was coming.

They're going to behead us!

At twenty yards out, panic prickled Lori's scalp, and her knees nearly buckled. Video images flashed before her of the British aid worker on her knees, her captor clad in black, her exposed throat, the glint of the knife. The horror of Billy's impending death consumed Lori like an inferno and suddenly she was on the street in Santa Ana covered with Tim's blood. Then she saw Dan in his last moments, fighting back, saving them—*I'll be right behind you!*—before they shot him.

Ten yards away, every vein in Lori's body felt ready to burst. Her eyes bulged as she scanned their captors. Vic sat down to work on the laptop while Jerricko searched his backpack, pulling out a bottle of water.

Lori smiled at Billy as she approached him, her voice trembling.

"It'll be okay, sweetie."

Cutty positioned her next to her son. Percy, who stood guard, yawned and was not fully attentive as she surrendered her left hand behind her back. As Cutty began to bind her, Lori's mind still blazed with… *Tim's blood… I'll be right behind you… they're going to kill us now...nothing left but to fight for our lives...*and she exploded with lightning fury.

She pivoted and with all her might drove her right fist into Cutty's face. Before Percy could react, she plowed her fist hard into his groin. Then she grabbed Billy and rushed with him to the cliff side, jumping into the river twenty feet below.

As they fell everything whirred in slow motion.

Their captors cursed and let off a spurt of gunfire that missed while Lori prayed the water would be deep enough to survive.

The river swallowed them with an icy splash. They plunged to a muddy spot at the bottom. Lori held Billy, kicking until her feet found traction, thrusting them downstream underwater with the current as bullet tracks bubbled around them.

It took all of her strength to hold Billy, whose hands were still bound. She surfaced for air as bullets ricocheted on rocks. The killers were firing down on them while running atop the rugged treacherous terrain; its rocky walls reached some twenty feet up along the twisting river.

Lori worked hard to keep above the surface, so Billy could breathe, at the same time she had to avoid being slammed into jagged formations.

At first she thought Billy had banged his leg against a rock.

But Lori soon realized from the blood wafting in the water around him that he'd been shot. His face was white but his eyes were open. He was breathing. His wound was on the right side of his stomach.

They were floating too fast with the current for her to tend to him or pull them out. Electricity suddenly shot through her arm. She raised it and saw that a two-inch chunk of flesh, exposing bloodied tendons, was gone from the meaty part of her forearm.

She'd been shot.

Blood oozed from her wound.

As the distance between them and the killers grew Lori looked downstream for a sanctuary. But her vision was blurring, her strength waning as she battled to keep Billy and herself alive.

71

Coyote Mountains, New York

The small sneaker floated in the eddy among swirling foam tinged a pinkish red.

"I told you I got them—both of them!"

Percy held up Billy's shoe for the others who were standing with him in a valley at the river's edge. They looked at it, then looked downstream at the raging rapids, the rocks spearing the surface and spouts of white water.

"They're dead," Percy said.

"I say we go downriver and find the bodies to be sure," Cutty said.

"We don't have time. Look at this!" Percy held up Billy's shoe again. "I hit them. See the blood in the water? No way they survived."

"I agree. If they're not dead they will be soon. Forget them. They're done," Jerricko said. "We don't have time, we have to go!"

Vic took advantage of their location along the river and consulted his GPS compass. "We're not far from the meeting point." He looked up and down the river. "Our brother should be there waiting by the time we get there. We continue with the operation." He adjusted his backpack and pointed his gun. "That way."

72

Coyote Mountains, New York

A sickening sensation grew in the pit of Kate's stomach as Strobic drove them deeper into God knew where. The forest rolled by, taking them farther from the media center. Looking into the woods, trying to penetrate the darkness, she thought of the Fultons again.

Dan was in intensive care. Lori and Billy were missing with fugitives suspected of plotting a terrorist attack—if they were still alive. Kate's heart went out to the family.

Will my story make their situation worse?

Kate hadn't heard from Reeka or anyone at the desk but reception was bad, so that was a factor. She was struggling to control her rising anxiety when she caught a faint static-filled transmission spilling from one of Strobic's scanners.

"...hikers...reported...gunfire...sector..."

"Did you hear that, Stan?"

Nodding, he adjusted the scanner's volume and frequency. A series of static pulsations and squeals filled the cab as Strobic continued tuning the scanner for better reception.

"*...hikers just came out of Fox Ridge near the... need air support...*"

"Air support? Where? Near where?" Stan shouted at the scanner.

"*...we're sending people to Fox Ridge...at the northwest turn of the Bearfoot River...hikers... hearing steady automatic gunfire...*"

"Fox Ridge and the Bearfoot, I know it."

"Are we close?"

"We're close." He pressed down on the accelerator. "The best way in is seven or eight miles from here."

Strobic pushed his truck flat out. Kate gripped the grab handle above her door as the narrow road twisted left then right, climbing and dipping through the woods. At one point they rolled by an immense swath of charred trees and gnarled stumps, the aftermath of a wildfire from years gone by. Gradually, stands of deadwood gave way to thick, healthy trees.

Strobic and Kate listened hard to every dispatch as the road ascended and curled into forests so dense they obscured the light. They stayed on the fringes of the search perimeter to avoid any checkpoints.

Sometime later, he pulled off the road, turned and crawled into the dirt mouth of a forgotten trail. His truck was invisible from the paved road, concealed by the dense brush.

"This is the northwest entrance to Timber Point,"

Strobic said as they got out and went around to the back of the truck. "It's an old logging trail but it tapers off into some badass terrain."

Strobic lowered his tailgate, raised the door of the cap and began rooting through his gear.

"You'll need these." He collected boots, heavy woolen socks, jeans and a ball cap. "They're my wife's, but you're about the same size, I think."

Kate nodded and took the gear from Strobic.

"We'll take the trail. We might have to hike in a long way."

"Remember, they heard gunshots."

"I know."

A helicopter thundered above the treetops as it passed.

Kate stepped behind a tree with the clothes. After changing, she returned to Strobic, who waited with his camera bags and radios.

All suited up and ready to move, he passed Kate a fluorescent orange vest with the word PRESS in reflective lettering across the back. It matched the one he had.

"This is so we don't get shot at," he said. "You know the rules, Kate, same as in a war zone. Be watchful, be careful and be lucky."

Kate nodded. "Let's go."

73

Coyote Mountains, New York

Lori hung on to Billy as they shot along the rushing river.

They rolled and turned in the furious water as she struggled to keep Billy's head above the churning surface.

They slid over smooth stones, banged against jutting rocks. The river bounced them mercilessly from one boulder to another, faster and faster. At times they were on a collision course with massive rocks rising directly before them. It took every last bit of Lori's dwindling strength to raise her feet and avert impact.

Managing a glance at Billy, she saw that he was bleeding from the side of his head.

Has he been shot, or has he banged his head on the rocks?

She was hurting, her wounded arm nearly useless as the unrelenting river carried them still farther. Surely they were beyond the reach of the killers, she thought, growing dizzy, searching for

calm water and a safe place. Above the roar she
thought she'd heard a helicopter, but she couldn't
tell whether it was real or a hallucination, as the
sound faded along with her hope.

Most of the feeling in her body was ebbing. Her
strength was all but gone, her eyes closing just as
the river delivered them to a section of flat, slick
rocks and tranquil, shallow water. Lori lay for a
moment praying. Then she summoned the last of
her strength. Struggling with her numb, wounded
arm, she untied Billy's bound hands and ripped off
a section of her shredded shirt. Gritting through her
pain, she tore it into strips and used them to wrap
the wounds she found on Billy's stomach and head,
then took a moment to tend to her own.

Cradling her son's body, she could see that his
lips had turned blue. Panic flared inside her again.

"No! Stay with Mommy!"

She bent over his still body, starting mouth-to-
mouth resuscitation.

I can't lose you, too!

Breathing her last breaths into him, she col-
lapsed while voices screamed in the back of her
head.

*Don't give up! You've got to hang on! I'll be
right behind you!*

74

Coyote Mountains, New York

Trooper Larry Mattise stood at the checkpoint near Fox Ridge, his patrol car blocking the road as he directed drivers to pull to the side. Traffic trickled at this extreme edge of the dragnet, the junction of Birch Creek Road and Red Hawk Way.

A dog's bark pulled Mattise's attention to where a trooper, a Greene County deputy and a K-9 unit from Albany were searching the van of a family from Vermont. Next in line, an older man and woman in a Mercedes from New Jersey waited their turn. Behind them in a polished Lincoln was an arrogant, "Do you know who I am?" injury lawyer, who did TV commercials promising sky's-the-limit settlements.

Mattise's job was to ensure all civilian and commercial traffic was checked by the roadside search teams at his point. He was also directing every newly arriving law enforcement vehicle to go down Birch Creek Road, where resources were needed most. They were still setting up and expanding the search boundaries miles in every direction, pulling in people from across the region.

He studied images of the suspects on his phone. Most of the photos were crisp: Jerricko Blaine, from Dallas; Doug Gerard Kimmett, from Binghamton, New York; Jake Sebastian Spencer from Minneapolis; and a grainy head shot of Adam Chisolm Patterson of Chicago. As he reread the key facts and threat summary, an alert and photos from the FBI came through concerning a new, fifth suspect: Todd Dalir Ghorbani, of Springfield, Massachusetts, believed to be driving a 2014 red Chevrolet Malibu.

This case was busting wide-open on all fronts, Mattise thought as a fixed wing plane flew overhead for the first time.

Good, they needed more help in the air, since it was impossible to cover every road, back trail and private path in this corner of the state. If you took in the Coyotes, the Blackheads and the Catskills, you were looking at something like a million acres to search. Sure, the report of gunfire near this end of Fox Ridge gave the SWAT teams a focal point for convergence, but man, these guys could be anywhere.

Who knew? They could be long gone from here.

Mattise resumed studying their faces, lifting his head at the rumble of an oncoming vehicle. It was a marked New York State Police SUV. He didn't recognize it right off. The brakes emitted a gentle squeak as it halted and Mattise approached the trooper behind the wheel.

"Where you coming from, pal?"

"Hudson," the driver said. "What've you got going here?"

"Roadside search. And way up there along the ridge—" he nodded to the mountains "—they're trying to nail down a report of automatic weapons fire."

"That right?"

"Yeah, it was on the radio. And they just updated the mugs and info on the suspects."

"What do we have now?"

Mattise showed the driver the pictures on his phone. The new cop never removed his dark glasses. His jaw muscles bunched and he licked his lips a couple of times as he studied the five faces. He seemed to be sweating a bit. After a moment, Mattise pulled his phone back and asked: "You're here to help, right?"

The man nodded.

"Then you keep going down Birch Creek a few miles," Mattise said, pointing. "They'll assign you down there."

"No, I have to go down Red Hawk."

"Orders are to send everybody to Birch Creek."

A sudden wind kicked up and blew through.

"My staff sergeant will kick my ass if I don't do as instructed," the trooper said.

"Well, my lieutenant's orders are clear—I gotta send everyone down Birch Creek Road."

The dog searching the Vermont van barked and turned its head to Mattise and the trooper, who both glanced at it.

"Whose pup is that?" the trooper asked.

"Albany bomb squad. They haven't detected anything here so far. Listen, buddy, I'll call my lieutenant, get him to call your staff, sort this out."

The dog started barking again, as if he wanted to have a go at them.

"Yo!" the dog's handler called to them. "Everything okay over there?"

"We're fine!" Mattise called back, then to the new guy he repeated, "So, want me to call my lieutenant?"

"Naw, I don't have time for that," the trooper said. "And my boss will kill me. I've got to take Red Hawk."

"You're not hearing me. Nothing's going on there. It's outside the current perimeter. Nothing's set up yet. We need people at Birch Creek. I don't advise going down there."

"Well, that's where I'm headed anyway. If you get any trouble from your boss, just blame me."

Mattise stared at him for a moment, then stepped back.

"What's your name?"

"Hennesy. Carl Hennesy."

"Where're you from, Hennesy?"

"D troop, but for the last month I've been on assignment with K. Look, let's keep it simple and say we never talked. I gotta go."

"Fine. It's your ass, Hennesy."

The trooper offered Mattise a casual parting salute and wheeled down Red Hawk Way. Mattise was frustrated as he searched in vain for the troop and zone prefix marking on the unit, but he managed to lock on to Hennesy's license number.

He shook his head as the dog continued barking. *That's right, every now and then you encounter a prick,* he thought, staring hard at the SUV before it vanished down Red Hawk. *At least the jerk's out of my zone.*

But as Mattise walked back to his car, his disgust gave way to a feeling of unease that pinged in a far corner of his gut.

75

Coyote Mountains, New York

Undergrowth and branches tore at the four men as they moved double time through the forest.

The recurrent roar of helicopters told them with each pass that the search was intensifying, but Jerricko insisted that he had the operation under control.

He'd accepted that they'd made mistakes, that they'd failed to make the execution video. But it didn't matter now. Lori Fulton and her family of enemy combatants were as good as dead.

Jerricko's team had prevailed. They'd recovered the laptop. They had a quarter million dollars in cash. Their martyr videos were secure, along with the names of soldiers who'd join them on their path to glory. All they needed now was to meet up with the bomb maker and drive to their destiny.

As they descended a steep slope through dense growth, Jerricko dreamed of paradise.

Soon I'll see you again and together we'll bask in the brilliant light of God. Don't worry, Malcolm.

We'll succeed. Our mother will be so proud. Our glorious leaders will capitalize on our triumphant act. The world will bear witness to our victory over the murdering nonbelievers—over immorality and filth.

The death squad continued traveling at great speed, as if by instinct. Jerricko glimpsed at each member moving with determination and conviction.

Each one yearns to breathe their last breath for the glory of God.

Vic held up his hand, halting the group as he consulted his compass and calculations again, keeping his voice soft.

"We're on track, within a hundred yards, maybe less."

They moved over terrain that rose and dipped. They crossed a small stream to a tangle of brush and then they saw pavement through the branches reaching to a narrow highway where they caught a reflection of light on a windshield, a fender, a hood—the markings of the New York State Police. The patrol unit had pulled completely off the road and was parked amid a lush canopy of branches, concealing it from any passing traffic.

But there was none.

Jerricko took stock of the others before signaling to proceed. They tightened their hold on their rifles. Moving in silence, they surrounded the vehicle, weapons drawn and fingers on the triggers.

Jerricko crouched and advanced from the rear to the driver's door.

The lone occupant was behind the wheel. The window was down. Jerricko stood, pressed his gun to the trooper's neck.

Slowly the trooper raised his hands.

Jerricko asked: "What are the wedding gifts? The wrong answer means death."

"Clocks."

"What is your name?"

"I'm Ghorbani."

Relief washed over Jerricko and the others as they lowered their weapons.

Ghorbani got out of the SUV, exchanged hugs and greetings with the team. Like the others, Percy was impressed with the car and uniform.

"They look real, where'd you get this stuff?"

"A company in Brooklyn supplies props for TV and movie production. I convinced them I was a producer and made the purchases several months ago when we began planning the operation."

"And the gun?"

"The Glock's real." Ghorbani tapped his holster. "Now, we have no time to lose." He opened the rear door, lifted a canvas to reveal four backpacks. "Each device is ready. They can only be detonated by pulling this—hard." He showed the six-inch cord with plastic handle on the shoulder strap. "Dropping it won't set it off. The components guarantee a high kill rate."

The men studied the backpacks.

"Do you have what I need?" Ghorbani asked.

Jerricko pulled the laptop from his backpack and handed it to Ghorbani. He motioned toward his team and each of them brought forward a sports bag and placed them in the back of the SUV. Jerricko unzipped one of the bags, showing Ghorbani the bricks of bundled cash.

"The laptop has our videos and information on new believers we've recruited. The bags contain two hundred and fifty thousand in cash to fund operations," Jerricko said.

"Good. You've done well."

"We didn't produce the execution videos," Jerricko said. "As desirable as they were, we'll still succeed without them."

"Agreed," Ghorbani replied. "Quickly, bury your rifles and use these." Ghorbani moved the canvas, uncovering more Glock pistols with several magazines. "To be less conspicuous."

"Why do we need to be inconspicuous?" Cutty asked. "Aren't you driving us to Manhattan? We should keep our guns."

"We face obstacles," Ghorbani said. "There's a lot of heat and checkpoints."

"But you'll get us through in this," Jerricko said. "This is our backup plan."

"I've already been challenged." Ghorbani shook his head. "I'm telling you, it's not good. They're circulating your pictures, *my picture*. I saw it at the last checkpoint."

"They already know who we are?" Jerricko asked.

"They're moving faster than we expected," Ghorbani said. "We'll have to think of another way to get you to New York, but for now, bury your weapons."

Using deadwood, they stabbed and scraped the soft soil. After they buried their weapons and took up the handguns, they got into the SUV. Jerricko took the laptop, sat in the front and they started down the road.

"This is the wrong way." Vic consulted his GPS. "Go south."

"There's a very active roadblock at the Birch Creek Road junction," Ghorbani said. "I think the sniffer dog picked up something on this SUV, possibly the explosives. We can't risk going back that way. I threw them off the first time, but I have a strong sense that they're watching for this vehicle."

"Why?"

"I had an exchange with a trooper there and I think he suspects something was up. We have to take Red Hawk Way before they seal it at the extreme end."

"How far do we have to go to get out?"

"Another ten or twelve miles will bring us to the state route. Then we should be out and clear. We'll take a longer way to New York City, but we'll get there, brothers."

Jerricko exhaled deeply, moving closer to the windshield to look up as a helicopter passed overhead.

"We'll do whatever you have to do to get out."

The five men had gone about five or six miles when they came to a short stretch of road with a large Adirondack cabin clinging to the roadside. The rooftop sign identified it as Jenny's Mountain Gas & Diner.

It had a two-pump gas island out front. A few lonely cars and pickup trucks dotted the parking lot.

"No cops," Cutty said when they passed. "That's good."

During the next few miles, clicking sounds filled the interior as some of the team checked their handguns. Jerricko was using an earpiece to watch their martyrdom videos, his heart bursting with pride.

We'll give our lives for the glory of God. We'll bring swift justice against the nonbelievers.

As they rounded a sharp, narrow bend, Ghorbani slowed reflexively upon spotting an oncoming tour bus. Air brakes hissed and the grind of diesel growled as the bus whizzed by in the opposite direction. The SUV shuddered in the wake.

"Not much room on these roads."

Other than the bus and a few cars, they hadn't encountered much traffic, and, with the exception of the faint sounds of aircraft, there was little activity. The team grew optimistic that it was the fringe of the search.

"We should be hitting the state route intersection any minute now, then we'll be clear for sure."

Ghorbani suddenly came to a full stop.

Emergency lights pulsated several hundred yards in the distance, where Red Hawk Way met the state road. Several police vehicles were moving into position and blocking the intersection.

"Dammit," Ghorbani said.

"Is that for us?" Jerricko asked.

"Could be, or it could be they're expanding the search boundaries."

"Can't we just drive through? If they stop you, say we're with you and you're taking us to another checkpoint."

Ghorbani shook his head. "Too risky, given what happened at the last checkpoint."

"Well, we can't sit here!"

Eyeing his rearview mirror, Ghorbani backed up slowly until the SUV dropped out of sight behind a rise. Then he wheeled around hard, accelerating in the opposite direction. Eyeballing his mirrors, he dragged the back of his hand over his mouth.

"I've got an idea that will get us out."

76

Coyote Mountains, New York

Strobic took big strides as they hiked deeper into the woods.

Kate had no trouble keeping up with him because she ran three times a week and used hotel treadmills whenever she was on the road.

They moved well together, covering a lot of ground as the forest rose high around them, cutting them off from the world. Hours before, Kate was working in one of the world's largest cities. Now she was isolated in this enormous wilderness.

She wondered if they would encounter searchers or police. She was then consumed with the terrifying possibility the fugitives were out there, watching them, taking aim at their glowing vests.

The dull roar of a river distracted her.

"That's the Bearfoot," Strobic said, raising his voice over the rush. "We want to follow it north, this way."

They walked along the cliff that twisted some twenty feet above the water. Kate thought the river was beautiful, its rapids and rocks breaking the surface and creating powerful spouts and rainbowed curtains of white water.

What a pretty and lonely place to die, she thought, thinking of the Fultons.

Strobic and Kate's progress slowed when they reached a perilous section of water-slicked ledges. That area evolved into a rugged stretch of craggy formations. As they emerged, Kate glanced downriver and gasped. Through a screen of leaves she'd spotted small dollops of color.

She tapped Strobic's shoulder and pointed.

They stopped. He took out his long lens, found a steady position on a tree branch and focused.

"Amazing!"

He showed Kate, who squinted behind the viewfinder to distinguish the details of a head, an arm... another head.

"I don't believe it!"

But it was true.

There, about seventy-five yards downstream, a woman and boy were lying in an eddy. Kate and Strobic covered the distance between them so fast she barely remembered traversing it as they navigated their way down the cliff side to the riverbank below.

Kate knelt beside them.

The woman was bloodied and moaning. The boy's lips were blue, his skin was white. His head was bleeding. He was unconscious but breathing. Both had makeshift bandages around their wounds.

"Hang on!" Kate said. "We're going to help you!"

She had first-aid training and did what she could.

With Strobic's help they first moved them from the water to dry land. Then Kate yanked off her vest and jacket.

"Give me your vest and shirt, Stan! We've got to keep them warm!"

Kate pulled off the woman's and boy's wet clothes and wrapped them with the dry garments.

Strobic reached into his bag for a small radio.

"What's that?" Kate asked.

"A PLB!"

"A what?"

"A Personal Locator Beacon. I've just activated it. It's got GPS and sends out a signal. The search team should pick it up and come to us!"

The woman groaned and Kate leaned closer.

"Help's coming!" Kate took the woman's hand. "Are you Lori and Billy Fulton?"

The woman squeezed Kate's hand.

"You're safe now, Lori. Help's coming!"

"Stop…them…must…stop them…"

"Police are taking care of it," Kate assured her.

"They killed…husband…shot Dan… Murderers…going to attack…stop them…killed… Dan… he's dead…"

Kate shook her head. "No, Lori! Dan's alive! He's hurt but they found him! He's in the hospital."

Lori squeezed Kate's hand, hard. Her eyes flicked open to Kate.

At that moment, they heard the approaching thump of a helicopter.

77

Ghorbani's knuckles whitened on the wheel as he drove.

Reeling from the deteriorating situation, he faced the terrible truth: his plan wouldn't work. Anything he tried at this point would be a risk.

At MIT he was considered a genius. Yet, here he was, at a loss with so much at stake. But he wouldn't give up because he'd always believed that for every problem, a solution existed for those who sought it.

"What are we going to do? What's your idea?" Jerricko asked.

"I'm thinking! Let me work it out."

"We don't have time! We need to do something now."

Ghorbani racked his brains for another option and continued praying with each passing mile. When they came back upon Jenny's Mountain Gas & Diner, the answer revealed itself to him in the form of the Canadian Travel-Ride tour bus that was parked at one side of the lot.

The same bus they'd seen earlier.

It's dangerous, but it could work.

Ghorbani pulled into a far end of the parking lot, turned off the car, popped the hood and got out.

As he looked at the engine, the others joined him, puzzled.

"Come on, Ghorbani! What're we doing, stopping for tea?"

"Listen to me, here's what we're going to do…"

The engine ticked down and Ghorbani quickly outlined the risky plan, Jerricko and the others exchanging nervous glances with each other.

"It's the only chance we have," Ghorbani said.

"Let's do it," Jerricko said.

Taking their backpacks from the back, the men ensured their handguns were concealed as they entered the busy diner. Nearly every table was occupied. Small lines formed at the restrooms. The air was heavy with aromas of bacon and coffee, the clink of cutlery and dozens of conversations.

As Ghorbani took stock of the room, Jerricko and his team found an empty corner table and put their backpacks under it as they sat down. Ghorbani hung back, stopping at a table where he'd picked up snippets of conversation of four grandmothers nattering about their grandchildren.

"Excuse me, ladies, are you with the tour bus?" Ghorbani asked.

A woman with auburn-tinted hair and stylish glasses smiled up at him.

"Why, yes, Officer. Are we under arrest?"

The other women giggled.

"Not this time," he said. "Could you please direct me to your driver?"

"That handsome man over there," she answered, nodding in the direction of a white-haired man in his sixties sitting on a bar stool at the counter.

"Thank you."

Ghorbani made his way over to the man, who was hunched over a coffee.

"You're the driver of the tour bus?"

The man turned to Ghorbani, taking in his uniform.

"I am. Is there a problem?"

"We need your help. Where're you coming from and where you headed?"

"From Ottawa, Canada. Headed to Manhattan—hotel's near Times Square."

"How many passengers? This a seniors' tour?"

"I got forty passengers, all ages, seniors and students. It's a scenic charter package. Mind telling me what's going on, Officer?"

"We have an active dragnet in the area for several armed suspects from a bank robbery and shooting out of Queens, New York. Maybe you've heard about it on the news?"

"Holy cow! My company did put out an advisory about some sort of police action on a robbery and shooting around New York City. I never realized it was this far out. Jeez, should've paid closer attention."

"Well, you just drove into the fringe of it. Did

they stop you back at the state road before you got on to Red Hawk?"

"No. It was all clear. I saw one patrol car just before we got here."

"Did you pick up any passengers once you entered the US?"

"No, this is a solid all-Canadian tour group."

"Well, you're going to be stopped and searched at the checkpoint at the junction with Birch Creek. It'll mean a big delay."

"That's going to frustrate my passengers."

"We may be able to help each other out. My patrol car's engine just quit, those darned computer systems. You can't trust them. My dispatcher said it could be a long wait before the service truck comes. My problem is I got to get these volunteer searchers—" Ghorbani nodded across the diner to Jerricko and the others "—up to the next search point, back beyond Red Hawk."

The driver nodded.

"So how can I help?"

"Let us ride with you. I'll let my people know your bus and passengers are clear, seeing how you just arrived, and you're leaving the edge of the search boundary. You go back on Red Hawk to the state route and take the long way to the Thruway and New York."

"You think we should go back and take the longer way?"

"In the end, it'll save you time. We'll get off when you reach the search point we need beyond the state route."

The driver rubbed his chin. "Think that will help?"

"Definitely."

The driver nodded. "Okay, I'll let my company know. But you gotta let us finish up here. People need to eat, and this is a scheduled stop arranged with the diner."

"How long you figure?"

"Forty-five minutes?"

"And you got seats for us on the bus?"

"How many again?"

"With me, five."

"Yes, you're good."

"Thank you," Ghorbani said. "That's what we love about you Canadians. You always step up."

After slapping the driver on the back, Ghorbani joined Jerricko and the others at the table. Keeping his voice low, he updated them.

"In about half an hour, we're joining the bus tour which is going to Times Square. At some point, we'll own it and forty hostages. We'll order him to park it the Square. One of you will stay aboard. The others will take their places at Grand Central, Penn Station and the Staten Island Ferry. Once all the networks and online feeds go live with us, we'll detonate everything." He smiled broadly, clapping Jerricko on the back. "We're not going to achieve our original goals—we're going to exceed them."

78

Twenty minutes after the jackass had pulled away from his checkpoint, Trooper Larry Mattise was still pissed.

Something about that guy troubled him, beyond the fact he was a jerk. He kept staring at the five suspects on his phone: Blaine, Patterson, Kimmett, Spencer and Ghorbani.

Todd Dalir Ghorbani, of Springfield, Massachusetts.

He looked harder at the last man—examining his mouth, his chin and ears.

That's it!

That trooper looked like Ghorbani. A lot like him, now that Mattise thought of it. But it couldn't be him. People looked like other people all the time. He was talking about another cop here, not a suspect. He was just pissed at the guy. He needed to calm down, let it go so he could focus on the job.

A patrol unit eased up alongside Mattise.

"Larry," the trooper at the wheel said, snapping

his gum. "Sarge sent me to spell you for a short break."

"Roger that."

"Go make a coffee run. I like mine black."

Mattise started his car, slid the transmission into Drive and rolled off.

He had two choices for coffee. Mumford's gas was down Birch Creek, but would likely be swamped from all the search activity in that sector. Jenny's was down Red Hawk a bit farther, but Mattise decided it would probably be quicker if he avoided the search crowd.

Along the way, his unease about the new trooper came back.

I couldn't read his patrol number, his troop or his zone. Nothing marked on his car. Was he a special? Or with the governor's detail?

Mattise had noticed the guy's plate and thought he'd check it out as he drove. He punched it in, requesting dispatch to run it.

It still bothered him that the cop had insisted on going down Red Hawk. Why give him so much trouble?

And, damn it, he looks like one of the suspects.

The dispatcher responded to his request.

"Negative on your tag."

Mattise keyed his microphone: "What'd you mean?"

"Nothing comes up, Larry."

"Is it a special or something?"

"Negative. That plate is not registered with the state."

"Thanks. Ten-four."

Mattise took a breath, tightened his grip on the wheel and, for the next few miles, tried to downplay what was building in the back of his mind. Then he came to the section for Jenny's Mountain Gas & Diner, which stood at the roadside about sixty yards away.

"Holy crap, I don't believe this!"

He braked hard and pulled to the shoulder, using a large rock formation and group of pine trees for cover. There, in the lot with the tour bus, the cars and pickups, was a marked state police unit with its hood up.

A trooper was looking at the engine.

That's gotta be him.

Four civilians were next to him.

Mattise reached under his passenger seat for his binoculars, raised them to his eyes and adjusted them. The trooper was the first face that came into view. Mattise scrutinized the mouth, the chin, the sunglasses.

Is that Ghorbani? Damn, it can't be him!

Mattise steadied the binoculars and focused on the other men one by one, checking them against the images on his phone.

His stomach knotted. *It's them.*

The view went dark for several seconds as a car passed by on a long angle, blocking Mattise's view. Then he saw the men walk into the diner with their backpacks. He took the tour bus and other vehicles into consideration. His breathing quickened as he sent his dispatcher a secure text.

Five suspects sighted at Jenny's Mountain Gas & Diner, on Red Hawk Way, Mile 35. Request SWAT and backup to secure building ASAP. Potential hostage situation. Maintain radio silence.

The dispatcher acknowledged.

Mattise knew Columbia County's SWAT team and Ulster County's Emergency Response Team were near.

A moment later the dispatcher alerted all law enforcement involved in the search of a report that the suspects had been sighted, followed with the location and an advisory for marked units to stay clear of the hot zone.

Mattise's cell phone rang.

"This is Billich," his lieutenant said. "You're certain you've sighted the suspects? All five of them, Larry?"

Mattise sat a little straighter.

"Yes, sir, pretty certain."

"Pretty certain? Listen up. We've just received a report that the two hostages, the mother and the son, have been rescued on the Bearfoot River in Fox Ridge. We're concentrating our SWAT people in that sector, so if you think we need to divert resources, you'd better be more than 'pretty certain,' do you hear me?"

Mattise understood there'd be hell to pay if he was wrong here, but his gut told him he was doing the right thing.

"I swear to you, sir, it's them."

79

Reggie Hunter popped some breath mints in his mouth.

It'd been sixteen years since he'd quit, but he'd kill for a smoke right now as he gazed down at Jenny's from the SWAT command post.

Two weeks from retirement and wouldn't you know it, fate dropped this beauty in his lap. Hunter led Columbia County's special ops section, but in thirty years of law enforcement he'd never seen anything like this.

They had a count of fifty, maybe sixty potential hostages in the diner.

Lord, help us.

Luck had put his SWAT team and Ulster County's Emergency Response Team within four miles of the building when the call came in. They'd moved fast and undetected by those in the diner to get deputies and troopers to block the highway and seal the area.

Nothing went in or out as SWAT people took positions.

They had hunkered unseen near the restaurant's windows and strategic locations around the building. Snipers took up points out of sight in the woods, or from behind parked cars, trucks and the tour bus.

Peering inside the diner with high-powered telescopes, they made visual identities of the five suspects and whispered updates over their headsets to Hunter at the command post. His phone vibrated nonstop with calls from the state police, FBI, ATF and Homeland people demanding status reports.

Critical new information came in from Massachusetts, arising from the FBI's investigation of Ghorbani's residence in Springfield. A lease had led them to a rural property where they'd found Ghorbani's Chevy, photos of a decommissioned New York State Police vehicle—the car parked at the diner—and trace evidence indicating Ghorbani had manufactured several IEDs.

Hunter got a new call from his captain.

"Reg, we're getting leaned on from Albany and Washington. These guys attempted to murder a family and are behind an impending attack. You're authorized to take them out the first opportunity you have."

"Doug, we've got a lot of innocent people here."

"Do whatever you have to do to terminate the threat, Reg. No one leaves that parking lot until it's done."

Tension had numbed Hunter's neck and shoulders. He resumed crunching on his mints, time ticking down as he ran through his scenarios.

Storming the building would cost many lives. Calling in to negotiate would prompt the suspects to take hostages and that would also cost lives. Lives were at stake with every turn. One option was for SWAT snipers to pick off each suspect once all five exited the diner.

"Devon? Bobby?" Hunter whispered to his squad leaders. "Do we have a lock on each target, clear to take the shot?"

"We do, Reg."

"Affirmative, Reg."

"All right, this is what—"

"Heads up!" Devon Sorrell interrupted. "Major activity! People are leaving! Stand by!"

"Wait until all five are out!" Hunter said. "Watch their hands—they've got IEDs! When all five are out, you have a green light."

Ghorbani and the driver led the passengers as they began flowing from the diner into the parking lot.

Jerricko and the others were behind him, mixed in with the other passengers.

Once the bus got to Red Hawk's intersection with the state road, Ghorbani would inform troopers there that it had been searched and cleared at Birch Creek and was leaving the area.

It's going to—

Ghorbani froze. A boot and camouflage pants reflected in the door of a polished pickup truck. For a moment, Ghorbani couldn't believe or understand what he was seeing. As more people streamed from the diner, it suddenly became crystalline.

Police SWAT!

"Police! This is it! God calls now! Detonate now! Detonate *now*!" Ghorbani yelled to the others as he slid his arm around the surprised driver's neck and placed his gun to his head. In that instant, the air cracked and Ghorbani dropped dead to the ground before he could pull the trigger. A police sniper's bullet had ripped through his brain.

In that moment, with nearly all passengers outside, one of the suspects, upon seeing Ghorbani die, hooked his arm around Trevor Williamson, a seven-year-old boy from Ottawa, Canada, who was on vacation with his mom. The suspect was wearing his bomb-laden backpack. His fingers gripped the detonation cord as a police bullet tore through his neck, while another drove through his frontal lobe, killing him.

"Police! Everyone on the ground now! Now! Now! Get down!"

With the yelling and gunfire, conversations stopped, smiles faded into confusion with shouting and screaming. Some people tried to run and bumped into others.

While on his knees a suspect lifted his backpack to heaven and as he reached for the cord police fired upon him, bullets drilling through his head and chest, killing him.

"Get down! Everybody down!"

Passengers lowered themselves, huddled on their knees, hugged and comforted each other; some people panicked and ran while another suspect eyed a cluster of SWAT members behind a car, and at the side of the tour bus, slid on his backpack, rushing with blinding speed toward them, his finger's grappling the detonation cord. His body was hammered by shots as he yelled: *"Glory to God!"* charging them, swinging between parked cars and the bus, yanking the detonation cord.

A blinding flash of light. The air spasmed.

Boom!

The shock wave lifted the cars, shattered glass and whip-sprayed bloodied visceral matter in all directions. The blast ignited small fires around the twisted cars and bus, which had absorbed much of the explosion.

People screamed, cried out.

It was hard to tell if they were injured from the bomb, or in shock after being splattered with blood. In the chaos, some people tried to run as SWAT team members and other officers swooped in from all directions, forcing everyone to freeze. They pinpointed the fifth suspect, who was uninjured, handcuffed him at gunpoint, then took him away.

Police teams rushed into the diner from the rear and front, ordering people to the floor, securing the building. The burning air reeked as it filled with smoke from the fires and the wailing of sirens.

80

Coyote Mountains, New York

Kate and Strobic hiked faster out of the woods than they did going in.

Fueled by adrenaline at having helped rescue the Fultons, they were driven to get the story and photos to headquarters. Trotting and leaping over rocks, they sailed through the rugged terrain.

With each step, Kate composed her story in her head, while in her heart her prayers went with Lori and Billy and the thought of the helicopter hoisting them skyward in the rescue basket.

I hope they make it! They've got to make it!

Arriving breathless at the pickup truck, they set out to work. Strobic called up his strongest photos and began adjusting and cropping them. Kate began writing on her phone, fingers blurring as she concentrated on every detail of how they found the Fultons, their condition, their surroundings and Lori Fulton's words.

They worked at top speed while the radios crackled.

"We've got a solid signal, are you ready to file?" Strobic said.

"Ready."

Kate sent her story to New York without proofing it. Better to send raw copy in while they could and let the desk clean it up. Strobic showed her the dramatic pictures he'd sent.

After Strobic read Kate's story, he said: "Looks good. Another exclusive for Newslead. Want to go to Albany, try to get the family in the hospital?"

"I think the story's still here—"

They both jumped at a sudden transmission squawking from the scanner.

"...explosion at Jenny's Mountain Gas & Diner, on Red Hawk Way, Mile 35...multiple injuries... Columbia SWAT on scene...request fire and all available EMS..."

Strobic pushed his Silverado hard.

Six miles from the diner they'd caught up to a fire truck, sirens screaming, lights flashing as it roared to the scene with Strobic behind it.

The area still afforded a good signal and Kate's phone rang with a call from Reeka in Manhattan.

"Where are you, Kate? We've got reports from our stringer of an explosion and gunfire with fatalities at a gas station, Jenny's—"

"Jenny's Mountain Gas & Diner, on Red Hawk Way!" Kate shouted over the siren. "We're on it! About five or six miles—no wait—Stan says now we're two or three miles from it!"

"Good. Nice job on the rescue story and pics you just sent. Is it exclusive?"

"Totally."

"Excellent. Keep us posted on the diner. We heard people have been killed. We need to confirm the toll, so get back to me ASAP!"

They'd gone another two miles when the fire truck in front of them slowed.

Up ahead in the distance they saw the diner and the havoc—tangles of emergency vehicles' lights wigwagging, a tour bus surrounded by a smoky haze, and police choppers overhead.

Immediately in front of them a state police car blocked the road. It moved, allowing the fire truck to pass, then returned to obstructing entry. A trooper standing at the point raised his hand, halting Strobic.

Kate shouted that they were news media.

"Park it on the side, go up to the tape!" the trooper said.

Strobic pulled the pickup to the shoulder alongside the dense forest. He and Kate grabbed their bags. They hurried down the road to the yellow tape, catching the smell of gas and burning plastic from the destroyed vehicles.

"Looks like a war zone," Strobic shouted over the circling helicopters as he raised his camera and shot the scene.

Kate walked the full line of the tape, searching for a spokesperson or official. She saw no one. Paramedics and firefighters were tending to a dozen bleeding people outside the diner. Investigators in plain clothes were talking to other civilians while taking notes. K-9 units were probing the luggage in the tour bus storage compartments. Studying the mayhem, Kate continued walking all the way to the far side where she spotted Nick Varner talking to a county commander and an older man who looked like he was the tour bus driver.

Varner was taking notes.

Kate waited until his attention shifted, then gave a little wave with her notebook. Varner glanced at her then resumed working.

Determined to talk to him, Kate stood her ground.

Several long minutes later, Varner went to Kate at the tape.

"Did you get them? Is it over, Varner?"

"We're still sorting things out."

"Bull. You know what happened here. What's the toll?"

"I told you, we're still putting it all together."

Kate tapped her notebook to her leg.

"Come on, Nick. I held back on reporting that you had intel about a planned attack. I played fair with you. And we helped find Lori and Billy Fulton."

"I heard that. We still need a statement from you."

"It's in the story I just filed. I'll show you, on the condition you tell me what happened."

Varner's jaw tightened. Kate could only imagine the words running through his mind.

"Show it to me," he said.

"Are you going to help me?"

"Show it to me."

She cued up her story on her phone, and he read through it.

"Well?" she said.

Though he was reluctant, Varner kept their deal and cooperated, summarizing how a trooper had identified one of the suspects and how it led to the discovery of the others at the diner; how the suspects planned to board the Canadian tour bus bound for New York and elude the dragnet with upwards of forty passengers as hostages or victims. He outlined how SWAT teams moved into place and took out three suspects.

"Unfortunately, one suspect managed to explode his device."

Kate wrote fast as Varner continued.

"About ten civilians were injured, three critically, and others suffered minor flesh wounds from shrapnel. Four of the five suspects were killed, the fifth is uninjured and in custody. One suspect charged at SWAT team members in suicide fashion, detonating the device. Fortunately, it went off between parked cars, which absorbed most of the blast. It could've been worse. Bomb techs have removed other unexploded IEDs from the dead suspects."

"So it's over, Nick?"

"We're still investigating, but, yes, we think it's over, Kate."

81

Catskill, New York

Within an hour of the explosion, the surviving suspect was handcuffed and thrust into a hard-back chair in a barren holding room of the state police barracks in Catskill.

During the drive from the scene he'd refused to answer questions.

Now sitting across the table was NYPD detective Marv Tilden and FBI special agent Nick Varner. The *snap, snap, snap, snap*, akin to laying down playing cards, was sharp as Varner set down four color photos: Todd Dalir Ghorbani, Jerricko Titus Blaine, Jake Sebastian Spencer and Doug Gerard Kimmett.

"Do you recognize these men?" Varner asked.

"They sat near me at the diner. Is that why I'm under arrest?"

"We have witnesses who say you sat *with* them, that you were with them?"

"They're wrong. I never saw them before today."

Varner stared hard at the suspect. He was white,

in his early twenties, had thick brown hair and a wispy beard. Varner cracked open the Canadian passport they'd seized from him.

"What're you doing with Thomas Randall Thompson's passport?"

"That's me. It's my passport."

"The Royal Canadian Mounted Police tell us this passport was reported stolen two months ago at Chicago O'Hare."

"That was me. I lost it and reported it stolen, but I found it later in my bag when I got home."

"The RCMP and Canada's citizenship people have no record of the passport's recovery."

"Well, I didn't think I needed to call them once I'd found it."

Varner snapped a new and final photo on the table then jabbed it with his forefinger. "That's you, right here!"

The suspect looked at the new photo and shook his head.

"The bus driver doesn't remember you as a passenger," Varner said.

"I sat at the back with my hood pulled up. I slept most of the way."

Tilden leaned forward, slammed down his palms. The suspect flinched.

"Cut the crap!"

Tilden jabbed the photo, too. "You're Adam Chisolm Patterson, of Chicago, and we know you're in this deep. You're one of the Young Lions, and, buddy, you're facing enough charges to lock you away for all eternity. If you want us to put in a good word with the US attorney, you'd better cooperate."

"Cooperate?"

"We want the network," Varner said. "Names, contacts, codes—everything."

The room went still as the air-conditioning cycled off.

The suspect began shaking his head and sniffling. His handcuffs clinked as he raised his hands to brush his tears.

"Here's the truth. I swear. In my backpack, there's..." He grew apprehensive, reconsidered, stopped and lifted his head in defiance. "I know my rights. You haven't Mirandized me yet. I want a lawyer, and I want to inform the Canadian consulate in New York or the embassy in Washington that you've detained me."

Tilden shook his head in disappointment.

"Don't you think we already know what's in your backpack?" Tilden said. "Why're you making it hard for yourself with this bullshit, Adam?"

"I refuse to answer any questions."

The investigators stared hard at him for a moment, exchanged glances, then left.

Tilden and Varner entered the adjoining room.

Pierre Norbert, the tour bus driver, stood at the one-way glass, studying the suspect as he was taken from the holding room to a jail cell.

"What do you think, Mr. Norbert?" Varner asked.

"I believe the man in that room is the man in

the pictures you showed me—Adam Patterson—
and I saw him sitting with the others before the
explosion."

"And you don't recall seeing him on your bus?"

"I don't."

Varner nodded to a trooper.

"Thank you for your cooperation. You're free to
go, Mr. Norbert. Your bus company will be sending another bus and a fresh driver to help with the
other passengers. We have their statements."

After Norbert left, Varner, Tilden and investigators from several other agencies huddled at the
room's table for a case status meeting. Varner had
been informed that the FBI director in Washington
was awaiting an update and wanted the Bureau to
issue a written statement release ASAP.

"Here's what we know." Varner started the meeting, flipping through his notes. "Ten passengers—
seven Canadian nationals, two German nationals
and one US citizen—were injured in the explosion.
Three have lost limbs and are in critical condition.
The others received various minor injuries. The
critical ones have been sent to area trauma centers, the others are being treated in a hospital in
Catskill."

Varner flipped a page.

"Todd Dalir Ghorbani of Springfield, Massachusetts, who posed as a state trooper, is confirmed
dead. We obtained his prints from his employer.
Our intel points to him as the bomb maker.

"Jerricko Titus Blaine is the suspect who charged
SWAT and detonated the backpack IED. His re-

mains failed to yield enough for us to recover fingerprints. DNA analysis will take time. One SWAT team member identified Blaine as the suicide bomber, while another was uncertain. However, one reported seeing Blaine touch a newspaper box in front of the diner during the walk out seconds before the explosion. We recovered a print from the box that is consistent with Blaine's. DNA comparison from toiletries Blaine left at his cousin's apartment will confirm the suicide was Blaine.

"Jake Sebastian Spencer of Minneapolis, Minnesota, is also deceased, as is Doug Gerard Kimmett, of Binghamton, New York. In both cases confirmation came after local PDs in Minnesota and Binghamton managed to secure fingerprint records, which were originally unavailable, for comparison."

Varner turned to another page.

"Now, we don't have any record for Adam Chisolm Patterson. The photo we obtained from Illinois was of poor quality. No fingerprints, no criminal history, nothing. We've sent the surviving suspect's photo to our FBI office in Chicago, and they're working with Chicago PD to circulate and confirm his ID with his former college, so we can proceed with charges."

Varner looked around the room.

"We haven't yet determined where and what their intended targets were, but we're determined to learn the full extent of the plot by questioning the survivor and the hostages," he said. "Now I'll turn it over to Marv."

Tilden touched the tip of his finger to his tongue and read from his notes.

"The bomb techs located two unexploded IEDs in backpacks at the scene and removed them for examination and detonation. ATF people tell us that early on-scene analysis of the bloodied clothing, fragments and debris, collected from the explosion, are consistent with evidence collected at sites linked to Todd Dalir Ghorbani."

Tilden double-checked something on his phone.

"The gas station's security cameras were not working. Last week an RV clipped the exterior cameras, knocking out the system. It was to be repaired tomorrow. And…"

Tilden found another note.

"We also discovered at the scene, concealed in the fabric of a backpack, a pound of cocaine."

Varner's phone vibrated. He read and relayed the message.

"The director wants a full press conference at the media center within twenty-four hours to answer all outstanding questions wherever possible."

A ripple went around the table to acknowledge the underlying role of political optics in high-profile cases.

"And we've just learned that Dan Fulton's condition has deteriorated. Doctors do not expect him to survive."

82

Albany, New York

Lori Fulton was surfacing.

Floating to consciousness, as her senses awakened to medicine and antiseptic smells mingling with freshly laundered linen.

She was groggy, her body stiff and heavy. She could feel bandages on her arms and face. She opened her eyes to see a nurse standing near, adjusting her IV. A uniformed female officer sat in a chair near the window.

It was evening.

"How are you doing, Lori?" The nurse keyed notations into her chart.

"Where are Billy and Dan?"

"Here, in this hospital. Billy's right there. He's asleep and doing fine."

The nurse whizzed the dividing curtain open so Lori could see his bed across from hers. Glimpsing her son's face and hair, she struggled to get up as the nurse gently pushed her back.

"Take it easy. You need to rest."

"No, I need to go to him!"

Lori struggled to a sitting position and began swinging her legs weakly but with determination to get out of the bed.

"Okay, hold on. We'll get you over there, Mom." Turning to the officer, she said, "Could you get the wheelchair in the hall for us?"

The officer got the chair and helped the nurse get Lori into it. After affixing her IV bag to the chair's pole, they wheeled her to Billy's bedside.

Lori took one of Billy's hands in hers then caressed his cheek and hair. His head was bandaged. His face laced with cuts and scrapes. She nearly leaned out of the chair as she reached to kiss him and whisper as he slept.

"It's over, sweetheart. You're safe. We're all safe."

A woman entered the room. Her hair was in a ponytail, she wore glasses, a white coat and had a stethoscope collared around her neck.

"I'm Dr. Beth Valachek. How're you doing, Lori?"

"Tired and sore." She continued holding her son's hand. "How's Billy? Will he be okay?"

"Yes, he's going to be all right. He's got a gunshot wound in his lower abdomen. Miraculously, the bullet passed through without damaging any organs. He also suffered a concussion, but no major damage is evident. It took over a dozen stitches to close his head wound and he's lost some blood, but he should recover nicely after some rest."

Lori nodded her thanks.

"You," Valachek said, "will need some surgery on your arm to repair the damage from your wound. But you'll regain full use in a few months."

"And Dan? I want to see Dan."

The nurse and police officer looked at the doctor.

"Lori," Valachek said, "Dan's not doing well."

Lori covered her mouth with her hand.

"What—is he—"

"He's in the ICU and he took a bad turn earlier today."

"I need to see him!"

"I don't think it's a good idea right now."

Lori gripped the handrails on the wheels and began pivoting her chair. Valachek gripped the chair, lowered herself, removed her glasses and looked directly into Lori's eyes.

"Lori, listen to me. He's in critical condition. He was shot six times. He suffered a number of compound fractures to his ribs and legs. He suffered exposure and he lost a lot of blood. He's had several setbacks. By all measures, he shouldn't be alive right now."

"Then I need to see him! I need to see him before…"

Valachek took Lori's hands in hers.

"Lori, let's wait. He needs to rest. The next few hours will tell us how he's doing."

"I want to see him now!"

The doctor gave it a moment, then nodded once. "Okay, I'll take you." She wheeled Lori to the elevator, then up to the intensive care unit. Before entering, she helped Lori as they put on protective smocks, hair nets, masks, gloves and foot covers.

The light in the room was dim, making it tranquil with the soft beeping and hum of the monitoring equipment. A nurse, who'd been keeping vigil, stepped aside.

Lori stared at Dan as the doctor moved her closer.

He was unconscious. His hair had been shaved off, and his scalp was webbed with stitches. His swollen face was bruised and laced with cuts. An IV line ran from his left arm, while a sensor clipped to his right index finger ran to a monitor. A clear oxygen tube looped under his nostrils.

Lori found Dan's hand, entwined her fingers with his.

Using her free hand to steady herself, Lori stood and leaned into her husband, kissing his cheek tenderly.

"It's Lori, sweetheart. I'm here, Dan. Billy's here, too. We're both safe because of you, because of what you did."

Valachek watched the equipment monitoring Dan's heart rate, blood pressure and breathing.

"You have to keep fighting, Dan. We need you. Don't leave us, please. Keep fighting. We're here with you. We love you, we need you."

A beep sounded.

"Okay, Lori." Valachek nodded to the nurse. "We need to take care of him now."

"Please, let me stay."

The beeping grew louder, more insistent.

"You really should leave, Lori," she said. "Nurse, please help Lori into her chair and back to her bed."

The beeping grew to an alarming level.

"Dan!" Lori called. "Stay with me!"

As the nurse wheeled Lori out, other emergency staff rushed in.

Lori demanded she be allowed to remain on the ICU floor, to stay as close to her husband as possible.

The nurse agreed to take her to an empty lounge area where Lori watched all-news channels and their coverage of the case. She sat alone at the end of a hallway in the darkened lounge, bathed with the light of the television mounted in a high corner. During the commercials and sports reports she took stock of the IV tube in her arm and all she'd endured.

Was this real?

Her life blazed before her...the first time she'd met Dan, falling in love; the tears in his eyes on their wedding day; his smile when Billy was born; her agony over Tim's death; how Dan had helped her every painful step of the way, his smile, his resolve to save her when she was lost.

The TV flickered with a news bulletin showing the aftermath of chaos, gunfire and an explosion at a mountain diner. Lori stared in disbelief.

All of the suspects, except one, were dead.

Tears streamed down her face as she shook her head and prayed for her husband's life.

83

Coyote Mountains, New York

The Early Light Motel hadn't changed since the 1970s, when it was established by a retired navy cook.

Sheltered by maple trees, it stood about four miles from the media center where the FBI would hold its press conference the next morning.

Looking at the neon No Vacancy sign, Kate was relieved that she'd reserved two rooms when she and Strobic had first arrived in the area.

As a veteran reporter, she'd learned that when you're on the road, you've got to think ahead. News crews from New York, New Jersey, Connecticut and Pennsylvania filled the lot.

"The FBI presser's at nine, so I'll meet you for breakfast at seven-thirty in the motel restaurant," Strobic said as Kate unlocked the door to her unit, which was next to his.

Her room was utilitarian and "shipshape," like the website said.

The knot in Kate's gut had not yet relaxed. As

she sat on the bed, her body aching for sleep, she smiled at her phone's screen and the faces of Grace and Vanessa. It seemed a lifetime had passed since she'd seen them.

Kate pressed the number for Nancy Clark.

"Hi, Nancy, it's Kate. Hope I'm not calling too late to talk."

"Hi, Kate. No, Grace's getting into her pajamas and Vanessa's at a night class. So how're you holding up?"

"Good, just a bit tired."

"We read your story, how you found the Fultons. I'm so happy they rescued everybody and stopped those psychos. It could've turned out much worse."

"It could've been far worse."

"Are you on your way home?"

"Not tonight. The FBI's holding a press conference here in the morning, so I'll be back tomorrow, likely in the afternoon."

"Would you like to talk to Grace? She's right here."

"Yes, thanks. And Nancy, as always, thank you for doing this."

"You don't have to thank me. Here she is."

"Hi, Mom!"

"Hi, sweetie, how did school go today?"

"Well, my friend Lilly and me saw Lucas Parker try to kiss Madison on the mouth! Eeeww!"

"Oh, my."

"He tries to kiss all the girls on the mouth. We said, 'Lucas, you're spreading germs!' But Mia Schendaller kissed him back! Eeeww! Right?"

Kate laughed. "Right."

"Mom, when're you coming home?"

"Tomorrow. I was thinking that you, me and Aunt Vanessa could all go out shopping and then go to your favorite restaurant."

"Yes!"

"I'm so sorry I've been working a lot, sweetie. I love you so much."

"I love you, too, with a million hugs and a million kisses!"

After Kate ended her call, she texted Vanessa.

Miss you, sis! See you tomorrow and we'll all go out.

A short time later her phone chimed with a text.

Love you, too, Kate! Be safe!

For a long moment Kate stared at her phone, tracing her finger lightly over Grace's and Vanessa's smiles. Then she flipped on the TV, surfing quickly through the twenty-four-hour news channels and checking her phone to see if any competitors posted any breaking angles online.

No one had anything new.

She searched her bag, glad she always carried a small emergency overnight travel kit with toiletries and underwear. She grabbed it and headed for the bathroom when something on TV stopped her in her tracks.

Cell phone footage of the immediate aftermath

of the explosion had been captured by a Canadian tour bus passenger. The short, dramatic images had been obtained by CNBC, working with a Canadian network.

The knot in Kate's stomach tightened again as she got in the shower.

As steam clouds rose around her, the day replayed with memories and moments that had pierced her and pulled her through her tragedies.

Lori and Billy Fulton bleeding in the river. Billy, only a year older than Grace. Holding Lori's hand, the way she'd held Vanessa's all those years ago in that mountain river where death nearly took her.

Lori closed her eyes and let the hot water soothe her.

84

Coyote Mountains, New York

At 9:06 a.m. the next morning, the assistant director of the FBI's New York Field Office sat at the table on the dais in the media center.

He was joined by officials from several other agencies.

Microphones with network and station flags were heaped before him, catching the flash of still cameras and the blinding glare of TV cameras. More than one hundred and fifty news media people had crammed into the old church. All major networks were broadcasting live and streaming online.

As she took her seat near the front, Kate recognized faces from the New York City press corps. She spotted Nick Varner and Marv Tilden standing in the wings. Strobic was moving about freely for the best vantage point.

After the assistant director made a round of introductions, he got down to business, reading a statement from prepared text.

"Let me begin by saying that minutes ago we

were informed that Dan, Lori and Billy Fulton, of Queens, New York, will recover from their injuries. As you know, Dan Fulton was listed in critical condition, but doctors at the hospital have advised us that in the past twelve hours, he's shown dramatic improvement. And we've also been informed that all passengers injured in the explosion are expected to recover. We're thankful for that."

An FBI agent then unveiled a display board showing photographs of the five suspects. The word *Deceased* ran under four of the pictures. The last image was an enlarged grainy image of Adam Chisolm Patterson of Chicago with the words *In Custody* under it.

After letting a moment pass, the assistant director continued by listing the time line of events that began more than forty-eight hours earlier with the invasion of the Fulton family home in Roseoak Park, Queens, and ending with the deaths of four of the five suspects at Jenny's Mountain Gas & Diner on Red Hawk Way at the edge of the Catskills.

"As indicated, we have one suspect in custody," the assistant director said. "This incident is detailed in the background sheets we've distributed to each of you here and posted online. Because we're still prosecuting the case, you'll appreciate that we cannot provide all information or answers in many areas at this time. Bearing that in mind, we'll take a few questions."

"Nate Brewbaker, *Washington Post*. Can we get the latest death and injury toll?"

"The four fatalities, all are the suspects, noted

on the board. As for injuries to the tour bus passengers, we have updated our original list. We now have sixteen passengers—eleven Canadian nationals, two German nationals, and three US citizens—injured in the explosion. Three have lost legs, two have lost arms. Two have lost eyes. Those serious cases are in critical but stable condition. The others received various minor injuries. The critical ones have been sent to area trauma centers. All will recover. Some have indicated they are willing to talk to the press. This does not include the Fulton family. Dan, Lori and Billy are recovering and will make a statement at a later time. Of course, at this point, all of the victims have been removed from the scenes. Our agents have been, or will be, at hospitals to continue interviewing all victims as witnesses."

"Neena Perelli, *New York Post*. Sir, was this a terrorist plot?"

"Yes."

"What's the basis for your conclusion?"

"One of the suspects we identified in the invasion robbery raised a flag with national security officials. Subsequent investigation linked the suspect and his associates to intercepts of chatter by known extremist groups concerning a planned attack on US soil."

"Chad Mortimer, FOX News. Are all the suspects American citizens? And is this a case of homegrown, or self-radicalized, terrorism?"

"All are American citizens, yes. We believe they were self-radicalized. They expressed their views online, which attracted extremist factions over-seas."

"Would you say they were coached and directed by those factions?"

"Yes."

"Sally Langston, *New York Times*. Can you please address reports by Newslead and the *LA Times* on the connection of suspect Jerricko Blaine to Lori Fulton's time as a California police officer? Is it true she was involved in the shooting of Blaine's brother? As well, can you speak to the belief that their mother is associated with the extremist group known as the Young Lions?"

"We aren't prepared to speak to that at this time, as it is all under investigation."

"Are you denying the alleged links?"

"Neither denying nor confirming. It's all under investigation."

"Chad Mortimer, again with FOX. Sir, will there be US-led retaliatory military strikes against those factions overseas?"

"I can't speak to that. That's for the Pentagon to address."

"Seymour Abrams, Associated Press. Are there locations in New York City that were being targeted for attack?"

"We can't name specific targets at this time. We mined a damaged laptop recovered in the explosion at the diner. So far we've only retrieved bits of information. It's a difficult, painstaking process."

"How certain are you that there aren't more suspects or explosives still out there?"

"As I've indicated, though this is an ongoing investigation, we're confident we have all the major players in this operation. The SWAT action and explosion at the diner was a horrific and chaotic situation. There was a lot of confusion. Fortunately, innocent casualties were minimal. Our technicians are still on the scene, but we believe we've stabilized the situation. However, given that this is still an ongoing investigation, we are appealing to the public, if anyone has any information concerning any part of this case, they should call the FBI or local law enforcement."

"Melissa Sanchez, *Wall Street Journal.* Were there any warnings—any signs that this was coming?"

The assistant director hesitated, glanced at the other officials at the table, then cleared his throat.

"I cannot discuss much detail, but as I indicated earlier, a huge number of assets and agencies worked together in a short period of time to connect a lot of what appeared to be disparate dots. They worked hard and fast to make the connections. Lives were saved because of them." The assistant director paused. "That's all. Thank you all very much."

Kate noted his final words, and, as she moved to the table to collect her recorder, she signaled to Varner that she needed to speak to him.

"Meet me outside at the back in ten minutes," he said.

In that time, two networks approached Kate and requested short on-camera interviews concerning

Newslead's role in finding Lori and Billy Fulton on the riverbank in the woods. She agreed to speak to them later, then made her way to Varner, finding him near the FBI and state police helicopters. One had completed its preflight checks and started the engine.

"I don't have much time," Varner said as the rotor blades began turning. "We're going to the Albany hospital to talk to Lori Fulton."

"I wanted to tell you that I'm glad this all worked out, even though you were a hard-ass most of the time."

Varner gave her a deep, sincere smile that she liked very much.

"It's my job. Besides, you're one hell of a journalist. I've never met anyone like you, Kate."

She blushed then shifted the subject to work.

"Would you mention to Lori Fulton that I'd love to get the first interview with her?"

"Sure, on one condition."

"What's that?" She spoke louder over the chopper.

"You agree to have coffee with me some time."

They smiled at each other.

"It's a deal, Varner."

85

New York

Kate smiled as Strobic guided the Silverado south on the Thruway, keeping it within the speed limit.

Her story and his pictures had been filed.

It was over.

They were going home, and the tension melted with each passing mile, allowing Kate to relax as she watched the scudding clouds filtering the sunlight over the sweeping forest hills.

"It was a helluva story," Strobic said, smiling at her. "You did some nice work, Kate."

"You, too, Stan."

"What're you going to do when we get back?"

"I'm going to have a girls' day out on the town with my daughter, my sister and friend. What about you?"

"I'll log my overtime and mileage, maybe get Yankees tickets. Hey—" He reached for the radio. "How about some country music? I know deep down you love it."

She shook her head, smiling.

"Sure, Stan. Whatever."

Dan was going to make it.

In the hour before dawn, when he'd squeezed her hand, opened his eyes and gave her a tiny smile, Lori knew she had him back.

Billy was going to make it, too.

We're going to be okay.

Lori held on to that assurance later when Varner and Tilden arrived.

With Valachek and a nurse nearby, Lori sat up in her bed and told the investigators everything, from the night of the invasion by the four men, to Dan's heroic action, to her last memory of being rescued at the riverbank.

Varner's and Tilden's phones vibrated with messages but they ignored them as Lori continued, telling them of her connection to Jerricko Blaine and his brother. She recounted the abduction and how the suspects intended to record their beheadings as part of the planned attacks.

"It was all on their laptop, the targets were—the Staten Island Ferry, Times Square, Penn Station and Grand Central Terminal. They'd made martyr videos condemning the US government and Americans. They were using the money from Dan's bank to fund other operations and had a list of homegrown radicals to share with their leaders."

"Hold on, Lori," Tilden said. "You said the targets were the Staten Island Ferry, Times Square, Penn Station and Grand Central?"

"Yes."

"You're absolutely certain?"

"Yes. I saw their file on their laptop."

Tilden threw a glance to Varner.

"That's four targets, Nick. We can only account for three IEDs."

The Silverado's headlights gleamed on the white-tiled walls of the Lincoln Tunnel.

Strobic guided his pickup along one of the two eastbound lanes that curved under the Hudson River from New Jersey to Manhattan.

Kate was looking at Grace and Vanessa on her phone, estimating how much longer before she'd have a few days off to spend with them.

"So," Strobic said, "we'll go to the newsroom first. Wrap things up there?"

"Yeah, let's do that."

"Okay, then I'll drive you home."

"Sounds great, thanks."

Daylight was glowing as they neared the end of the tunnel.

"You're certain there were four targets?"

"That's right. Four," Lori said.

"Didn't that trooper say he saw them carry four backpacks into the diner?" Tilden asked.

"I thought he wasn't sure," Varner said.

Tilden turned to study messages on his phone as Varner continued questioning Lori.

"Did you see the press conference, Lori? It was broadcast live earlier this morning?" Varner asked.

"No, I didn't watch it."

"Okay, I'm going to show you some photos."

Varner started with a photo of Todd Dalir Ghorbani.

"I've never seen him before."

"We've confirmed him as deceased at the diner. He was the bomb maker from Springfield, Massachusetts."

Varner showed Lori photos of Doug Gerard Kimmett.

"Yes, that's one of them," Lori said.

"He's deceased at the diner."

Then he showed her photos of Jake Sebastian Spencer.

"Yes, he's one of them."

"Deceased at the diner."

He then showed her photos of Jerricko Titus Blaine.

"That's Jerricko Blaine."

"He's also deceased. He detonated the IED."

Then he showed her the last photo, a clear picture they'd taken of Adam Chisolm Patterson while in custody.

"Who's that?" Lori asked.

"Adam Chisolm Patterson of Chicago, one of the four men who abducted you."

Lori looked again, then shook her head.

"No, I've never seen him before."

"Are you sure?"

"Their faces are burned into my memory. Trust me, I'm sure."

"Nick, look at this." Tilden held his phone to Varner.

The message said that the forensic techs found a finger at the scene and had obtained an impression from it. Chicago FBI and Chicago PD were able to compare it with a latent found in Adam Chisolm Patterson's last known Chicago address.

"Nick, the guy who detonated the IED was Patterson, not Blaine. And look at this supplemental message from Canada. The kid we have in custody—the RCMP confirms his identity as Thomas Randall Thompson!"

Varner's gut heaved.

They had the wrong guy.

Jerricko Titus Blaine was missing, along with one bomb.

After leaving the Lincoln Tunnel, Strobic headed for Newslead's headquarters.

He'd wheeled on to West Thirty-Third Street when the rear cab window slid open, and Jerricko Titus Blaine stuck his arm through it and held a Glock pistol to Strobic's head.

"I've got a bomb strapped to me that I can explode in one second!"

"Okay! Take it easy!" Strobic held up one hand. "What'd you want?"

"You'll drive where I tell you!"

"Okay!"

"You!" Blaine pointed the gun at Kate. "Get back in here with me!"

All the saliva dried in Kate's mouth and her skin prickled as she looked at Strobic without moving. She screamed and spasmed when the cab exploded with muzzle flash as Blaine fired a shot into the console.

"Get in the back now!"

Kate unbuckled her belt, climbed into the back, squeezing through the rear window.

"Drive to Forty-Second and Sixth Avenue!"

Strobic nodded.

"Okay, okay! Forty-Second and Sixth! Okay!"

Kate had to force herself to breathe.

In the back she saw that Blaine was wearing a backpack that bulged and what looked like a pull cord dangling from the shoulder strap.

"Why are you doing this? Why did you pick us?"

Blaine stared at Kate as if she were something to be scraped from the sole of his boot.

"I didn't pick you. Fate chose you!"

"I don't understand."

"After my brothers died as martyrs, God led me into the woods along the road into the first safe vehicle. Back here, I heard you talking. You're infidel press! You print lies to support your murdering American government! It is my destiny to kill you and all nonbelievers!"

"No, please." Kate kept her voice soft. "Don't do this!"

A bright light flashed and pain shot through her brain as Blaine smashed the gun to the side of her head.

The destination was less than ten blocks away.

Strobic searched the traffic and streets for a solution. It was futile. This was not a Hollywood script. Blaine had the upper hand. He had a bomb, he had the gun. He had Kate. He had control and he was going to kill people.

There was no escaping this without deaths.

"Don't do this, buddy!" Strobic said.

"Shut up!"

Blaine dug his free hand into his pocket then something clinked as he snapped a metal handcuff to Kate's wrist before locking the other cuff around his own. Blood webbed down her cheek as she regained her senses with the horror that she was now chained to Blaine.

A few minutes later, Strobic pulled along Forty-Second Street and Sixth Avenue.

"Turn down Forty-Second."

The street was lined with empty school and charter buses at the edge of Bryant Park. Some five thousand schoolchildren from all five boroughs were on the lawn before the stage for a special Broadway in Bryant Park event. The cast of one of Broadway's running hits was performing a shortened version for free.

Music and singing boomed, reverberating off the nearby skyscrapers.

"Stop beside a bus!"

Strobic stopped.

"Put your emergency lights on, come back and let us out!"

Strobic froze, his knuckles whitening on the wheel.

"Do it now! Or I'll kill her and I'll kill you and detonate this bomb!"

"No!" Strobic refused.

Kate screamed as Blaine fired another round into the floor of the pickup's bed, prompting Strobic to get out of the cab. As he trotted to the back, he saw two uniformed NYPD officers standing thirty yards away. Strobic waved frantically and whistled.

Unsure they saw him, he opened the cap and tailgate of the Silverado.

Blaine charged out, dragging Kate with him.

Strobic backed away, hands up, yelling: "He's got a bomb!" Then Strobic dove at Blaine.

Kate screamed as Blaine shot Strobic, sending him to the pavement of Forty-Second Street.

The disturbance caused the two police officers to turn just as Blaine ran with Kate into a park entrance.

Officers Rita Muldowney and Elonzo Lang saw the glint of the handcuff, the gun in Blaine's hand and his bulging backpack.

"Freeze! Police!"

Blaine cut through the lawn with Kate, running, stomping on the small feet and hands of children sitting on the grass, watching the stage show. Using Kate as his shield, Blaine headed to the center for maximum impact as she struggled against him.

Muldowney was fast, gaining on them, reaching for her weapon.

"Everybody down! Police! Get on your stomach! Now! Now!"

Children screamed and got down as flat as they could while some, thinking it was part of the show, giggled and clapped. Kate saw the officer raising her gun, finger on the trigger, then saw Blaine reaching for the cord.

"Down! Down!" Muldowney was ten yards away.

Kate smacked her hand on Blaine's, then dropped to her knees as Muldowney fired rapidly, hitting Blaine's head, chest and shoulders.

Blaine and Kate fell on to two boys from Brooklyn.

Blaine was dead before he could detonate the bomb.

The show was stopped.

The NYPD sealed the area and evacuated the park.

The bomb squad used bolt cutters to free Kate from Blaine's corpse and defuse the IED.

Later, she was still in shock when they took her to the same hospital where they'd taken Strobic. He'd been shot in the thigh and would recover, a nurse told her.

"That's good," Kate said, gazing out her hospital window, listening to the never-ending wail of sirens echoing through the city, trembling as tears rolled down her face. "That's good."

Epilogue

As soon as she could manage, Kate called Grace, Vanessa and Nancy from the hospital to let them know that she was "a little shook-up, but okay."

In the hours after the failed attack, Varner and Tilden arrived and took detailed statements from Kate and Strobic.

By the time Kate's family got to the hospital, the enormity of what had happened was the nation's top news story. Grace locked her arms around her mother and never let go during her entire visit.

Later, doctors gave Kate a sedative, kept her overnight for observation and arranged counseling sessions for the posttraumatic stress she would likely experience after the event.

In the days after her release, Kate and Strobic agreed to Reeka's request to give their account of their ordeal to Newslead. Reeka assigned their best writers to weave their dramatic experiences with the interviews Newslead had obtained with Lori and Billy Fulton—a major Newslead exclusive on the planned attack against New York City by homegrown extremists. Kate was the lead writer on the feature, which was presented in a compelling four-part series that was picked up by subscribers across the country and around the world.

In the wake of the incident, editorials, blogs and news network political talk shows addressed the issues of detecting and preventing attacks by domestic self-radicalized loners, vulnerable to be guided by overseas factions. The *New York Times* and Britain's *Guardian* newspaper investigated Blaine, his mother, Nazihah, and their links to senior extremist leaders in Iraq, Syria, Afghanistan and Yemen. Within two weeks, the US, using intelligence arising from its investigation of the attack by the Young Lions, launched drone strikes destroying extremist compounds hidden in mountainous border regions.

A month after the events in Bryant Park, the story had faded and Kate was happy things were returning to normal. She had declined most requests for interviews and speaking engagements, with the exception of one.

It came about six weeks after the event.

Kate was at Newslead working at her desk when a news assistant handed her an envelope.

"This just came for you, hand-delivered by some government guy in a suit. He said it was to be considered 'a priority.'"

Kate opened the envelope to find an elegant card with beautiful calligraphy that began: *The President requests the pleasure of the company of Kate Page at a ceremony to be held in honor of the citizens whose extraordinary acts...*

Kate was stunned as she scanned the words over and over. It was an invitation under the presidential seal! Her phone rang and soon she'd learned that Grace, Vanessa and Nancy had also received individual invitations. Later she learned that the Fulton family, Stan Strobic and his wife would also attend.

Preparing for the event was exciting as Kate, Grace, Vanessa and Nancy shopped for what to wear and received advance protocol advice from White House staff.

The day at the White House was like a fairy tale.

Dan Fulton was in a wheelchair and still bore the scars of his ordeal, as did Lori and Billy. It was heartwarming to see that Sam, Billy's dog, was allowed to participate. Word was that the president, having learned Sam's role in Billy's recovery, insisted his dog be present.

NYPD officer Rita Muldowney, the officer who had shot Blaine in the park, was also there, along with many of the tour bus passengers. Officials from the FBI, Homeland Security, the Justice Department, the New York State Police, the NYPD and more than a dozen other security agencies also took part.

During the ceremony, the Fultons, Strobic and Kate sat on the riser, listening to the president's remarks.

"We're here today because these people behind me, these ordinary American citizens, selflessly placed themselves in harm's way for the safety of our country. They took unusual risks and steps to protect others. Through their courage and sacrifice, they bravely thwarted a major attack on New York City. They demonstrated unimaginable resilience to disrupt the plans of those who would wish us harm. A great many lives were saved because of them, and on behalf of a grateful nation, I thank you."

At the reception that followed, Kate was thrilled to talk to the president and other officials. But one of the most meaningful moments was when she talked with the Fultons and introduced her family and Nancy to them.

Grace liked petting Sam, who seemed to be enjoying the doggy treats in a bowl with the presidential seal.

Later, as things wound down, Kate was surprised to hear a familiar voice and turned.

"Agent Varner, I didn't see you here!"

"I was at the back with my boss and didn't want to intrude. You seem quite popular today."

"As my daughter says, it's been awesome."

"I was just waiting for the right moment to ask you, Kate."

"Ask me what, Nick?"

"About that coffee?"

* * * * *

Acknowledgments

Every Second was, in part, inspired by a number of terrible but true events that took place in Australia, Canada, France, the United Kingdom, the United States and other countries around the world. It is not in any way a criticism of any faith or group. This story is above all and entirely a work of fiction concerning ordinary people confronted with life-altering circumstances.

I want to give special thanks to the agents at the FBI's New York Field Office, who provided exceptional help when I visited them in Manhattan.

In my travels to New York City I also struck up conversations with some New York City police officers. I kept in touch with a few. They'd requested anonymity but helped me with technical and procedural aspects of my work.

If *Every Second* rings true for you, it's because of the kind help of the FBI and the NYPD. If this story fell short, blame me, the mistakes are mine.

My thanks to the amazing Amy Moore-Benson.

Many thanks to Emily Ohanjanians and Michelle Meade, and to the incredible editorial, marketing, sales and PR teams at Harlequin and MIRA Books in Toronto, New York and around the world.

Wendy Dudley, as always, made this story better.

Very special thanks to Barbara, Laura and Michael.

It's important you know that in getting this book to you, I also relied on the generosity of many people, too many to thank individually here. I am indebted to everyone in all stages of production, the sales representatives, librarians and booksellers for putting my work in your hands.

This brings me to what I hold to be the most critical part of the entire enterprise: you, the reader. This aspect has become something of a creed for me, one that bears repeating with each book.

Thank you very much for your time, for without you, a book remains an untold tale. Thank you for setting your life on pause and taking the journey. I deeply appreciate my audience around the world and those who've been with me since the beginning and who keep in touch. Thank you all for your very kind words. I hope you enjoyed the ride and will check out my earlier books while watching for my next one. I welcome your feedback. Drop by at www.rickmofina.com, subscribe to my newsletter and send me a note.

Rick Mofina

www.facebook.com/rickmofina
www.twitter.com/rickmofina

RICK MOFINA

32948	IN DESPERATION	___ $9.99 U.S.	___ $11.99 CAN.
32901	SIX SECONDS	___ $7.99 U.S.	___ $9.99 CAN.
32638	VENGEANCE ROAD	___ $7.99 U.S.	___ $8.99 CAN.
31745	FULL TILT	___ $7.99 U.S.	___ $8.99 CAN.
31609	WHIRLWIND	___ $7.99 U.S.	___ $8.99 CAN.
31500	INTO THE DARK	___ $7.99 U.S.	___ $9.99 CAN.

(limited quantities available)

TOTAL AMOUNT $ _____
POSTAGE & HANDLING $ _____
($1.00 for 1 book, 50¢ for each additional)
APPLICABLE TAXES* $ _____
TOTAL PAYABLE $ _____

(check or money order—please do not send cash)

To order, complete this form and send it, along with a check or money order for the total above, payable to MIRA Books, to: **In the U.S.:** 3010 Walden Avenue, P.O. Box 9077, Buffalo, NY 14269-9077; **In Canada:** P.O. Box 636, Fort Erie, Ontario, L2A 5X3.

Name: _____
Address: _____ City: _____
State/Prov.: _____ Zip/Postal Code: _____
Account Number (if applicable): _____
075 CSAS

*New York residents remit applicable sales taxes.
*Canadian residents remit applicable GST and provincial taxes.

MIRA®

www.MIRABooks.com

MRM1015TALLBL